NEVER
BLOW
A
KISS

NEVER BLOW A KISS

THE SECRET SOCIETY OF GOVERNESS SPIES

LINDSAY LOVISE

FOREVER

New York   Boston

Forever
Hachette Book Group
1290 Avenue of the Americas, New York, NY 10104
read-forever.com
@readforeverpub

First Edition: January 2024

Forever is an imprint of Grand Central Publishing. The Forever name and logo are trademarks of Hachette Book Group, Inc.

The publisher is not responsible for websites (or their content) that are not owned by the publisher.

The Hachette Speakers Bureau provides a wide range of authors for speaking events. To find out more, go to hachettespeakersbureau.com or email HachetteSpeakers@hbgusa.com.

Forever books may be purchased in bulk for business, educational, or promotional use. For information, please contact your local bookseller or the Hachette Book Group Special Markets Department at special.markets@hbgusa.com.

Print book interior design by Taylor Navis

Library of Congress Cataloging-in-Publication Data

Names: Lovise, Lindsay, author.
Title: Never blow a kiss / Lindsay Lovise.
Description: New York : Forever, 2024. | Series: The Secret Society of Governess Spies ; 1
Identifiers: LCCN 2023036588 | ISBN 9781538740521 (trade paperback) | ISBN 9781538740545 (ebook)
Subjects: LCSH: Governesses--Fiction. | LCGFT: Spy fiction. | Romance fiction.
Classification: LCC PS3612.O8746 N48 2024 | DDC 813/.6--dc23/eng/20230908
LC record available at https://lccn.loc.gov/2023036588

ISBNs: 9781538740521 (trade paperback), 9781538740545 (ebook)

Printed in the United States of America

LSC-H

Printing 1, 2023

To my mother, who always knew I would.

In the Secret Society of Governess Spies there are rules one must follow, along with things one must *never* do. First and foremost...never blow a kiss.

Chapter 1

May 1838

Emily Leverton was a hopeless governess. She played the pianoforte with the grace of an elephant, her arithmetic was appalling, and the last time she'd read *A Lady's Guide to Etiquette and Manners* her eyes had nearly crossed with boredom. The only thing at which she excelled was something no gently bred woman should know.

Alas, Emily was no gently bred woman.

Emily handed her youngest pupil a sheet of stationery. Although it was true that Emily's ability to teach accomplishments such as needlework and dancing was nearly nonexistent, she was an *expert* in deceit.

"The first rule of spying," she instructed, "is to act as if you are entirely uninterested in the conversation around you. Jot that down, Morris. You will never best your twin sisters if you do not take this seriously."

The seven-year-old neatly wrote the first rule at the top of the stationery. Late-afternoon sunlight slanted through the school-room window and caught in his hair as if it were a halo and he an angel. Morris truly was the dearest child, which made him an easy target for his conniving older sisters. Fortunately, Emily's true talents were... *unconventional.*

When he finished, he lifted earnest brown eyes. "What is rule number two, Miss Leverton?"

Emily crouched beside him and touched his shoulder. "Rule number two is that you must never base your worth on what others think of you. None of us are perfect. Some of us are not even what we seem."

The dinner gong rang, and Morris smiled shyly before tucking the paper in his trouser pocket. "Thank you, Miss Leverton."

"We will finish tomorrow!" she called at his departing back.

Emily spent a few minutes tidying the schoolroom before she set off for the Mottersheads' library. As the governess of the house she was neither servant nor nobility, which made dinner arrangements awkward. She had solved the problem early in her assignment by retreating to the library until the Mottersheads had finished their repast, and then taking her supper alone in the breakfast room.

Emily stilled in the hallway and cocked her head, her baser instincts buzzing. Had she heard a sound? Everyone should be dressing for dinner, including the latest addition to the household—the children's uncle, the Viscount Charlsburn. The tyrant had arrived the week before, and his sour demeanor had the entire estate on edge. Unhappy with everything from the state of the silverware to the architecture of the stables, he lorded over the house as if he owned it himself, his hooked nose sniffing out Cook's imperfections and his crafty eyes appraising the value of each object. No anomaly escaped his scrutiny, and that included Emily.

Satisfied she was alone, Emily continued toward the library. She rounded the corner and shrieked with dismay when she nearly collided with the viscount, who *had* to have been walking silently on purpose.

"What is the hurry, Miss Leverton?" he asked, his fingers clawing into her upper arms even though she was in no danger of falling. His oily voice reminded her of her former husband's.

"No hurry." Emily's tone was light as she stepped back, forcing him to release her. "Is there something I can help you with, my lord?"

Shrewd gray eyes fell on her mouth. "Indeed. Remind me from where you hail, Miss Leverton?"

"Monmouth."

"Yes, that is what I thought. I have a dear friend in Monmouth. I wrote to him within a few days of my arrival. To his knowledge, no Leverton family resides in the township. Odd, would you not say?"

Emily had suspected Charlsburn knew she was not what she seemed, and this confirmed it. She was experienced enough to know when a con had gone south.

It was time to move on.

He closed the distance between them and reached for a dark curl that had fallen from her pins. Emily dodged his hand, but he advanced again. "Stay still, my pet. Do you know how I have dreamt of this moment?"

Emily's stomach clenched. With a smattering of unfashionable freckles and hair so curly it disobeyed pins on the regular, she'd considered herself neither pretty enough to draw attention nor ugly enough to do the same. She was ordinary. Plain. And aside from her rough hands and sunburnt nose, she'd thought she'd successfully pulled off the role of respectable governess. Even her imitation of the upper class's posh accent was spot-on.

The viscount had clearly seen past her act. Had she aroused his suspicion with the watercolor incident? He'd recently come across her teaching the girls to paint a watercolor of the horses in the field, except the art session had taken a cheek-reddening turn into a lesson on reproduction. How was she to have known the mares were in heat? Surely any governess could have made that mistake.

"You must excuse me, my lord," Emily said, pressing her hand to her stomach. "I am not feeling well. You had best move before I—" She retched. Violently.

Lord Charlsburn paled.

"I believe I ate some poor fish," Emily continued, and covered her mouth just in time to muffle a loud belch.

Charlsburn took a hurried step back. "You must return to your chamber at once! A more unladylike display I have never witnessed."

Emily nodded in agreement, but rather than turning away she stumbled toward him and gagged. With horror etched on his face the viscount scurried off, muttering about filthy servants and the plague.

Once he was out of sight, Emily resumed her walk to the library, her footsteps lighter than before. Yes, she was going to have to skip town and find a new situation, but repelling the viscount had been immensely satisfying. Besides, she still had her forged letter of recommendation from the baroness, Lady Rosigan, who'd once spit on her in the street.

Emily entered the library, confident it would be empty. Her employer, Mr. Mottershead, was a genteelly impoverished man who squandered most of his income on items that made him appear wealthier than he was. This extended to the library, a sweeping room of rich woods accompanied by the scents of lemon polish and dust, the shelves stacked to the ceiling with classics and fashionable volumes that had never been cracked.

It was Emily's favorite place. Although she lacked knowledge in nearly every subject a governess ought to be versed in—mathematics, world geography, history, and classical music—her literacy and imagination were unparalleled. As a child she'd read a filched copy of *Prometheus Unbound* to shreds, and with it had discovered an escape from her dreary world.

The orange glow of sunset seeped through the open drapes, catching floating dust motes with its light and warming the library to a cozy temperature. To save on overhead, the Mottersheads had been cutting back on staff, letting their gardener go months before and several maids since. That meant the only time the library was entered, other than by Emily, was when it was stocked with new books or dusted once a month.

She leisurely browsed the shelf of Mr. Mottershead's newest acquisitions, running her fingertips over the leather spines and settling on the one she'd most anticipated seeing: *The Pickwick Papers*.

With the evening stretching before her, Emily sank into her favorite chair, the one that faced the wild tangle of orange, white, and violet blooms that lined the flagstone pathway in the garden, and bent to sniff the book. It smelled of leather and fresh ink.

She sighed contentedly. Her time with the Mottersheads was rapidly approaching an end, but Emily had learned to slow down and bask in the good moments while they lasted.

When she flipped open the front cover, the spine cracked and a piece of paper fluttered to the floor. Emily untucked her legs and plucked it from the carpet. She could tell it was a note by the slanted, neat script. She shouldn't read it; it was obviously intended for Mr. Mottershead.

Feeling virtuous, she was about to slip the note back into the book when she spotted the name *Esther* through the back of the paper.

Her *real* name.

With numb fingers, Emily unfolded the paper. Her eyes raced across the text.

I have been watching you for some time, Esther Lewis. Is the life of a country governess fulfilling? Or do you dream of something more?

You can be more. I can help.

If you are interested, meet me at the church at midnight.

—The Dove

Emily stared at the words for a full minute, reading and re-reading them again before crushing the paper in her fist and lifting her eyes to the window. No one peeked at her from the garden; no glass glinted from a faraway telescope.

Someone out there knew her true identity. Even more worrisome, this person knew how to reach her. Knew, somehow even before she did, that she would choose this book to read.

Impossible.

She ran across the room and pulled down the next book on the shelf. An identical note fluttered to the ground. Every book on the new-acquisitions shelf, once opened, contained the same message for her.

Surrounded by the abandoned books, Emily clutched the stack of letters, her heart thumping. She suspected this was a precursor to blackmail; not for a moment did she consider the note's promise of a brighter future. She was lucky to have come *this* far, to have tricked her way into a living that provided food and lodging and safety from her former life. Who cared if she languished with cruel pupils? What did it matter if she had to dodge immoral men? She was alive. She was safe.

Or she had been.

The papers had become tacky with sweat. Emily wasn't giving up this life. She would meet this person and hear out his demands.

Then she would devise a plan.

Chapter 2

St. Peter's chapel in Aston-by-Sutton was constructed of Runcorn sandstone and flanked by an assortment of poorly tended graves. Dandelions sprouted between headstones, and the scents of warm grass and pollen still lingered in the air. A cupola atop the tower boasted an embedded clock in the stonework, and in the cloudless light of the moon, the black hands hovered a few minutes to midnight.

Emily surveyed the quiet churchyard, its silence disrupted only by the creeping rustle of grass on stone. Aston-by-Sutton was a hamlet with a tiny population of two hundred. Despite the scant number of residents, the church's doors welcomed nearly every one of them—apart from the Mottersheads—each Sunday.

Satisfied that the churchyard was vacant aside from the souls sleeping beneath the soil, Emily rounded the side of the building to the entry arch. The heavy wooden door was closed. She expected it would be locked, but when she pulled on the brass ring it swung outward.

Despite the warmth of the day, the white stone and black

marble floor held an earthen chill. Rows of oak pews faced a pulpit positioned beneath a sweeping white ceiling arch. Two single candles burned in slender iron candleholders on the altar.

Emily scanned the church, her eyes falling on a figure seated in a pew three rows from the front. She slid her hand into her pocket and curled her fingers around the hilt of her dagger. With a jeweled handle and scrolled metalwork, it was the nicest possession she owned. Her former husband, Lionel, had pickpocketed it from a rich duke, and then Emily had stolen it from Lionel. It had been the least she'd deserved.

She crept closer to the figure, unable to make out if the blue-cloaked head belonged to a man or woman. Her palm was solid around the hilt, although her heart beat a tattoo in her ears.

When she reached the pew, she stood at the end, ready to run if necessary. She'd packed her meager belongings earlier that evening and stashed the carpetbag behind a headstone in the graveyard. She could disappear within two minutes if she had to, and it would be as if she'd never been in Aston-by-Sutton apart from the note she'd left Morris. She couldn't abandon the little boy without a goodbye.

The figure crossed itself and drew its hood back, revealing a fashionable black hat with an attached mourning veil. The woman's hair was uncharacteristically loose beneath the hat, the strands a warm honey in the weak flicker of candlelight. Emily squinted at the short black veil that ended at a half-smiling mouth. She couldn't make out the woman's full features through the sheer black fabric, but she thought her nose was straight and patrician, her mouth slightly too wide, her lips a tad too thin. Despite the shroud of anonymity, the gloss of the woman's hair and the fine quality of her cloak told Emily that her mysterious summoner was not only beautiful, but also wealthy.

Emily's confusion multiplied. What on earth could this woman know about her? And why had she wanted to meet her here?

"Esther?" The woman's voice was smoky and slightly mocking as she lifted her face to Emily. She knew very well who Emily was.

"My name is Emily now. What do you want?" Emily's response was harsh, although she didn't let her posh accent slip. Not yet.

"You do not trust me."

"Why should I?"

"You should not. I approve. I approve of a lot of things about you, Emily."

"I am not looking for your approval."

The woman laughed. It wasn't the dainty, tinkling laugh girls were taught that ground on Emily's nerves, but a robust, chesty sound that spoke of genuine enjoyment. "Regardless, there are many characteristics of yours I admire. There are few dirt-poor thieves who could fit in with the English aristocracy as seamlessly as you have."

Emily's hand squeezed the hilt of the knife. "How do you know about my past?"

The woman took a moment to respond. "There is not a governess in England that I do not know about."

Emily sensed that wasn't the whole truth. "What do you want from me?"

"I want to make you an offer."

"I have nothing of value a person such as yourself could desire."

The woman made a soft clucking noise. "Do not sell yourself short, Emily. I have a new position for you. I understand Lord Charlsburn has become tiresome in his pursuit."

Emily's lips parted. How could she possibly know that? "Who *are* you?"

"Come, have a seat. I am tired of craning my neck."

Emily slid into the polished pew, the wood smooth and worn beneath her palm. She angled herself to face the woman, leaving several feet of distance between them. She caught a whiff of vanilla and peony: an expensive combination.

"They call me the Dove, and you may do so as well."

"They?"

"The network of women I employ." The Dove paused, and Emily tried to peer through the net over her eyes. She could just make out their shape—slightly tilted and feline—but everything else remained in shadow. "Do you know much about the police?" At Emily's look the Dove laughed softly. "I strongly believe the Metropolitan Police of London, and the even newer police forces of the Royal Boroughs, are necessary to protect the people of England and deliver justice."

The police were anathema to Emily. Had she been lured here so the woman could have her thrown into prison like the man Emily had called father?

"They are fledgling agencies without established rules and customs. The finances are yet shaky, as are the expectations for the policemen and the public. The police forces are, as expected, entirely male."

"What does any of this have to do with me?"

"I have a vested interest in seeing the policing network succeed. Too many criminals have gone free in the past, especially in the upper echelons. It is time we all abided by the same laws despite social class."

Emily couldn't help her stunned snort. "That will never happen."

"It will happen," the Dove replied, her voice steely with promise. "Maybe not in our lifetimes, but the foundation will be set now. Aside from the problems I have already mentioned, the current police forces are mostly working class and have zero entrée into the world of the *ton*, defeating the entire purpose of holding all classes to the same standard of legality."

"Right. So they are stuck holding the working class and poor to the law, while the rich get away with breaking it. Like always."

"Like always," the Dove agreed.

Emily was surprised by the woman's response. "But you are one of them, one of the wealthy."

The Dove tilted her chin in interest. "Why do you say that?"

Emily shrugged before she could stop herself from the common action. Not that it mattered, since the woman already knew who she was. "Sorry, lady, but you're an easy read: quality fabric, expert stitching and cut, that discreet emerald pin in your hair, the softness of your hands, the way you hold yourself. You are upper class through and through."

The Dove's lips quirked. "I knew I was right about you. You are going to be an excellent asset."

Emily fidgeted. "I still do not understand what you mean by all this."

"Quite right. In an effort to even the odds, I have decided to give the police a helping hand. There is an entire network of women who live in the houses of the *ton* and hear the fights, witness the scandals, and watch the servants clean up the blood— metaphorically speaking. They know where to point the finger for certain transgressions, and this information can be invaluable to the police."

Emily sucked in a breath. "Governesses. You mean to say you use governesses as a network of spies within the *ton*?"

The thought of spying on the *ton* stirred to life a guilt Emily had borne for six excruciating years. Perspiration beaded at her temples. She sincerely hoped the Dove did not ask her to take part. She would not. She *could* not. Spying was amusing when it was a game, but she had learned too late that in real life, eavesdropping could be fatal.

The Dove considered Emily's words. "Yes, I suppose that is close enough to the truth. The governesses work for me first and foremost, their hired family situation second. If I need a governess in a new situation, I move her. I *do* run the most prestigious governess agency in all of England."

"Perdita's Governess Agency?"

"You have heard of us."

Emily certainly had, but she hadn't ever considered applying to the agency. It supplied the elite upper class with governesses, and she'd known she'd never pass closer scrutiny.

She studied the Dove with new regard. Why would a woman of wealth and standing run a governess agency, à la spy network? What was this *vested interest* she had in seeing the police force thrive? Why the focus on justice within her own class?

There had been a time when Emily had trusted the ruling class at their word—a folly she would forever regret. She would not make the same mistake again.

"The information my governesses report back to me is extremely valuable, and we have been able to ruin several men who would have otherwise been left free to continue with rape and murder."

Emily's brows lifted, and the darkness stirring in her soul settled. *If* the Dove's motives were as pure as she claimed, could this be Emily's chance to atone for her past?

"This is not a game," the Dove continued. "At times I put my governesses in dangerous positions, and the women take greater risks than some policemen. Their reward is twofold: the knowledge that they helped stop a monster, and the pay."

Emily knew it was unladylike to ask about wages, but then she'd never been a lady, had she? "What do you pay?"

When the Dove told her, she nearly fell out of the pew.

"That is for active, dangerous situations. If you are in a normal household collecting blanket information, the pay is far less, although added to your wages as a governess is quite adequate."

Even an eighth of the price the Dove had listed would be more than what Emily made in a month with the Mottershead family.

Emily wasn't a fool. When something seemed too good to be true, it always was. "What do you get out of it?"

"I would have been disappointed if you had not asked, Emily." The Dove absently stroked her bare ring finger. "Someone dear to me died because a man held too much unchecked power. The man was untouchable, and he was not made to pay for what he did."

"Revenge." Emily sat back and nodded. "You've built this system not only for justice, but also for revenge."

The Dove tilted her head. "Is that not the most powerful motivator of all?"

That and love, Emily supposed. Although she still did not entirely trust the Dove, the woman's answer had satisfied some of her skepticism.

Emily considered what she'd learned. A network of female spies! In theory Emily believed in justice, although in reality she hadn't seen it practiced very often. The money was an alluring part of the offer. If she made enough to stash away, she would never have to worry about living in poverty again.

Then there was the possibility that *maybe* she could ease some of the black guilt she bore like a stain on her soul.

"What if the family questions my qualifications? I am not actually a good governess. I can read and write and spell, but that is about it. And there is no way I would say and do all the proper things. It would be obvious I do not fit in." Emily may have fooled the Mottersheads all the way out in Cheshire, but she'd never pull the wool over the eyes of a highly educated family of the *ton*.

The Dove stiffened in mock offense. "They would not *dare* question the qualifications of a Perdita girl. And by the time you have graduated my school, you will be one."

"How can you trust me?" Emily asked bluntly. "Don't you expect me to steal the silver candlesticks from the family you position me with? Seduce the husband? Smother the grandmother? I am a thief by trade."

"You spent your youth stealing to survive. When was the last time you took something that was not yours?"

Emily thought about it. "I do not know. But I lied to get the position I have."

"Lying is a different matter entirely," the woman assured her.

"I took my former husband's dagger."

"The one in your pocket? I know of your former husband, Emily. He deserved far worse. I have no worries."

"How do you know so much about me?" And more important, did she know about Emily's deepest shame?

"I think I have shared enough secrets tonight. There remains only one question: Are you ready to join us?"

The choice was obvious. Emily could either bounce from situation to situation, praying no one would discover her lies, or she could become a spy and make more money than she'd ever dreamed possible.

"I'm in."

Chapter 3

2 Months Later
July 1838

Zachariah Denholm stood at the edge of the ballroom counting all the ways he knew to kill a man—and none of them was painful enough for his friend Deputy Commissioner Wright Davies. Wright had begged Zach to attend an intimate dinner party at Exeter House, where his sister was the newly minted marchioness. The four-hundred-person ball Zach had discovered upon his arrival was many things, but intimate it was not.

After that blasted article in the society pages that morning, the last place Zach wanted to be was at the Season's most successful crush. When he saw Wright, he was going to . . .

"It has to be him!" a young woman squealed to his right, interrupting his fantasy of socking Wright. "His eyes are as cold as the Arctic, just as the article said." She shivered theatrically.

"It also said he is not a man to be toyed with," her companion hissed. "It called him 'frozen and merciless.' I do not think you should ask for an introduction, Ainsley."

Zach's surliness multiplied.

"Your countenance is frightening my sister's guests."

Zach didn't bother turning at Wright's voice. "What did you expect when you lied to me?"

"It was a simple misunderstanding, Denholm."

Zach did look at him then, and Wright appeared entirely too pleased with himself. He sported a thick, dark mustache and a head of hair that was already thinning. Pads were sewn into his coat to bolster sloping shoulders that at times seemed to carry the entire weight of the force now that he was the deputy commissioner of the Metropolitan Police.

"Do not be cross, Detective Constable. My sister begged me to invite you. Apparently, as a 'wealthy playboy with a policing hobby,' you are the Season's most *ineligible*—read mysterious—bachelor."

"When I discover the identity of that columnist, I am going to break every one of his pen nibs."

Wright handed Zach a flute of champagne. "Look around you, Denholm. Every young lady here is vying for an introduction."

Zach swallowed half the glass. "I am not searching for a wife, and even if I were, I sure as hell wouldn't find her here. These people think of me as something hairy that weaseled its way into their exclusive coop. Sons of butchers are not generally considered marriageable."

"But filthy-rich railroad investors are. Most folks are willing to forgive your past for your present." Wright popped a monocle in his eye. "They're not a fascinating lot, I'll give you that. Before word circulates that the Season's most *ineligible* bachelor has arrived, did you read the article in the paper this morning?"

It had been hard to miss. The headline had screamed: EVANGE-LIST STRIKES AGAIN! The "Evangelist," as the sensationalist press had dubbed him, had murdered three streetwalkers in the Bethnal Green slum of London. The article had gone on to detail the incompetence of the fledgling Metropolitan Police force, declaring them inept and incapable of stopping the latest scourge to society.

There was pressure from the public to solve the murders, although nothing compared to the panic the Silk Stalker had raised eight years prior. Then, the targets had been upper-class ladies, and those with deep pockets had been frantic to identify the man who strangled his victims with a silk cravat. When the Silk Stalker had been unmasked as a peer, the shock waves had been felt to the Americas. The Evangelist was different. Since he seemed to have a taste for streetwalkers, the *ton* read reports of the murders with salacious interest rather than fear.

Not Zach. He'd been raised in poverty, understood that many of the women who prostituted themselves did so out of desperation to survive or provide for their children. That someone was preying on those who were already so vulnerable made a cold, white rage sweep over his body.

"I read it."

"The commissioner is breathing down my neck. He wants to know if we have any leads on the identity of the Evangelist."

And *that* was one of the many reasons Zach had insisted on the rank of detective constable. With his income he could have easily placed higher in the police hierarchy, as Wright had. Wright hadn't understood Zach's refusal to do so at the time, but Zach suspected he was beginning to. Before Zach had made his fortune investing in the railroad, he'd spent a decade leading men in the Anglo-Burmese War and the Portuguese Civil War; he was more than happy to let Wright pass down the orders these days.

"The commissioner isn't the only one I have to answer to in this blasted position. The home secretary is wondering why he went out on a limb to found the Metropolitan Police when we can't manage to unearth even a single clue. He has made it clear that we need to prove our usefulness to the public, or *else*."

A vaguely familiar gentleman accompanied by three sour-faced women started across the mahogany parquet floor, their eyes locked on Zach. A stream of ladies robed in pastel and lace whirled between him and the approaching entourage, breaking the party's line of sight. Zach pinched the bridge of his nose. "What about your secret informant? He hasn't come through with anything?"

"Nothing. If I want to save the Metropolitan Police, I am going to have to create a task force to root out this so-called Evangelist."

Zach finished the contents of the flute, the bubbles sliding down his throat with a burn. The heat of the ballroom combined with the heavy scents of perfumes and the approaching headaches—plural—made him wish he were home reading a book in front of the fireplace instead of preparing to disappoint a house full of strangers as well as his friend.

"No," Zach said. A servant whisked his glass away.

Wright sniffed. "I was not asking you to head it. I am going to suggest Taylor take the lead."

Zach's steady gaze met Wright's. "Robert Taylor?"

"Yes."

"He is an idiot."

"He is competent. You don't like him because he drinks."

"No, he is a drunk. There is a difference."

Wright conceded the point by lifting a hand. "Who would you suggest?"

Zach ran through a list of names in his head. There were several good men in service, but for one reason or another they all failed to meet the requirements it would take to lead a task force.

He bit back a sigh. He'd walked right into that one. "Fine," he growled. "But I have conditions."

Wright was smiling widely. "Name them."

"I want full discretion when deciding who joins the task force. I will not report to anyone but you, and I will report only when I have something to say. Otherwise, don't bother me."

"Consider it done."

"I also want you to get me the hell out of here."

Wright slapped him on the back. "It is too late for that, my friend. You are about to meet Mrs. Hill." He nodded at the woman steamrolling toward them, draughting her two daughters in her wake. "You are going to need all the luck you can muster."

Chapter 4

"M r. Denholm, I am Lord Moore." The man introducing Mrs. Hill and her daughters had watery eyes and an obsequious tone that set Zach's teeth on edge. "I am sure you remember me from Knottingham's."

That was why he'd seemed vaguely familiar. Moore was a member of one of the clubs Zach had joined and visited twice, simply because he could.

"Not really."

Lord Moore laughed, and it came out in high-pitched wheezes. "Just so, just so. I would like to introduce my sister, Mrs. Hill, and her daughters, Miss Hill and Miss Jane."

Mrs. Hill was as thin as her brother with the same weak blue eyes. Her brows were drawn onto her forehead in a startling arch, and her nose was slightly upturned like that of a dog Zach had once seen. She bared her teeth in an approximation of a smile and shoved her elder daughter forward.

"Mr. Denholm, my brother says you enjoy reading, and so does my darling girl," Mrs. Hill crooned. "Dear, tell Mr. Denholm what it was you read recently that had you in stitches. Really, we did not read as much in my time. I was too busy perfecting my needlework and pianoforte, but girls these days have such independent and clever minds. I cannot seem to stop her from consuming every written word in the house!"

Zach forced a smile. It wasn't the girl's fault she was being thrown at his feet like an offering. "What do you enjoy reading?" he asked dutifully, silently vowing to sic the Hills on Wright as soon as he had the chance.

Miss Hill appeared horrified at being addressed. She was a voluptuous girl in a way that Zach appreciated, but had the sickly pallor of her mother and uncle. Furthermore, she seemed completely tongue-tied and incapable of answering. Zach wondered if she was stuck for trying to think of a single title.

"The Bible!" Miss Hill blurted.

"Since when have *you* read the Bible?" sneered her sister, Miss Jane.

Mrs. Hill stomped on Jane's foot, causing her to yip like a puppy.

Zach caught a glimpse of movement in his periphery: a woman, slipping like a shadow along the edge of the ballroom. She was dressed as a governess or perhaps a nursemaid, and therefore invisible to the patrons of the ball. She would have remained unseen by him as well if she had not stopped to view his predicament with visible glee.

He stared at her in direct challenge. Instead of blushing and turning away, she boldly met his eyes, her own dancing with amusement. Her hair was richly dark and so curly that even pins couldn't keep the unwieldy locks from tumbling down her neck. Her cheekbones were high and slightly reddened, although he was sure it was due to the heat of the room and not a rouge palette. Her cheeks and nose were sprinkled with freckles from too much sun. A modest, unadorned navy dress concealed her from chin to wrist, but nipped in at a slender waist, giving her a curvy, athletic figure. Somehow, in her simplicity, she made more of an impression on him than all of the bosoms and jewels displayed in the room.

Or perhaps it was her completely inappropriate enjoyment of his discomfort that sparked his interest. Who was the woman? And what was she doing sneaking along the outskirts of the ball mocking poor, unsuspecting men?

"I also like poetry," Miss Hill said shrilly in an attempt to reclaim his attention. "Shall I recite my favorite?"

"No, I think it best if—"

Miss Hill folded her hands together and closed her eyes as if she were about to sing in a choir. *"Peonies are pink and love is true/ My heart is blue when I do not have you/Jasmine is white and will not take a fright/Because it has a knight, just like you."*

The governess's face blossomed into a grin, and Zach felt as if he'd taken a hit to the stomach.

"Lovely darling, just lovely." Mrs. Hill sighed. "Was that Browning?"

"That was by one Miss Olivia Hill," Miss Hill said proudly.

Mrs. Hill clapped white-gloved hands together. "Splendid! You are a true rare diamond, my dear. That was poetry for the ages, do you not think so, Mr. Denholm?"

"Hmm? Yes, that is a poem I shall never forget. If you will excuse me."

Zach didn't dare take his eyes off the woman lest she disappear before he had a chance to confront her. He started toward her, blocking out the squawks of dismay behind him and nearly mowing over a tiny dame dripping in jewels so heavy that a good gust of air would have toppled her anyway.

The laughing minx allowed him to almost reach her, and then she *blew him a kiss* and turned on her heel, scurrying along the perimeter and sliding through bodies as if she were a ghost walking through walls.

Like hell was she getting away. She may have had the advantage when it came to squeezing through small spaces, but Zach hadn't become an army colonel by lacking strategy.

Chapter 5

Idiot, idiot, idiot. Emily berated herself on a loop as she dashed between the backs of two gentlemen in exact shades of black. What had she been *thinking* antagonizing that man? She'd always had impulse control issues, but really, this was a step too far. She'd be lucky if he didn't catch her and turn her in to her employer, and then she'd be in an awful pickle. She'd been placed with her employer for a reason, and she'd just jeopardized the very mission she'd been sent to accomplish by being an impulsive fool.

The problem was he'd looked so comically trapped and long-suffering while that dog-faced woman had tried to pawn her clearly vapid daughter off on him, that Emily had been seized by an intense curiosity to stop and watch. She'd wanted to see what he would do. He wasn't a traditional fop; she could tell that with one look at him, even though he wore an expertly tailored jacket that brought out the shot-silk cobalt of his eyes. He was taller than most of the men in the room, with broad shoulders and an easy muscular build that she was used to seeing on farmers who used their bodies for a living. She could tell he was a powerful man by the way he held himself and how the other men in the room reacted to him, but there'd been something that set him apart from the other nobles. He'd seemed *earthier*. As if he were a real man cut of human sorrow and triumph rather than a man who watched it all unfold from above.

When he'd met her eyes, there had been such intensity and heat in them that her heart had skipped. Then he'd started toward her, and she'd been frozen with indecision. She wanted to meet him, talk to him, see those eyes up close and focused on her.

Then reality had returned with a whoosh, stealing her breath. She was a governess and a common-born thief, while he was obviously an important man. She was being not only ridiculous, but dangerously stupid.

Except then she'd *blown him a kiss* before dashing off, and honestly it had been worth it to see the look of astonishment cross his face.

She ducked through the servants' entrance and headed toward the exit. The eldest sibling of her new charges, Lady Minnie, had left her reticule at home and Emily had been dispatched to deliver it to Exeter House as it held Minnie's fan, and Minnie had been working *so* industriously on her seductive fan flutters.

Emily hadn't minded the order. It was a short walk to Exeter House, and the night was warm with just enough nip in the air to be refreshing. If Emily had been in the countryside, she would have tilted her chin back and drunk in the sparkling blanket of stars, but instead she was in London where smog smothered the sky. So she'd filled herself on the sights in the streets: the bad-tempered hansom drivers with cigars dangling from their mouths, tipsy men stumbling from one club to another, and then later, the fine satin gowns of the women entering the private ball.

She'd only been at Eastmoreland House for a fortnight, but

already she could tell their situation was night and day from the impoverished Mottersheads. The staff was full, the furnishings rich and polished, the food fresh and prepared with pomp and circumstance. The children had wardrobes so expensive the cost could have fed a small town for an entire winter, and Emily's quarters even had a small receiving room and fireplace.

Now that Emily had graduated the Dove's school she felt more confident in her skills as a governess, even if her French remained rudimentary and her watercolor paintings still made her blush with the memory of the horse faux pas. She'd been pleasantly surprised to discover that the Eastmoreland children were bright and even-tempered. There were six of them, from the eldest, Minnie, to Charlie, the youngest at four years old.

Their parents were Robert Enfield, Earl of Eastmoreland, and Clara Enfield, Countess of Eastmoreland. The dowager countess lived in a separate wing of her own, and by all outward appearances they were a proper, well-respected family.

Appearances, Emily well knew, could lie.

There was something a shade off about the family, a sense that not all was quite so darling within the richly appointed walls.

Emily could not put her finger on what made her so sure the Eastmorelands were hiding secrets. Was it the tense quiet among the servants when the lady of the house was in residence? The way the children actively avoided their parents? Mayhap it was the odd comment the head housekeeper had made before depositing Emily in her quarters on her first day: "See to it you do not find yourself alone with the master."

Or was it simply that one liar knew another?

No wonder the Dove had placed her there. In Emily's experience, there was no such thing as the perfect family.

Emily rounded Exeter House, keeping her eyes straight ahead and ignoring the whistles and invitations from the coachmen and footmen waiting with the carriages. Once she'd passed them and was farther up the street, she exhaled. She'd been stupid to walk through the throng of waiting servants. She'd been off the streets less than a year and already it seemed she'd lost some of her edge. There were men who wouldn't blink at taking advantage of an unescorted woman, especially someone as lowly as a governess.

Lowly governess she may be, but Emily could have been walking on the moon rather than the filthy London roads. A year ago she'd been caught in a pattern of abuse and poverty from which so few ever broke free. Now she was waltzing down the streets of Mayfair and stashing money in the stockings hidden in the carpetbag under her bed—more than she ever thought possible. She was eating three times a day. Her sheets were clean, she owned more than one dress, and she existed in an entirely different world now—one where hope and poetry still existed.

Even more, she was part of a team of women who worked together to keep the *ton* honest. She was going to make a difference. An honorable difference. She would never be able to atone for her past, but she could take pride in trying.

This life that she'd fibbed and forced her way into was worth everything, and she would do anything to protect it.

That was why her impulsive stunt at the ball was unacceptable. If she wanted a steady, unexciting life—and she truly did—then she needed to keep her head low. A reformed thief concealing a dark past was best left in the shadows.

She turned onto Norfolk Crescent and screamed in alarm when a dark figure leaning against a lamppost spoke to her.

"Took you long enough," the figure said, and stepped into the light. Emily startled with a thrill of both angst and anticipation when she saw it was the gentleman with the ash-blond hair and intense blue eyes that she'd taunted at the ball.

He towered over her, the shadows of night and flame throwing oddly shaped silhouettes across his face, and yet Emily wasn't afraid. It must have been that she never traveled without her trusty dagger. There was no other explanation for the bizarre sense of safety that enveloped her in his presence.

He smelled deliciously of nothing but clean soap—no cloying cologne. His scent was almost intoxicating, and Emily had to stop herself from leaning in and giving him a good hard sniff.

"You followed me," she accused. Better to be on the offensive, especially since someone of his status could ruin her life with a snap of his fingers.

"How is that possible, if I was here before you?" he asked. His voice was deep and smoothed up her spine like a sensuous touch. "Rather, it appears that *you* must have followed *me*."

Emily scowled at his reasoning. "What do you want with me?"

"Your name."

"You left that glamorous ball and followed me into the streets for my name? Why?"

"I thought we had established that you followed me? And yes, I left that stuffy, boring ball to discover the name of the woman who dared blow me a kiss."

Ah, pickled pig's feet. She was in for it now.

"You must be mistaken. I would never be so forward. Perhaps you saw me starting to say the word—" She grappled for a moment. "—noodles."

His mouth quirked, revealing clean, even teeth. "You were saying the word *noodles*?"

Emily crossed her arms beneath her breasts and lifted her chin. "That is correct. Noodles. It is a German pasta."

"I know what it is. Pray, tell me in what context you used the word when I saw no companion with you?"

"Well, see, I was saying it to myself."

"You were talking to yourself."

"Right." Emily took a moment to reflect that if there were an earthquake at that very moment, she'd be relieved to sink into the ground. "I say noodles as an oath." She edged away from him and pretended to stub her toe on a rock. "Oh, noodles!" she exclaimed.

He burst into laughter.

Emily hadn't thought it was possible to feel any more foolish, but apparently she was outdoing herself that night. "Your merriment over my pain is quite indecent, sir."

"My deepest apologies." He sketched a mocking bow, and Emily's heart thundered at the vision of someone like him bowing to someone like her, even if it was in jest.

Suddenly the mockery disappeared, and the look he gave her was so intense that she took a half step back before she stopped herself and held her ground.

"In your haste to exit the building after your oath," he said, closing some of the distance between them, "it seems you made the mistake of walking through the dozens of men waiting with the carriages, many of whom have been drinking."

She swallowed. She knew it had been stupid, but it rankled to have him point it out. "I thought you weren't following me?"

"I looked behind. I would suggest you take care the next time you think to shortcut through a crowd of drunks, or an alley, or a waterfront slum. There are men who lack scruples, especially when it comes to a beautiful woman."

She'd been about to tell him it wasn't any of his business where she went, when his last words sank in. Her lips parted in surprise, and she almost missed him advancing another few inches. Was he calling her beautiful? Her, Emily, a governess in a gown that would have pleased the nuns?

"Now, you have very neatly avoided telling me your name thus far."

He was close, so close she could have stretched out her hand to touch him. Emily lifted her chin to meet those cobalt eyes, and for the first time in her life found herself speechless.

"Do not make me beg," he said softly.

Her name tumbled from her lips before she could stop herself. "Miss Emily Leverton."

"Emily." He lifted his hand as if to touch one of the curls that lay on her neck but stopped himself, his fingertips hovering over her bare skin for a moment before dropping.

Emily was disproportionately affected by the almost-touch, her skin tingling as if he'd actually brushed his fingers over her sensitive throat, her lungs filling with sharper bursts of air than usual. She swallowed and tried to regain focus. *Be on the offensive,* she reminded herself. She'd learned early on that it was better to attack than to wait and defend.

At the liberty he'd taken with the use of her given name, Emily forced her chin forward and demanded, "And you are?" It was impertinent for a governess to ask the name of a gentleman. In fact the entire exchange was beyond inappropriate for her station. Then again, *he'd* started it.

A trio of drunks staggered past, their off-key song stinging the air. Emily barely noticed. She saw only the man in front of her, felt only the heat of his body and the hair-prickling nearness of unmistakable power.

"Mr. Zachariah Denholm. Zach, to my friends and cheeky governesses."

Cheeky! The nerve. Why she ought to—well, she had been a *bit* cheeky in the ballroom. "No title, Mr. Denholm?"

"None. I am a common man."

She nodded. "Oh, of course you are. Lady Exeter often invites commoners to attend her private balls."

"It is the truth. I am a bobby."

She studied him, trying to discern his motive in toying with her. He gazed steadily back without so much as a twitch of amusement on his face. Certainly he wasn't serious. Was he?

She sincerely hoped not.

"Where are you employed, Emily?"

The mention of employment shredded the intimate, two-person world he'd woven around them. It was late and she still had two of the children's historical reports to look over. At this rate she'd be awake into the early-morning hours, and the Eastmoreland household—at least the servant and governess part of it—started early.

Emily took several steps back, inserting distance between them. "I have to leave. Do not follow me again."

He slid his hands into his pockets. "I did not follow you the first time. Do not be a stranger, Emily. Stop by the Metropolitan Police station sometime and say hello."

"It is Miss Leverton, and I most certainly will not!" Imagine voluntarily visiting a police station!

At his impudent grin, she spun on her heel and walked away with her chin held high.

Chapter 6

Emily was awake until one o'clock in the morning marking the children's reports, and even after she blew out her candle and laid her head on her pillow she had trouble falling asleep. She replayed her encounter with Mr. Denholm—Zach—over and over again. He'd been amusing and charming and she could never, *ever* see him again. Nothing lay for her in that direction. Despite his claims of being a bobby, the quality of his clothing and his mingling with high society said otherwise. A man like that could only want one thing, and it wasn't marriage to a thief masquerading as a governess.

Besides, Emily had already been married and she'd found it extraordinarily lacking. She was quite content on her own, thank you very much.

Resolute, she promptly fell asleep.

Emily typically ate her breakfast alone after washing and dressing for the day. She expected her young charges to be in the schoolroom at 9:00 a.m. sharp, which gave her a leisurely hour to breakfast and stroll through the Eastmoreland courtyard in solitude.

Emily walked briskly down the servants' hall and was largely ignored by the maids, who didn't consider her one of them. Outdoors, she let her shawl fall to her elbows and enjoyed the warm touch of sun on her face and neck.

Lord, she missed it. She craved the fresh air and the sweet grass she'd come to know as a child traveling between small country villages. Emily, her mother, and her younger sister hadn't moved to London until Emily was twelve. By then, their laundress mother had stolen enough garments from the local women to be forced to seek employment in the city. Emily had longed for the country ever since.

Emily's daily walks in the Eastmoreland courtyard, a small paradise of greenery and blooms in the midst of the city, were her salvation. The space had been converted into an artistic tumble of plant life that made use of every square foot. A crushed-seashell pathway looped through the vegetation until it reached a marble statue of an angel. There, four scallop-carved marble benches faced each of the four directions.

That was where Emily was headed when she heard raised voices through a first-floor window the maids had left open. Her first inclination was to withdraw and give the unidentified parties privacy, but she hesitated. Eavesdropping was technically part of her job description.

Whether or not she shared the information with the Dove was a different story. She wasn't blindly following orders. Not anymore.

Emily flattened herself to the brick wall and glanced in both directions. No one else was in the courtyard. The window was less than a foot to her left, and she made some mental calculations of the layout of Eastmoreland House. It must belong to the informal ladies' drawing room. The voices were clear, although no longer raised. The speakers had to be very near the window.

"How dare you allow her here?" a woman hissed.

Emily strained to recognize the speaker. Could that be Lady Eastmoreland? She'd never heard the countess speak with anything but stiff politeness.

"I know you have a soft spot for trollops, but you have overstepped this time."

Emily expected Lord Eastmoreland to speak in his defense, so she was stunned when instead she heard the wavering voice of the elderly dowager countess. What the peonies was happening here?

"You will not speak to me in this manner, Clara."

"*I* am the mistress of this manor now and I will speak to you however I please. I will not have her kind darkening my doors again. Do I make myself clear?"

"Robert—"

"No." The word was scalpel-sharp. "Robert will not be told of this. He carries enough on his shoulders without having to deal with his mother's sordid extraneous activities."

"A woman with your title and wealth has a philanthropic duty to those less fortunate. Have you no compassion?" The elderly woman's voice shook with repressed emotion. Whoever the "trollop" was, she obviously meant a great deal to the dowager countess.

"You are here, are you not?"

Ouch. That was cold, Emily thought.

There came the rustling of taffeta skirts from within the room;

a bird trilled in the garden. Suddenly a pair of slender hands popped outside the window. Emily swallowed a gasp and pressed herself farther into the brick, her rib cage expanding with panicked breaths.

The hands paused, then clasped the wrought-iron inserts of the windows and swung them shut with a slam.

Emily's pulse gradually slowed. She forced herself to wait three minutes to give the countess and dowager time to disperse, and then she dashed back into the servants' hallway, up the stairs, and to her room. While the conversation was fresh in her memory she jotted it word for word onto a slip of paper, cursing each time the pen blotted in her haste.

When the Dove had placed Emily in Eastmoreland House, she'd assured her it was a safe, routine situation. Even so, the other woman had stressed that should Emily see or hear *anything* about prostitutes, she was to report it straightaway. The Dove hadn't needed to tell Emily her interest in prostitutes sprang from the Evangelist murders. The protocol was to send a note to Perdita's asking, *Would you care to visit at teatime?* The Dove would reply with further instructions.

Never in a hundred years did Emily think she'd actually be using the protocol, and only two weeks into her situation!

Emily paused halfway through folding the note. Was she overreacting? She scanned the transcript. At no point did either the countess or the dowager actually mention the word *prostitute*, only *trollop*. Their conversation hadn't made much sense to Emily. Would it make sense to the Dove?

She hesitated, her duty to the Dove warring with her determination not to repeat the mistakes of the past. After a moment she made the decision to send the note. She would wait on the Dove's response and then reassess the situation and her role in it.

Emily nearly shrieked when she noted the time and hurried downstairs to find an errand boy to deliver her message. Then she raced back to the schoolroom just in time to catch George pulling on Jonathan's ear. Sighing, she pasted on her most serious schoolmarm expression and marched into the room.

Chapter 7

Zach's day was rubbish.

He'd slept poorly the night before, his dreams plagued with images of the cheeky governess—Emily. He'd chase her out of the ballroom, and when he'd catch up to her he would discover she'd morphed into a horde of desperate mothers bearing down on him, waving letters of their daughters' accomplishments.

He'd woken in a sweat, cursing the sense of responsibility that had compelled him to return to the ball after his run-in with Emily and thank his hostess, Lady Exeter. He'd meant to pop in, kiss Lady Exeter's hand, and pop back out. His plans had been foiled almost immediately when he'd had to fend off one simpering debutant after another. It seemed the tides were turning and society was finally coming around to the idea that although they considered him inferior, his money spent as well as theirs.

Either that, or Wright had been correct when he'd claimed the article labeling Zach unmarriageable would only make him more enticing.

Zach wasn't interested in acquiring a noble-blooded wife, especially not one whose accomplishments included yessirring him to death. In fact, Zach had never been interested in wedging his way into the *ton*'s esteem. He didn't give a damn what they thought of him, and it was rather convenient *not* to be invited to social events. If he were to ever settle down, it would be with a woman who stirred his blood.

A woman who made him laugh.

An image of Emily cursing *Oh, noodles!* flashed in his mind just as Adam shouted, "Look out!"

Zach dodged the ham-sized fist and with the flat of his hand struck his attacker in the throat. The man stumbled backward, clutching his seizing windpipe.

"This has been a delight," Zach said, bending on one knee beside the man, "but I am rather busy. Let me save us both time and make myself plain: Take care of your girls or you will have more than a crushed windpipe to contend with. Your job is to protect them, not only leech off them. There is a psychopath killing prostitutes. Do not let the next corpse be another one of yours. Do you understand?"

The pimp wheezed and glared, but nodded his head.

Unsatisfied, Zach let the violence in his soul surface to his eyes, and his gaze bore into the other man's. The pimp shrank back. "Spread the word. You tell every rat you know that Zachariah Denholm is coming for the Evangelist."

He stood and without a backward glance strode out of the alley with Adam at his side. Adam was one of three men he had chosen for his task team. He figured the fewer people hunting the Evangelist, the more likely they were to actually catch the monster. Men in uniform tended to find a way to let their egos gunk up the works, and Zach didn't have time for pissing contests. The

Evangelist had struck his second victim fifteen days after the first, the third victim twelve days later. If the pattern continued, they could expect to find another dead prostitute the next morning.

They hadn't even begun yet and they were already running out of time.

"Remind me not to get on your bad side," Adam muttered.

"Are you good with patterns?"

"Yes."

"I'm sending you back to the office. Find a street map and go through the three murder files with a fine-toothed comb. I want you to mark the locations of where the bodies were found, along with where the girls should have been working. Catalog the times they were last seen and compare that with when the bodies were found."

Adam nearly vibrated with excitement. "You think the killer has a method, don't you?"

"You will have to tell me."

Adam circumvented a pile of horse dung. "All three pimps of the murdered prostitutes claim not to have seen anything."

Zach and Adam had run into the same walls with each pimp. First the men had resisted talking to them. Then, once Zach had convinced them it would be in their best interest to cooperate, they'd been sullen and insistent that they didn't know "nothing." They'd been worse than useless, but Zach had to start somewhere, and his colleagues who'd initially "investigated" the murders had declined to get their hands dirty by talking to any of the pimps and prostitutes actually involved.

"They do not speak for their girls. We will need to interview them. All of them."

"Mark and Sidney won't like that."

"Tough." Zach surveyed the waterfront street as they walked, his keen senses taking in the positions and movements of the individuals around them. Filth clung to the residents as surely as to the roads. Slimy fish, human waste, horse dung, coal smoke, and rot all mingled into a pungent odor that marked the slums as damnably as perfume marked the wealthy.

Children clothed in rags, most barefoot, sidled along the buildings, watching the two men pass with hungry eyes. They'd observed Zach work over the past several hours and kept their distance—there were some men they knew better than to pickpocket.

It was early afternoon, but already the pubs were crowded and street whores advertised their wares on corners. Most of the women were diseased, with missing teeth and thick coats of makeup.

It was getting worse, Zach thought. With the advent of industrialism, the rise of factories, and the influx of workers into the city, the slums were growing denser by the day. Children worked long hours instead of playing or learning, widows sold their bodies to buy bread, and men died of disease and accidents long before their time. Despite all their efforts, they still starved and froze and lived in filth.

Zach donated to several church-run charitable organizations that worked in the worst parts of the city, but as he and Adam left the wharf behind, he realized he was going to have to do more.

The peers' political sway and seat in Parliament was the one thing he envied about nobility. The laws needed serious amendment, especially when it came to child labor, and he was certain most of the men pompously filling their seats in the capitol didn't know the first thing about life for the working class.

"You are making a target of yourself," Adam said. He adjusted his spectacles and made an odd throat-clearing sound. Adam was a tall, gangly man with a nasally voice that bordered on annoying.

"How so?"

"That message, about coming after the Evangelist."

"I *wish*. It would make things much easier if the Evangelist showed up on my doorstep."

"Not just him. Those pimps hate you."

"I do not care if they hate me so long as they fear me. Fear is currency here."

"How do you know so much about the slums?"

Zach thought about what to tell the other man. Information was power, and he preferred people didn't have that power over him. Yet his poor beginnings and investments in the railroad were somewhat common knowledge. No one knew the details, but that didn't stop them from gossiping in clubs and drawing rooms across London.

"I was born in Whitechapel," Zach said. "My father rented a butcher shop and spent every penny he had paying the landlord for the privilege of eventually owning the garbage heap, only to discover it wasn't built to last longer than it had to."

Adam fiddled with his glasses again. "But I heard you sold it for a lot of money?"

"I sold it for five pounds."

The other man gaped at him. "Five pounds? How did you get so rich?"

It was an inappropriate question, but Adam lacked common social skills. Zach questioned how much was due to Adam's innate awkwardness and how much the man put on.

"Gambling," Zach replied succinctly. "I added it to my officer's salary and over the course of three months made enough to invest in the railroad when everyone else was scoffing at the idea. From there it was simply a question of how to best diversify my investments."

Adam shook his head. "Bloody brilliant. So what's the plan, boss? If your timeline is correct, the Evangelist will take his next victim within twenty-four hours."

At the reminder, fingers of rage tapped at the backs of Zach's eyeballs. "You will head to the station to put together the information I asked for. I'm going home for a few hours of rest. Tonight, I will be in Bethnal Green."

"We don't know where to look for him."

"No, but I will be there regardless."

Chapter 8

When the children took their midday dinner in the nursery, Emily wandered into the kitchen to forage her own repast. While arranging a hunk of bread and a bowl of soup on a tray, she listened intently to the kitchen maids' gossip. If the dowager countess had had a "trollop" in the house that morning, the servants would know about it. And they would certainly be talking about it.

She lingered longer than usual and her patience was rewarded when Lucy, one of the more flirtatious housemaids, entered with swinging hips and a wink for the newest footman.

The cook arranged a plate of sliced roasted chicken on a platter and shoved it toward Lucy. "You'd best hurry. The dowager asked for this nigh two hours ago except the chicken hadn't been slaughtered."

Lucy scowled and ignored the tray. "Why does she get to sit up there like a queen while I work myself to the bone down here? She isn't any less common than we are. Just look at what happened this morning!"

There were gasps of shock from the other servants. Cook, a rotund woman with soft gray hair and squinty eyes, swiped at Lucy with a wooden spoon. Lucy dodged it in time to avoid red sauce splattering on her white apron.

"How dare you speak about your betters that way?" Cook demanded. "You ought to be released from your position for such talk."

Lucy sniffed and fingered a curl she'd purposely let dangle from her pins. "It's true, though. Everyone is thinking it, only I have the nerve to say it. You saw that tart standing at the kitchen door just as I did, demanding to see the dowager countess."

Feigning ignorance, Emily turned to a housemaid pouring tea beside her and whispered, "What is she talking about?"

The housemaid was young and plain, but kinder than any of the other servants had been to Emily. "You haven't heard?" Her eyes rounded with surprise. "You really are out of the loop, aren't you?"

"No one speaks to me except the children," Emily admitted.

The maid finished pouring the tea, and with some relish at being the first to spread the news said, "This morning a woman showed up at the kitchen door. She was a...a *woman of ill repute*. You could tell with one look. She wore a torn satin gown that went out of fashion a decade ago and it had a big black streak down the front. Her bosoms were nearly falling out, I tell you. She had caked on rouge and was wearing lipstick as bright as an apple skin. At eight in the morning if you can believe such a thing! It was entirely scandalous.

"She walked right up the steps and knocked on the door and said the Countess of Eastmoreland sent for her. Cook told her to scurry off and not darken the door of a respectable house again, but she refused to budge, and when the butler tried to have his footmen remove her, she screamed!"

This time Emily's eyes bugged out. "She didn't!"

"She did! Well, the head housekeeper was at her wit's end and about to call the police when Lady Eastmoreland, who'd heard of the commotion, came down to investigate. The wench looks at her and says, 'Naw, it ain't you I's here for. She be an old lady wit' gray hair who asked fer me.' No curtsy, no proper address! Emily, I've never seen anything like it in all my days."

"What happened next?"

"Lady Eastmoreland was as cold as ice, she was. She asked Cook to give the girl a loaf of bread and then told the wench in no uncertain terms that she was not welcome to return or she'd call the police. The bread was more'n the trollop deserved in my opinion. How dare she show up at such a fine residence and act so coarsely? A shame it was."

Emily's heart lurched at the description of the woman being given a loaf of bread and then sent away. She had experienced the rage entwined with gratitude for another human's scraps, and she'd burned with the humiliation at being treated like filth.

She'd been frustrated at being turned away from a door she'd been told to visit.

Emily shoved the memories aside. "Did she leave then?"

The maid nodded vigorously and lifted the silver tea tray inlaid with a tiny rosebud pattern. "You likely haven't had a chance to see Lady in one of her moods, and pray you never do. When she gets icy like that, there's no man or woman who can stand her down. The wench had no choice but to turn tail and beat it. Lucy swears the air frosted when Lady Eastmoreland spoke to the tart, but of course that's disrespectful nonsense."

Yet she'd repeated it, Emily thought, which meant she'd found the comment apt.

Emily *had* heard Lady Eastmoreland's cutting temper, and the maid was right: She'd never want that ire directed at her.

She was about to leave the kitchen with her own tray when the errand boy she'd dispatched to deliver her message that morning rapped at the back door and handed her a response. She passed him a coin from her pocket and clutched the missive in her hand.

"Well, aren't we important, getting messages hand-delivered when we should be educating young minds," Cook snipped.

Emily ignored her and hurried out of the room. When she was alone in the corridor, she broke the fancy wax seal and quickly scanned the Dove's response:

Tonight 9:00 p.m. Kensington Gardens, Hyde Park.

Emily crammed the note in her pocket, her heart beating faster with anticipation. Her hunger forgotten, she returned to the schoolroom to prepare for her watercolor lessons with the girls, her mind already at Hyde Park.

Chapter 9

Emily palmed her dagger as she hurried along the darkened streets. Her meet with the Dove had been uneventful. The woman had already been waiting when Emily had arrived at the gardens half an hour early. *Never be the last to a meet.* That was a simple street rule. How had the Dove known to do the same?

The Dove had been cloaked in midnight black to fit the occasion, her hood concealing her honey-brown hair and the half veil covering the upper part of her face. Emily might have worried for the woman's safety—she doubted a lady of the *ton* could handle a thug the way she could—except the hairs on the back of her neck had lifted when she'd reached the Dove. Humans, Emily had come to learn, could scent danger as well as an animal. One would have to be a fool to tangle with this woman.

Or to trust her.

Emily had passed her what she'd written down after Lady Eastmoreland and the dowager's exchange that morning. She'd then relayed the kitchen gossip she'd heard that afternoon, carefully watching the Dove's mouth as she did so. The man who'd betrayed Emily six years ago had been able to turn his emotions on and off at the drop of a hat: easy charm one moment, blank-faced rage the next. Emily no longer trusted any person who could manipulate his feelings so easily.

The Dove had bit her lip as she'd contemplated what she'd heard, then she'd instructed Emily to keep a strict eye on the situation and contact her immediately should any other information come to light.

"Surely it does not have anything to do with the murders," Emily had said.

The Dove had agreed. "It is doubtful. However, the fact that a prostitute was involved means it is worth watching. You never know what snippet of news will make the difference in a case."

Emily had nodded and risen to go when the Dove's gloved hand had settled on her wrist.

"You may not trust me, Emily, and that is understandable," the woman had said, her voice as serene as the unruffled leaves on the hedge, "but do not let your past grievances blind you to the future. Lives of women are at stake. Withholding information could mean the difference between life and death for someone."

Emily tugged her wrist away, her heart beating so fast she thought it might fly out of her breast. *No. She could not be responsible for another's life again.*

Although the Dove could not know what demons haunted Emily, the line of her mouth had been sympathetic. "You must make a choice, Emily. You do not have to fully trust me, but you must trust me enough to do your job."

Emily hadn't withheld information *this* time, but once again the Dove's insight was unnerving. "I will consider it," Emily had said abruptly.

"You do that."

Emily had felt the Dove's eyes on her back as she'd walked away.

It was nearing ten o'clock and the moon was cutting a persistent swath of light through the ever-present blanket of smog. The streetlamps were lit, pushing back the darkness in dancing radiuses. Perhaps it was the feeling of foreboding she'd had since leaving the Dove, or mayhap it was the shadows that had Emily taking a second look at the figure hurrying out of Eastmoreland House.

Emily squinted. The slight figure was wrapped in a dark cloak, and the way the person moved was familiar. When the figure reached the carriage bearing the Eastmoreland crest, Emily's fear was confirmed.

She sprinted forward and grabbed the girl's arm just as she began to ascend the steps to the carriage. The girl cried out, and her hood fell back as she swung around. When she saw Emily, she gasped in dismay.

"Lady Minnie!" Emily exclaimed. "Where do you think you are going?"

The eldest Eastmoreland child appeared petrified for a moment before lifting her chin and stating regally, "That is none of your business, Miss Leverton."

"In fact, it is, as I am responsible for the virtue of your younger sisters. Maidens do not sneak off in the middle of the night unescorted. Now tell me what you are doing dressed like a commoner! Where did you even get those clothes?"

Minnie considered for a moment and then said, "I am meeting my friend, Miss Priscilla Winegartener."

"And pray, tell me where you and Miss Winegartener think you are going?"

"Slumming."

"Slumming!" Minnie could have blown her over with a sneeze. "What does that mean?"

"Oh, Miss Leverton, everyone is doing it. It is all the rage. Nobility dress in commoner clothes and head to the slums for the night."

The upper classes did the oddest things! Most people were trying to climb out of the slums, and here they were riding into them. "Why would you ever want to do that?"

"I do not know. It is interesting, I suppose. You are supposed to see things you would never see in proper society. Ladies of the night, drunks, gambling, saloons, pistol fights, everything!"

"And you planned on secretly 'slumming' in your father's carriage with the Eastmoreland crest on it?"

Minnie flushed. "I had not thought of that."

Emily put on her sternest voice. "Lady Minnie, step out of that carriage. I forbid you from going."

"I am sorry Miss Leverton, but you cannot stop me."

"I can. I will wake up Lady Eastmoreland this very minute if I must."

Minnie gave a bitter laugh. "Good luck. She took her sleeping potion hours ago and she is dead to the world for the night. Father left for his club half an hour ago. Unless you plan on having the butler forcibly carry me indoors, I am going."

Emily studied the girl's determined face. She knew rebellion was part of the adolescent experience, but she wished Minnie's rebellion could have been along the lines of refusing to learn French, or kissing a stable boy. This was more than foolhardy; it was outright dangerous. A young, naive, obviously genteel girl among drunks and gangs was a recipe for disaster.

Yet how could she stop her? Minnie was right. Short of politely asking the young lady to wait, running inside and waking the butler, then having him drag the girl out of the carriage, there was nothing she could do.

Except go with her.

Emily groaned. The last thing she wanted was to play sitter to a spoiled heiress on the hunt for illicit entertainment, but there was no way she could watch Minnie drive off and ever have a clear conscience again. The girl would be eaten alive within minutes of her arrival in the slum.

"Fine," Emily said. "I'm going with you."

"By no means—"

"Either I go with you, Lady Minnie, or I really do wake every blasted servant in the house *and* your mother. They will catch up with you before you are three streets over."

Minnie pouted for a moment, her plush lower lip poking out like a toddler's, and acquiesced.

"We are not taking the carriage with the earl's crest. Step away."

Minnie huffed but obliged. She was, somewhat expectedly, very small, with a delicate bone structure and almost fragile slenderness. Where Emily's hair was luxuriously thick and curly, Minnie's was so fine and blond that pins slipped right out of it. Her hazel eyes were red-rimmed from constant allergies, as was the tip of her nose. Despite Minnie's weak constitution, Emily had discovered the girl was headstrong, often in subversive and sneaky ways. Although no longer part of the schoolroom now that she had been presented to society, Minnie usually found her way to her younger siblings during the day, giving Emily ample opportunity to observe her.

"Come, we will walk a few streets over and catch a hansom cab," Emily ordered. She was grateful she'd brought her dagger to the meeting with the Dove, but she wasn't otherwise dressed to venture into the slums. As a general rule she wore bland, neck-to-wrist gowns, but she'd inexplicably chosen to wear her favorite day gown to her assignation with the Dove. Something about the pale-green and rose-studded dress had called to her, and she'd bought it with her saved wages without hesitation.

Now, she reflected sourly, the cleanliness of the two women's clothes and Emily's pop of pastel among the more serviceable colors of the lower class would draw unwanted attention. Worse, what Minnie didn't understand was that she could dress in rags and she would *still* stand out as nobility simply because of the way she conducted herself. It had been bred into her, and no coarse dress would change that.

"I am sure I do not have to remind you that not only is this in poor taste, but if you are caught your reputation and the reputations of your sisters will suffer severely," Emily warned.

"Then please do not."

Emily bit back a sigh and wondered what she had thought would be so bloody wonderful about being a governess.

Directly on the heels of that thought was the memory of her former husband, Lionel the Pig, throwing her only flower vase at her head.

Emily lifted her chin. Slumming it was.

They caught a hansom cab on Grosvenor Street, and when they climbed in Minnie's cheeks flamed red with excitement. This was probably the girl's first ride in anything other than the plush family carriage.

They picked Priscilla up on Weighthouse Street, where she was loitering nervously on the corner dressed in a simple brown gown and cloak. She'd managed to pull off the "commoner" look better than Minnie, who had silver buttons sewn onto her dress. Minnie probably hadn't even realized that wasn't normal, Emily thought with resignation.

Priscilla was a plump girl with iron-red hair and a jolly temperament. She was surprised to see Emily, and Minnie quickly explained that Emily had invited herself along and she hadn't had a choice in the matter. Priscilla took it in stride, and the girls giggled and shrieked with excitement as they gave the driver instructions to take them to Bethnal Green.

Chapter 10

The hansom cab dropped the women off outside Red's Tavern, a stone's throw from the largest weaving factory in Bethnal Green. The street was crowded with bodies, horses, and carriages; the scents of stale ale, horse manure, and garbage mingled in the air. The chatter of voices, shouts of drunks, clatter of horse hooves, and whistles overwhelmed Emily the moment she stepped down from the cab.

"Yer sure this is where ye want to be?" the driver asked, eyeing two men trading blows beneath the flicker of a streetlamp.

"No," Emily replied, "but this is where *they* want to be." She handed him one of her precious coins and said, "There is more of that if you stay here and wait for us."

He shrugged and lit a pipe. Emily took that as a yes.

Emily was afraid the girls might want to go inside the tavern, but apparently they weren't *that* foolhardy. Instead they clutched each other's arms and navigated the crowded street, taking in the sights with eyes as wide as saucers.

A child wearing half trousers ran up behind Minnie and

bumped into her. He murmured an apology and was about to take off when Emily, who was trailing behind, snatched his arm.

"Sorry," she said. "I cannot let you do that."

His face was sullen when she pried open his fingers and removed Minnie's purse. Fishing out a coin, she handed it to him and then tucked the purse into her own bodice. The boy didn't bother thanking her; the coin disappeared quicker than free ale at the pub and he ran off.

Minnie, unaware of the exchange, continued giggling on Priscilla's forearm.

A whore called out from a doorway ahead, and a drunken man who couldn't have been older than twenty peeled off from his friends and headed toward the woman. The girls gasped in horror and Emily tried not to judge them. It wasn't their fault. They'd been kept innocent and insulated because delicate upper-class women couldn't be trusted with such things as knowledge of sex and how the rest of the world operated.

In that moment Emily's attitude about slum tourism changed. Suddenly she was glad the girls had broken out of their neatly hemmed constraints. It would do them good to see that for most of London, life was hard work, disease, and starvation rather than sleeping until noon and planning dinner parties.

Emily was so busy keeping an eye on every person that came near the girls that she forgot to watch where they were going. Suddenly the girls halted and shrieked in fright. Emily, who'd been looking over her shoulder at a balding man who appeared far too interested in their trio, jerked her head around to see what had startled them this time.

The girls had unwittingly turned into an alley littered with garbage and human feces. Before them stood two ruffians, dirty and leering. Behind them, the bald man Emily had been eyeing closed in.

◦❦◦

Standing across the street from Red's, Zach wasn't sure he could trust his eyes. Was that Emily, the governess, climbing out of a hansom cab? Impossible. A woman of her good standing in a position with an esteemed family would not be traversing the streets of Bethnal Green at eleven at night.

Yet there was no mistaking that slender form, the curvy hips, those dark eyes and unruly curls. It was Emily all right. But what in the blazes was she doing there?

The moment he spotted the two young girls with her, he understood. The girls were so clearly gentry they might as well have worn signs around their necks. One good guess was the girls wanted to explore the seedier side of London, and somehow the governess had been roped into chaperoning.

Foolish, he thought grimly as he crossed the street to follow them. They were like a trio of sheep wandering into a wolf's den. The governess was no more protection for the girls than a lamb was protection for another lamb, no matter how plucky she might be.

A young boy bumped into one of Emily's charges, and Zach thought it served the girls right to lose their purses. This wasn't a game.

When Emily caught the boy's hand with a catlike reflex and extracted the purse, Zach's eyes widened in surprise and then narrowed. Well, well. As far as he knew, they didn't teach pickpocket-deflecting skills at governess school. In fact, most governesses were as sheltered as the children they taught. There was definitely something different about Miss Leverton.

Zach's curiosity about Emily only expanded as he observed her eyes dart back and forth, cataloging every possible threat. She even noticed the thickly muscled thug who was looking her up and down as if she were mutton stew and it was suppertime.

In fact, Emily was so busy surveying the threats she didn't notice when her charges were skillfully edged down an alleyway and the thug followed behind.

Zach sped up, dodging a lonely shift worker and brushing past a prostitute who reached for his arm. He ran pell-mell into the alley and his heart thumped painfully when he caught sight of the two additional men waiting there, eyes gleaming and hands on the buttons of their trousers.

Zach assessed the situation with the rapid accuracy he'd honed in the military. The alleyway was a dead end, the stench overwhelming. By the looks of them, the two men waiting in the alley weren't experienced bruisers, but opportunists. The bald thug was the one who concerned Zach. He was the ringleader, the one who'd organized the trap, and this obviously wasn't his first time doing it. A nasty scar ran through the man's top lip, nearly separating it in two. He'd been in his share of knife fights.

"We'll take yer purses," one of the two men said to the girls.

His partner leered and added, "Then lift yer skirts. If yer real quiet-like, we won't make it hurt. Too bad."

The girls began to sob and wail, their screeching so high-pitched that everyone, including Emily, flinched.

"Shut it, or we'll shut yer mouths for ye."

The girls' cries continued, albeit somewhat quieter.

Zach moved soundlessly behind the bruiser, who still hadn't sensed his presence. He was strategizing how to take down the man without creating a hostage situation when Emily spoke. Her voice was clear and surprisingly calm.

"I will give you one chance to rethink, gentlemen," she said, boldly meeting the eyes of both men. "You obviously do not know who you are dealing with. If you want to exit this alley *intact*, I suggest you stand down and let us leave at once."

The men were stunned into silence for a moment and then guffawed and elbowed each other.

"She's got spirit, eh? I'll take that one. Ye kin take the scrawny one."

His companion scowled. "I don't want the scrawny one. I want the fat one."

"Which one do I bloody care ye take?"

As the two bickered, Emily slipped around her charges, placing her body between them and the men. Zach's throat tightened. The men were too busy quarreling to notice.

The bald ringleader was leaning with one shoulder against the brick wall, watching his companions with a bored expression. Zach pulled his pocket watch from his coat and held the chain taut between both hands. The two inexperienced thieves were arguing so loudly they didn't hear the bark of surprise from the ringleader, or the gurgling noise that bubbled from his throat when Zach quickly and efficiently choked him into unconsciousness.

"The hell wit' it," one of the men finally snarled. "I'm takin' the gurl before we's get caught."

One grubby hand reached for Emily. Zach ran forward, opening his mouth to shout that he was the police, when Emily deftly knocked aside the man's hand. Before the man could react, Emily's fist shot out and connected with his nose. Ten feet away Zach heard bone crunch and he instinctively flinched.

Blood spurted like a geyser from the man's face. Emily shoved the now disabled criminal against the wall and something sharp flashed in the moonlight. A dagger. She brought it to within an inch of the injured man's groin.

"You chose the wrong women," she said coolly. Then without removing her eyes from her quarry she snarled to the second thief, "Unless you want your partner to lose a piece of his anatomy, you'll back off. And tell the third guy creeping behind us to get lost as well."

"Get back!" the bleeding man howled. "The bitch is crazy!"

"Girls," Emily said, "I want you to run. Head straight back to the tavern. The hansom cab we arrived in is waiting. You tell him to take you home and you do not stop until you are at your front door."

Her two trembling charges didn't bother to protest or ask what would happen to Emily. They simply tumbled over each other, lifted their skirts, and ran straight past Zach, screaming the entire way.

Zach figured they'd be all right for a minute while he helped Emily finish cleaning up the situation, although it was rapidly becoming apparent that she was more than capable of holding her own.

This extraordinary woman was not a typical governess, and Zach was determined to discover just who she really was.

"Yer going to be sorry for it now," the bleeding man cried as his partner lifted a broken piece of board and swung it over his shoulder.

Zach scooped a chunk of crumbled brick from the street and hurtled it at the man, hitting him squarely in the throat. The man dropped the board and clutched at his windpipe. Zach effortlessly closed the distance and plowed his fist into the thug's face. The would-be rapist dropped like a sack of flour.

Emily's startled eyes met his. "Zach?"

"If you don't mind?" He gestured to the dagger. Emily obligingly stepped back, and Zach took immense satisfaction in incapacitating the final thief.

Emily slid the dagger into her pocket. "What are you doing here?" Her eyes narrowed. "Did you follow me again?"

Chapter 11

Zach swallowed a shout of laughter. "In a manner of speaking. Are you all right?"

She nodded, and when he scanned her for injury, he was impressed to see her hands were steady.

"Care to tell me what you are doing in Bethnal Green?"

"No." She gave a little jerk as she remembered her charges. "The girls!"

"I think I can still hear them screaming," he said drily. "I am sure they are drawing enough attention to ensure their safety."

Emily closed her eyes. "What an awful day."

"You're telling me." He offered the crook of his elbow and Emily wearily accepted. Instinctively he tucked her close, liking the feel of her hand on his arm.

They walked out of the alley together, and indeed they could hear the echo of the girls' screams farther ahead.

Emily groaned. "I tried to stop them, but they wanted to go 'slumming.' I had no choice but to come along and try to protect them. I didn't do such a great job." She paused, and then said stiffly, "Thank you for your assistance. I suppose we are fortunate you stalked me."

This time Zach did laugh. "I didn't stalk you. I saw you climb out of the hansom cab at Red's and I followed to make sure you were safe."

"What are *you* doing here?" Emily asked. "Slumming as well?"

"Official police work."

She scanned him up and down. "No uniform?"

"I did not want to stand out."

"Right." She didn't look as if she believed him.

He remained serious, and slowly her expression transformed from one of irritation to one of—fear?

"You meant it when you said you were a bobby outside of the ball. You truly work for the Metropolitan Police?"

"Truly."

"But you...you..." She flushed, clearly not knowing a delicate way to state her confusion over his position in the world.

"But I have a fortune? Yes, that I do. I have wealth and connections in the *ton*. The issue is that I have always worked for a living, and after making my fortune I quickly discovered a life of idle leisure was not for me. I offered my skills to the police force, and they accepted."

She tilted her head and looked him up and down again, assessing what skills he might possess. "Military," she said at last. "That is why you were able to handle those brutes in the alley."

He lifted a brow. "Precisely. And what past experience gave you the skill to do the same?"

She deftly ignored his query by exclaiming, "Oh! Are you here because of the murders? Do you think the Evangelist is present this very moment?" She looked wildly about as if she'd be able to spot the killer wearing horns and a spiked tail.

He could have lied to her but he saw no reason to. With the Metropolitan Police as tight as a sieve, it was likely everyone already knew he was working the case. "Yes, that is why I am here."

"It's terrible, isn't it? Those poor women. Life is hard enough without some cussed rotter preying on them." She clapped a hand over her mouth and paled. "Ah, I mean, without some lout preying on them."

Zach rubbed his chin and squinted at her in the mock study of a detective. "She is as mouthy as a sailor, carries a dagger, hits like a pugilist, and catches pickpockets red-handed. Methinks she is not all she claims to be."

If possible, Emily paled further. Concerned, Zach swung her to the side of the street. She met his eyes defiantly, just as she had across the ballroom the day before. Zach found his admiration of her tripling. This woman, whoever she really was, had more courage than half the men he'd commanded.

"Why did that make you nervous, Emily?" he asked softly. He slid one hand down her arm to clasp her elbow.

"That is not a very ladylike list. I have a strict reputation to uphold as a governess in the employ of—" She caught herself and said, "Well, you needn't know where I am situated."

"Where did you have your training?"

"Perdita's."

Zach lifted a brow and gave a low whistle. The riddle that was Emily complicated. Perdita's was exclusive: the crème de la crème of governess agencies, and its graduates abided by rigid standards.

For Perdita's to accept a woman as offbeat as Emily, it meant she must come from a very wealthy family.

He took in her flushed cheeks, bright eyes, and the curls that tumbled in disarray down her neck from the altercation. She was beautiful, brave, and quirky. If she were from a wealthy family of good breeding, why wasn't she married? Governesses were respected but generally pitied. It was often the only position left to an unmarried woman from a good family that had fallen onto hard times.

"Stop that," Emily snapped. "Stop trying to figure me out. You do not see me prying into your life."

He lifted his other hand. "I am an open book. Ask away."

Emily fluttered her eyelashes. "Except I have no interest in you."

Zach grinned.

"You are supposed to be insulted, not amused."

"I am ornery like that." He released her elbow and shoved his hands into his trouser pockets. "Shall we catch up with your foolish little charges?"

Chapter 12

Emily hurried beside Zach, dual emotions warring in her chest. The first was worry about his curiosity over her past. She'd certainly acted vulgar enough to set off anyone's alarm bells, much less a policeman's. She didn't know much about Zachariah Denholm, but her intuition told her he was the type of man who, once presented with a puzzle, didn't stop until it was solved. The Dove had overlooked Emily's thievery as a youthful indiscretion, but she hadn't known about Emily's deepest, most shameful secret. If Zach were to uncover it, there was no telling what the policeman might do.

Simultaneously, Emily was as intensely curious about Zach as he was about her. He had admitted to his wealth, and yet he chose to work as a policeman and walked the streets of Bethnal Green as if he belonged. He'd struck down all three men with the ease and skill of a man who was used to fighting, and fighting as dirty as necessary. That both thrilled and scared her. She'd been raised among mean men lacking self-control, although

Zach hadn't been wild or red-faced like her former husband, the Pig. In fact, he'd been so cool and methodical he'd nearly been emotionless.

It surprised her that although she walked alongside a man capable of greater violence than the Pig, she wasn't afraid of him. She felt as safe traversing the streets of Bethnal Green by his side as she did strolling in Mayfair in broad daylight. Perhaps it was because of the way he'd touched her: a gentle stroke down her arm before tucking her hand into the crook of his elbow. So far he'd been entirely gentlemanly in his actions, even if his blue eyes flamed with something indefinable whenever she met his gaze. Something potent and intense.

Emily shivered.

"Cold?"

"No."

Zach gave her a sidelong glance but didn't press the issue.

"Where do you live?" she asked. They were nearing the tavern, and she was suddenly curious to know all she could before they parted.

"I thought you were not interested in me."

"A proper lady ought to send a thank-you card to her rescuer."

"Alas, I only did half the rescuing. Who taught you to defend yourself? An older brother? A father?"

Self-taught and perfected on my mother's johns.

Emily sidestepped the question for a second time. "Is it a mystery where you live, then?"

He smiled as if he recognized the evasion but was choosing to let it slide. "The old Stanford House on Park Lane."

Emily couldn't conceal her shock. Stanford House was one of

the most richly appointed mansions in the Mayfair area. How on earth could a policeman, even a wealthy one, afford such a residence when many of the peerage could not?

As if he could read her thoughts Zach said, "Remember, I have connections. And money."

It would be unforgivably rude to ask how he'd come into that money, so Emily clamped down on the impulse; she'd been unorthodox enough for one evening. Regardless of how he'd made his fortune, it must have been *huge*.

"And you, Emily? Since you won't share where you are employed, will you at least tell me from where you hail?"

Everywhere. Nowhere. "Monmouth," she lied. "You?"

"Whitechapel."

She halted and met his flat, intense gaze, as if he expected an outcry of disgust or a gasp of horror.

Well, he was going to be disappointed, because Emily wasn't a simpering debutant. She'd grown up in the worst kind of poverty, helping her adoptive father con people she'd thought were his friends. After he was sent to prison, she'd spent her nights running off her mother's more violent johns. If Zach knew the truth about her origins, *he* would be disgusted.

Still, from Whitechapel to Mayfair? That was an unprecedented leap. She burned to know how he'd done it, but her curiosity would have to go unabated. She must exhibit nothing but the utmost decorum for the remainder of the night.

"There are the girls ahead," she said, standing on her tiptoes to see over a man passing in front of her. "Goodness, they are hopping from one hansom cab to the other. They cannot remember which one they came in." She shook her head over their foolishness. Why didn't they just *pick* one? She turned back to

Zach. "Thank you again for your timely arrival and rescue, Mr. Denholm."

"Do not start calling me that now. We are already on a first-name basis, *Emily*."

"It is not proper, *Mr. Denholm*."

"Neither was blowing me a kiss across the ballroom."

"Noodles!" Emily exclaimed. "Not a kiss. Noodles."

He stepped so close she could feel the warmth of his large body and smell the clean, citrusy scent that she recognized from the night of the ball. He dipped his head and said softly in her ear, "Fibber."

Emily's heart stumbled. She'd been called a fibber before, but it had never sounded like *that*, as if it were a gentle tease rather than an accusation. She lifted her face and met his cobalt eyes, her rejoinder sticking in her throat when she noticed how soft and near his mouth was. She'd never kissed the Pig, not once, and she wondered how it would feel to kiss a man like Zachariah. If she brushed her lips across his, would he pull her to his chest? She sensed Zach would be a complicated dichotomy of both hard and soft, demanding and generous. A man who was capable of icily incapacitating three brutes one minute, and then gently holding a woman's elbow the next, was a man complex enough to intrigue her despite her better senses. Emily knew what it was like to grapple with multiple facets of herself, and for the first time she suspected she'd met a man hosting equal inner turmoil.

Her gaze remained on his mouth, and her cheeks flushed at the direction of her thoughts. Zach's eyes darkened as if he could read her mind.

"You can kiss me anytime you want, Emily," he said, his low

voice sending shivers up her spine. "Whether you want to blow me a kiss or open your sweet mouth for mine."

A proper governess would be shocked. Certainly Emily should slap him or call him a cad. She barely knew the man! To suggest she wanted to kiss him was, well, it was just plain rude to acknowledge how she'd been openly staring at his mouth.

Emily had already put her identity as a maiden governess in question, and it was imperative that she recover her role now. "How dare you!" she cried with enthusiasm. Perhaps too much enthusiasm. "I am going to...I am going to slap you!"

The corners of Zach's eyes crinkled.

Emily nodded decisively. Yes indeed, she would slap him the way any other woman in her position would. She lifted her hand. He didn't shift away and he didn't flinch, he simply gazed at her with those deep, insightful eyes. She pressed her hand to his cheek and marveled at the rasp of his day-old beard against her palm and the heat of his skin beneath her own.

"That wasn't a slap."

"It is hard to strike a man who is looking at me as you are. Be a gentleman and close your eyes."

He obliged, his eyelashes fanning over his cheeks, and Emily found herself in the most extraordinary position of cupping the man's cheek while he made himself vulnerable to her. She certainly couldn't hit him *now*.

"That won't work, either. Open your eyes again."

When he did, the desire that surfaced in them was so potent her knees went weak. He encircled her wrist, his callused fingertips brushing her pulse point. "I'll wait."

Emily's breath escaped her lungs as she continued to cradle his cheek, his fingers lightly wrapped around her wrist. Whether he was waiting for her to strike him or for her to kiss him, she did not know. All she could think about was how generous his mouth looked and how loudly her pulse beat in her ears. "I *cannot* kiss you anytime," she murmured, perhaps more to herself than him. "You must know an unmarried woman cannot kiss a bachelor in the street."

"Can an unmarried woman be the recipient of a kiss?"

Emily wetted her bottom lip with her tongue. "I suppose if she did not see it coming…" Before she'd finished speaking he dropped his head and brushed his mouth over hers, his lower lip gliding across her own.

Emily let out a small gasp and swayed closer. It was all the encouragement he needed. His mouth returned to rub over hers, coaxing and easy, until his tongue traced the seam of her lips and they parted of their own accord. Zach slipped his tongue inside, stroking and swirling, the kiss languid and exploratory.

Emily had never had a man taste her as if she were the finest champagne, or hold her as if she were the crystal champagne flute. One of his hands cupped her neck; the other released her wrist and framed her face as he shifted angles, deepening the kiss. Emily melted into him, allowing him to brace her when she never accepted support. Unexpected heat worked its way through her belly, as thick and warm as honey. The way his tongue moved in her mouth was scandalous, maybe even taboo. She'd thought only the French kissed that way.

It felt…decadent.

After a few moments she tentatively returned the kiss, touching her tongue to his, pleased when she heard a satisfied rumble in his throat. Clutching the front of his coat, she forgot where she was, the sounds of the slum fading into the background, the smells receding beneath his cleaner, spicier scent. Every rational thought was consumed by the stunning intimacy of sharing the same breath as him, tasting him, feeling his lips capture hers with slow, simmering demand. She couldn't breathe. She was drowning. No, she was melting. It was too hot. She needed to get out of this suffocating gown. She needed…

Zach lifted his head, his eyes inky blue as his thumb stroked over her bottom lip. "That was much better than a kiss blown across a ballroom."

Even though the spell was broken, it took Emily several moments to regain her composure enough to step back. She pressed her fingertips to her swollen lips, feeling both stupid for falling into temptation and greedy for more. Had she really just allowed this man to kiss her in public? She glanced around, expecting to find disapproving stares and disgust.

Not a single person was paying attention to them.

"This is not Mayfair, Emily. I would never have kissed you like that somewhere that could ruin your reputation. But you can still slap me if it would make you feel better. You didn't see it coming, after all."

"I am not going to slap you and you know it. I…" She lost her train of thought as the blood drained from her face. She was seeing things. She had to be.

But no, that was in fact Lady Eastmoreland blazing at full steam toward the girls, who were still screaming.

Chapter 13

I have to go."

Emily didn't even try to explain; she simply took off, sprinting to reach the girls before the countess did. It was immediately clear to her what had happened: Although Minnie had made a clean escape from her house, someone must have spotted Priscilla joining Minnie in the carriage and tattled. The countess had then been woken to collect her daughter.

Lady Eastmoreland's arrival wasn't only bad for Minnie: It also meant Emily was about to be dismissed from her position.

Emily reached the girls mere moments before the countess.

"Lady Minnie, please, your mother..." she started, but Minnie took one look at her, gave a final scream, and collapsed sobbing into her arms.

A razor-sharp voice cut through the tearful cries. "Miss Leverton, what is the meaning of this?" Lady Eastmoreland's pale-blond hair was pulled into a tight coil at the nape of her neck, her silver eyes diamond-hard. She'd obviously rushed from the house because she was dressed in a simple day gown—hardly something she would have normally worn at this hour of the night. She lacked any of her jeweled adornments, and in her simplicity was even more fearsome. Streamlined, cold, and chiseled, the countess was like an ice sculpture given breath.

Minnie was blubbering so hard she couldn't catch her breath long enough to speak. When Emily tried to talk, Priscilla drowned her out with an excited roar.

"We were slumming and these men tried to rob us and we got away and awwwww my wooorrrrd I'm going to faint!" Then Priscilla did exactly that, slumping against the side of the cab.

Lady Eastmoreland cut her icy gaze to Emily. "Miss Leverton, you will help me load the girls into the cab and when we return to the house you will pack your belongings and quit our residence at once. I will write to Perdita's in the morning. You will never work as a governess in this town again. How dare you take two young, impressionable women to a place like this? Why, I ought to press charges against you."

Emily swallowed her disappointment. "Yes, my lady." There was no point in trying to muster a defense. She should have woken the butler and sent him after Minnie instead of trying to mitigate the girls' damage herself. She'd made a terrible mistake, and she would pay dearly for it.

Minnie dragged herself from Emily's arms and blew her nose loudly into her handkerchief. Her eyes were redder than usual and swollen and puffy. She was a frightful mess, and Emily was afraid she'd be traumatized by the night's events.

"M-mother," Minnie hiccuped before quailing under her mother's stony gaze.

"Hush, Minnie. You have caused enough trouble. I can only

thank the Lord that no one of consequence is here to witness your state."

Minnie nodded sullenly, then peeked at Emily. She seemed to draw strength from Emily's steadiness, because she pulled her shoulders back and said, "No, Mother. I will speak now."

Lady Eastmoreland turned back with arched eyebrows. "Pardon me?"

"You will not dismiss Miss Leverton."

A stiff wind could have knocked both Lady Eastmoreland and Emily over.

"Pray, tell me why I would keep on a governess who exposes my daughter to such danger?"

Minnie gulped but held her ground. "Because it was not her idea. I told her I was going slumming with Miss Winegartener and she could not stop me. Miss Leverton came with us as a last resort to keep us safe. Miss Winegartener and I wandered into an alley." Her voice wavered for a moment and her eyes watered. Then she stiffened her spine and continued. "These two men were going to steal our money and... and..." She coughed on a sob.

"It is okay, Lady Minnie." Emily rubbed her back. "It does not matter."

"No, it does! Miss Leverton defended us and told us to run while she was trapped. I thought she had died. She saved our lives, Mother, and it was all my fault. She never would have been here if I had not wanted to step out."

The countess studied her daughter with surprise. Emily guessed Minnie had never been so assertive in all her life. Frail and tender, she always allowed Lady Eastmoreland to bowl her over. She had had to grow up awfully fast that night, but instead of fainting like her companion, Minnie had drawn courage from the experience. Perhaps the girl had some character to her after all.

"Is this true, Miss Leverton?"

Emily nodded. "Yes, my lady."

"Well." Lady Eastmoreland seemed momentarily stymied. "I thank you for protecting my foolish daughter and her companion tonight. I will consider your employment in the morn."

Emily squeezed Minnie's arm. "Come along, Lady Minnie. Let us take you and Miss Winegartener home."

Chapter 14

The Dove sipped her brandy, studied her cards, and threw another note on the growing pile of goods at the center of the table. Her companions were deep in their cups, which was just as well: Although she was dressed in men's clothing, a sober man would have been hard-pressed to believe the illusion. She didn't worry about discovery, though. The gaming hell owner knew very well who she was, and he allowed her to come and go as she pleased.

She owned the banknote on the hell, after all.

Her earlier interaction with Emily Leverton troubled her. She had managed all types of governesses: the shy governesses who turned out to be excellent flies on the wall, the angry governesses who wanted to punish the *ton*, the whip-smart governesses who would have made excellent spies for the Crown, and every type of personality in between.

Emily Leverton was her favorite type: feisty, intelligent, and an unabashed upstart. The downside was that along with her positive attributes, Emily came with major baggage. She was distrustful and far too capable for her own good. The Dove worried that if she could not convince Emily to fully embrace her agenda, she might ultimately do more harm than good. And that would serve no one.

The man to her left puffed on his pipe and tossed the deed to one of his country estates onto the pile.

The Dove fought not to roll her eyes. Idiots. They were lucky she was not there to clean them out.

She ran a fingertip over the edge of her cards. Her husband had taught her how to play Baccarat, along with Vingt et Un, Whist, Piquet, Hazard, and a number of other games. He'd said it was important to know how to win—and how to lose. Powerful men let slip powerful secrets when playing at the tables, and if she was going to become a master of her occupation, she needed to be playing with the full deck.

He'd meant the pun. He'd been a goff like that.

The irony was that in the end, a powerful man with a steep wine tab and loose lips had led to her husband's untimely death. Her sweet husband, collector of absurdities, would have had something to say about that.

The Dove hadn't found it amusing. When it came to the people she'd loved, the *ton* had failed her time and time again.

Or perhaps it was she who had failed them.

She took another gulp of brandy and silently repeated the motto she'd adopted after her husband's death: *redemption and retribution*. She was beyond redemption, but she could put an end to the illegal and bastardly acts of the *ton*. They had too much power, too much wealth, and too little conscience. If no one else was going to hold them accountable, then she would.

"The Ainsworth Estate," she remarked casually, eyeing the deed on the pile. "I thought that place was rubble."

The man flushed. "Nonsense. I was just there. The hall is as majestic as the day it was built."

It was a heaping pile of brick, the Dove knew. She also knew Lord Durham, the man who'd offered up the crumbling estate, was so deeply in debt that his knees were probably quivering under the table. He'd squandered his wealth in a shockingly short amount of time, losing massive amounts of money to the tables and spending what remained at whorehouses.

"Really? I, too, was just that way," she said. The other players listened intently. Lord Durham's cheeks turned a deeper shade of red. "It was so run-down I rather thought it was an old Scottish ruin."

"You must be mistaken." He spoke stiffly and adjusted the lace on his sleeves. "Perhaps you visited Allensby. The names are somewhat similar."

The Dove made a humming noise in her throat. "Indeed. Perhaps I am mistaken." She nodded at Lord Fossey, who played Whist across the room, and tapped her forefinger on her glass. It was instantly refilled. "Gentlemen, I am looking for a new courtesan. Mine has begun to bore me. I would like to explore other...appetites."

The first rule of coaxing someone into talking about a topic they'd rather not was to introduce it as an escape to avoid a topic they disliked even more.

As she knew he would, Lord Durham eagerly grasped onto the new line of discussion. "What appetites are we talking about, Hallewell?"

The Dove, known at the golden hell only as Lord Hallewell, pulled a stack of banknotes from her breast pocket and absently played with them. The men's gazes fell to the veritable fortune in her hands. She'd begun to wonder if the Evangelist harbored sexual predilections outside the norm. Based on his targeted population and the baring of the victims' breasts in death, it was entirely possible. There were a number of establishments that catered to a variety of sexual desires, and the Dove intended to collect a roster of their clients.

"I think I should like to experiment before I choose a companion. Perhaps a brothel that specializes in humiliation to start."

Her companions exchanged knowing glances.

"Victoria's," one of the men said from across the table. He was fresh from the schoolroom and already a thousand pounds in debt.

"I do not want a cheap establishment with diseases," the Dove warned.

"She only caters to nobility," Lord Durham assured her.

The Dove lifted a brow, unconvinced. When he didn't expand, she stuffed the notes back into her jacket and said, "You insult me to suggest I do not know the difference between Ainsworth Estate and Allensby—"

"I know this," Lord Durham interrupted hastily, "because I personally know of several men who visit her establishment, and there are rumors of many more."

"I should like those references."

"Of course." Durham swallowed. "There are Lords Kendal and Carleton, Clapham and Marley."

"I heard Copeland," the young man added, losing his affected air of boredom. Gossip was as integral a part of the hells as the gambling.

"Yes," Durham agreed. "And of course Spalding and Eastmoreland."

Only years of training kept the Dove's face from registering her shock.

She tapped her cards to her chin and said, "Are you sure about Eastmoreland?"

"He's likely their biggest client!" Durham exclaimed, sensing he'd intrigued her despite her efforts.

Now that, the Dove thought, was very interesting.

Chapter 15

Once the Eastmoreland party had returned to the house, Emily was dismissed to her room while Minnie's maid attended to the distraught girl. Emily would have killed for a bath but had to settle for the washbasin. After she was clean she pulled her night rail over her head and lay on her hard, narrow bed.

Before she fell asleep she replayed every moment of her kiss with Zach. She'd been determined to put her mistake at the ball behind her, but fate had thrown Zach back into her life.

You can kiss me anytime you want, Emily, whether you want to blow me a kiss or open your sweet mouth for mine.

Emily pressed her knees together as heat settled between her thighs. Intercourse, in her experience, was highly unpleasant. So why her heart should thump and her breathing shallow at the thought of having Zach touch her in *that way* was an utter mystery. Sex was something men enjoyed and women endured, and she'd learned that for a fact.

But then the Pig had never made her feel the way Zach had with a single kiss. The night of their arranged marriage, a prettied-up term for what equated to Emily's mother selling her off to the highest bidder, Lionel had pushed her on the bed and lifted her skirts without any tenderness or finesse.

The heat faded as Emily remembered the experience. She'd been married two years, and in that time she'd done her best to keep the Pig from touching her. At times it had been inevitable. When she'd complained to her mother, her mother had sneered at her. Hadn't she spread her legs for years to feed Emily? How dare Emily complain about doing her duty? Besides, she was married to the man, so what he did was right and sanctioned. Emily belonged to him.

Emily squeezed her eyes shut. Not anymore. She belonged to herself, and herself only. She was no longer Lionel's, and in spirit she never had been. Her body was her own. Her mind was her own. Her soul was her own. And she would never allow another man the privilege of claiming her.

That meant that should she run into Zach again, and she suspected he would find a way to make that happen, she'd have to find a way to cool his interest for good.

❧

Zach had watched the events with Lady Eastmoreland unfold and had seethed at the injustice of it. He desperately wanted to intervene but was afraid it would only embarrass the countess and make the situation worse for Emily. He'd been relieved when Emily's young charge had defended her, silently applauding the girl for having the backbone to stand up to the Ice Queen of the *ton*.

And now he knew Emily was employed by Eastmoreland.

At least she had been. By Lady Eastmoreland's parting comment, that remained to be seen.

Now, seated at his desk, Zach looked down at the report Adam had spent the night synthesizing. Each of the Evangelist's victims had been last seen around 10:00 p.m. Their bodies had been found at varying times between 2:00 and 5:00 a.m., which meant they'd likely been murdered between 10:00 p.m. and 2:00 a.m. Each girl had been discovered a minimum of three streets over from where she typically worked. The bodies had been in alleyways and behind trash cans.

Out of the way. Unseen. Discarded like rubbish.

Did the Evangelist move the bodies after the murder? Did he lure each woman away from her post with the promise of money, and then stab her?

All three women had been taken from Bethnal Green, which meant the killer hunted in that area within a four-hour window.

Zach dropped the report on his desk, one of many clustered in the main station room. Noise whirled around him; men laughing, the scratching of nibs on paper, the clatter of objects being set down. The scents of tea and coffee made Zach's stomach grumble, but he ignored his body's request. He could have used the pickup after his paltry three hours of sleep, but he was too focused on Adam's report. He scrubbed a hand down his face, his eyes burning.

The Evangelist had not hit Bethnal Green last night. Zach's estimation had been off, but then he reminded himself the killer couldn't be expected to murder like clockwork. Life happened. Perhaps, if the killer were upper class like the Silk Stalker had been, he'd have had an engagement. If he were lower class, he may have set out to abduct a woman and then run into friends. Whatever the reason, Bethnal Green had remained untouched the night before.

Would terror strike that night?

Mark and Sidney approached, hats clutched in their hands, faces haggard.

"Boss," Mark said in greeting.

"How did it go?" Zach asked. He leaned back in his chair, feeling defeated and weary. His men looked how he felt.

"We interviewed as many prostitutes working the street last night as we could." Mark ran a hand through his thinning hair. "Not many would talk with us."

"Can't blame them," Sidney said. At just twenty, he was faring better from the all-nighter than his older colleague. He was a thin, pale redhead whose idealism hadn't yet been crushed by life. "We ain't exactly their best friends."

"Did you hear anything different from what the pimps reported?" Zach asked.

Mark nodded. "The girls are scared. There are a lot of rumors."

Zach perked up. "Rumors are good. What do you have?"

Sidney handed him a sheet of paper, and Zach scanned the bulleted points.

"There were two that we heard repeatedly," Mark said. "They're warning one another not to go with the man with the green cravat."

"And some had heard the killer was an underground pugilist named Roberto, or maybe Ronald. There wasn't consensus on the name."

"Description?"

"Maybe Greek or Italian. Tall. The way they described him he was as tall as this ceiling." Mark sighed heavily. "Couldn't get them to estimate a measurement, so let's say over six feet. Thick muscles, bald, mustache. A scar separating his upper lip in two."

Zach's blood chilled as if it had been put on ice. The description matched the thug he'd strangled into unconsciousness last night. Had he inadvertently incapacitated the Evangelist? Was that why the man hadn't struck?

But if he were the Evangelist, why had he targeted Emily and two upper-class women? It didn't hold with his pattern, unless the girls had simply been a fun diversion while he bided his time.

"Okay, thanks, men. Why don't you go home and get some rest? The Evangelist didn't strike last night, which means he may tonight. I don't know if we can stop him, but we can damned sure make him wary."

Mark's eyes brightened. "I'm all in, boss."

Zach knew he should follow his own advice. In his exhaustion he wasn't thinking clearly. If he wanted to be useful later that night, he needed a few hours of sleep, a bath, and a good hot meal.

When he entered Stanford House, his butler, Charles, hurried toward him and helped him out of his coat.

"Sir, we have been worried." The butler wrinkled his nose in disdain as he sniffed Zach's coat.

Zach had snapped up the old man after Charles's newly minted master had squandered the family fortune at the card tables. At the butler's age he'd had little choice but to accept Zach's offer. Zach knew Charles disapproved of his familiarity with the staff, his odd hours, and his insistence on holding such a common job. Yet Zach had once overheard the butler bragging, in his very modest way, to another servant about the generosity and decency of his master. So perhaps Charles wasn't completely unhappy.

Zach clapped the older man on the shoulder and said, "Thank you for your concern, Charles. I need to rest, but let my valet know I would like a hot bath when I wake."

"Of course. Sir, before you take your leave, you have had a number of visitors this morning."

Zach raised a brow. "Oh?"

Charles turned and lifted a silver tray from the table. It bore a literal pile of mail. "And far more invitations and calling cards. You have become very popular with the ladies, sir."

Out of a bizarre duty he felt not to disappoint his butler, Zach flipped through the stack of envelopes. He recognized some of the names, but many of them were unknown to him. Most looked to be invitations to soirees and balls. One was an invitation to attend the opera. There were half a dozen calling cards left by those who had stopped by to visit and found him not home. He grimaced when he spotted the names of Mrs. Hill and her daughters, Miss Hill and Miss Jane. They had ostensibly dropped in to visit Mrs. Denholm, even though that blasted article had taken great pains to point out that he ran a bachelor household now that his mother resided on the coast.

Zach dropped the cards back on the silver tray. "Choose two invitations for me to accept. Write my regrets to the rest."

The butler paled. "You want me to read your correspondence, sir?"

"Yes. And if anyone else should stop in, tell them I am not home."

"Very good, sir."

Zach took the stairs two at a time to shock Charles, whom he knew watched from below.

His chamber was in the right wing of the house. Stanford House was far too large for one man, consisting of fifteen rooms, a study, a library, a receiving room, a dining room, a kitchen, a ballroom, and servants' quarters, but then it was rather difficult to find a *small* dwelling in Mayfair.

Zach had decided that if he was going to have to buy a large house anyway, he might as well do it properly. Although Stanford House was not the grandest in Mayfair, it was in the top tier, and he found it amusing to watch the reactions of the *ton* when they learned that he, a butcher's son, occupied the coveted home.

As soon as he'd bought the house he'd had it stripped of its fussy moldings, the ugly scarlet-and-gold wallpaper, the dusty velvet drapes, and the heavy furniture that had reminded him of something that belonged in a medieval castle. The entire place had been coated in fresh paint, and he'd hired a decorator to outfit the house with simple, quality furnishings with clean lines. The result was unconventional—modern fashion required ostentatious displays of wealth—but Zach had always preferred quiet quality over gilded grandiosity.

His chamber reflected his unpopular taste for simplicity, with light wood pieces, a wide feather bed, and green, gold, and blue striped drapes. Zach pulled the drapes now, blocking out the insistent sunlight of midmorning, stripped off his clothes, and climbed into bed. He was asleep as soon as his eyes closed.

Chapter 16

E mily spent the morning on pins and needles as she taught the younger boys arithmetic, corrected the girls' poetry, and avoided Minnie's distraught gaze entirely. During the luncheon hour the children were dismissed, and Emily found herself confronted by the countess.

Lady Eastmoreland entered the schoolroom as Emily tidied the paintings and letter work. When Emily looked up, she nearly shrieked to find Lady Eastmoreland watching her with intense scrutiny. The lady of the house was dressed in a far more appropriate ensemble than she had worn the previous night, including perfectly pinned and curled hair, jewels at her ears and throat, and a gown made of the finest quality maroon satin.

Emily curtsied and waited patiently with her hands clasped behind her back as she'd been taught at Perdita's. Her stomach roiled, and she wondered if this was the moment where the countess told her to pack her bags.

"Miss Leverton," Lady Eastmoreland began. She scowled at one of her daughter's watercolors before returning her gaze to Emily. "As much as I would like to forget about last night's escapade entirely, it must, unfortunately, be addressed. While I appreciate what you did for Minnie, it was out of your purview to accompany my daughter to the slums."

Emily kept her gaze downcast, afraid she might burst into tears. She was done for. Where would she go? There was no way the Dove would place her in another house, not after Lady Eastmoreland finished destroying her reputation across London. And yet she couldn't go back home, *wouldn't* go back. Perhaps a factory would take her.

"However, Minnie has been adamant that you were left with no choice, and that you did indeed keep her and Miss Winegartener safe at your own peril."

Hope reared its tiny head.

"I have decided to allow you to stay on. However, in the future, should one of my children step out of the bounds of decorum, I expect you to notify the head housekeeper or myself immediately. Is that understood?"

"Yes"—Lady Eastmoreland's presence was so regal and overbearing that Emily just managed to stop herself from addressing her as *Your Majesty*—"my lady."

Lady Eastmoreland nodded once. "I do not wish to hear this topic spoken of again. I will expect your complete discretion in regard to last night."

"Yes, of course, my lady."

Lady Eastmoreland turned to leave but paused and waved a hand at the offending watercolor. "Who painted this?"

"Georgiana, my lady."

"Give her painting lessons twice a day until her form improves. This is an affront to beauty."

"Yes, my lady."

Lady Eastmoreland swept out of the room and Emily nearly collapsed with relief. After she stopped shaking, she picked up Georgiana's watercolor, which was dashed with wild colors and abstract images, and hid it behind her older sister's more stately and boring work depicting a field of daisies. Emily had liked Georgiana's creative painting. After all, the girl was only seven.

When the children returned, Minnie with them, the eldest Eastmoreland child sought her gaze until Emily met her eyes and gave her a slight nod. The girl's shoulders, which had been rigid with tension the entire morning, finally eased.

With the afternoon lessons completed, Emily's time was her own. She longed for a cool dip in a river or lake. Humidity had draped the city overnight—a wet, suffocating thing that made her feel as if her entire body were itching in her gown. When at Perdita's, the headmistress had been horrified to discover that Emily wore a flannel binding instead of a corset. She'd promptly fitted her out in one, and Emily hadn't taken a decent breath since. The heat made her want to throw it in the Thames.

For an early supper Emily sweet-talked Cook into giving her the leftover cucumber-and-butter sandwiches from tea. She was about to head to her room when a delivery boy appeared at the door holding a brown paper package.

"It's for you again, Miss Fancy," Cook bellowed, and eyed the cucumber sandwiches.

Emily shoved two in her mouth like a chipmunk before Cook could reacquire them, and took the package from the boy. She opened it in the kitchen to appease Cook's curiosity, which Emily suspected was the foundation of her ire. Inside was a small paper package filled with...noodles.

"Heavens!" Cook exclaimed. "Whatever do you need those for?"

"They are a gift," Emily said, grinning like an idiot. It seemed Zach had rightly deduced that she was employed by the Eastmorelands. She would have expected no less from him.

Cook didn't mistake Emily's glow. "In my day, men sent poetry."

Emily unfolded the note that had come with the parcel.

Will you join me for a stroll? I will be waiting for you outside Eastmoreland House at eight.

—Z

Emily clutched the note to her breast, her initial excitement waning when she remembered that Zach was above her station and therefore likely interested in nothing more than a quick, tawdry affair, and even if he were interested in marriage, she was not. More so, he was a policeman, and therefore dangerous to her.

An idea dawned. This walk could be her opportunity to discourage Zach. She could ignore the invitation, but if she did she suspected he would persist. If she met him, though, and she was successful with her budding plan, she could make him loathe her.

Chapter 17

W hen Emily appeared on the street two hours later, she
found Zach leaning against a lamppost, his hands in his
pockets and a hat tipped low over his eyes.

"Are you posing for me?" she asked.

He lifted his head, those sea-blue eyes of his sparkling with
humor. He opened his mouth to speak, but then his gaze dropped
to her outfit and whatever he'd intended to say abandoned him.

Emily had thought long and hard about what to wear. Obviously her governess uniform didn't bother Zach, and she suspected that neither would a commoner's gown. The one time she'd
seen Zach disgusted was at the ball with all of the fluffy pastel
gowns and fraudulent titters.

Daringly, Emily had asked Minnie if she could borrow one
of her old gowns. Minnie had been more than willing, especially after finding out that Emily was meeting a gentleman
friend. Although Minnie never would have been allowed to walk
alone with a gentleman at sunset, the same rules did not apply

to a governess of Emily's standing. As such, Minnie had been delighted to help, and had even let her borrow a matching pair of slippers.

"Are you sure you want to wear this?" Minnie had asked doubtfully. "It is from seasons ago."

"It is perfect," Emily had assured her.

She now stood in front of Zach dressed in an astounding confection of lace, tulle, and feathers. The gown had been designed for a young girl with too much money. There were tiers upon tiers of pink satin and tulle alternating with white lace. The matching hat was as pink as a pig's ear, with feathers that stretched nearly a foot high before drooping over, exhausted from the exertion. She looked like a giant walking cake. A fluffy, pink, hideous cake.

The blasted gown was heavy and hot, but the effect was worth the effort when Zach visibly leaned away from her.

Emily whipped out one of Minnie's practice fans and expertly applied it to her face, fluttering her lashes as if she had something in her eye. The air from the fan was actually a relief, as Emily was genuinely afraid she might pass out.

Zach's voice sounded strangled when he said, "That is an interesting dress."

Interesting was male talk for "ugly."

Emily tried to simper.

"Is something the matter? Your mouth is drooping a bit."

No more simpering.

Emily regally held out her elbow and Zach accepted, seeming confused by her apparent personality change.

They strolled down the street, garnering a number of curious stares. Emily stared back until she realized she was acting above her station and averted her eyes.

Zach cleared his throat after several minutes of silence. "I see you received my note."

"Yes, and the pasta. So nice of you to send a gift for Cook."

"The pasta was for you. A joke. Because of noodles."

"Noodles?"

"The first time we met. You stubbed your toe and said, 'Noodles.'"

Emily waved the fan so viciously that it flew out of her hand. Zach retrieved it for her. She noticed he didn't offer her his arm when he returned.

"Oh heavens, thank you. I do not remember anything about noodles. My goodness it is hot today. Would you like to walk to the park? It would be nice to breathe fresh air."

"Splendid idea."

Emily tripped in the monstrous, feather-decorated slippers. She caught the curse word before it left her lips, instead using her parasol to peevishly stab at the brick that had tripped her.

Zach widened the space between them. Feeling that she had sufficiently begun to alienate him, Emily sniffed and fluttered her eyelashes, but before she could speak he said quietly, "You have not been dismissed."

Some of Emily's zest waned. "'Twas not pretty, but I have been allowed to keep my position." Then she realized he'd handed her the perfect opening. She sucked in a breath and added, "Although ultimately it does not matter, as I have put in my notice anyway."

Zach's eyebrows lifted. "You have?"

"Of course, silly!" She gave a high-pitched laugh and swatted at his arm with her fan. Since he'd widened the space, she had to reach rather far to do so. "You made your intentions clear when you kissed me on the street, did you not? You said you have a fortune, so as the future Mrs. Denholm I see no reason to keep working."

Zach kept right on walking. He didn't halt in shock, sputter, or sprint away as a proper bachelor should. He remained utterly and completely silent.

"I am nearly worked to the bone as a governess. Surely you would not want that for your betrothed?" She fluttered her eyelashes again, but it was making her dizzy. She did not understand how debutants managed it so successfully.

Zach said absently, "Of course you may leave."

Obviously he wasn't listening to her. Emily ground her teeth together. "When should we set the date for the wedding? It will be a grand affair and we will need to procure a license. I will want the most expensive dress I can find." When he didn't reply, she said, "Pigs fly. Apples and potatoes."

Zach's face remained bland, even if his mouth did twitch. "If you are testing my hearing, I assure you I can understand you quite well. We can marry within the week if you like."

"*What?!*" Emily screeched, all of her breathy pretense disappearing. She pulled up short and gripped her hip. "Are you raving mad?"

"Darling, only one of us is dressed like a cupcake and talking about marriage."

Well, when he put it *that* way.

"We are *not* getting married. We barely know each other. And see how vapid and vain I am?" She waved her hand over her gown. "Do you really want to marry a governess who is only after you for your money? Have some pride, Zachariah."

He was full-on grinning now, his teeth impossibly white against the slight tan of his skin. "There is the Emily I know."

Chapter 18

"Why are you dressed like that?" Zach asked the quivering pile of lace in front of him. God, it really was hideous. She could barely walk in the thing, her stride a mix between a wiggle and a waddle.

The plume dipped over her face and she batted it away.

"I like it," she said defensively.

He didn't need a real answer. He'd already figured out she was trying to frighten him off. The question was why? He thought she enjoyed his company, and when they'd kissed they'd fit together like two statuettes carved from the same block of marble. Never had he felt such an all-consuming desire to simultaneously protect and ravish a woman as he had when Emily had all but melted in his arms in Bethnal Green. So why the determination to chase him away?

She was a complex puzzle that fascinated him as both a man and an investigator.

"Yes, it is a charming ensemble. Are you not hot?"

"Cool as a cucumber."

A bead of perspiration slid down her temple.

"Come on, Noodles, let us walk to the Serpentine. Maybe a brisk breeze will help."

Alas, when they arrived at their destination, there wasn't so much as a whiff of wind. The air was stagnant and as heavy as a blanket. Emily was literally panting, and he was afraid she might faint from dragging around the thirty-pound gown.

It was past the fashionable hour, yet several men on horseback and women riding in carriages passed, most likely doing their best to alleviate the oppressive heat, as he and Emily stared over the polluted lake.

"So about the wedding," Zach prompted.

Emily turned to him, her face solemn. "Stop jesting."

Zach reached forward and flicked the offending feather away. "Am I that unmarriageable?"

Clearly the little minx had brought up the topic of marriage with the hopes of sending him running, and to his utter astonishment he'd discovered that he sort of *liked* the idea of finding a wife as unconventional as Emily. She was a breath of fresh air from the steady parade of insipid society women throwing themselves at him. Yes, she was "only" a governess, but at one time he'd been only a butcher's son. Perhaps that was why he had never been able to seriously consider courting a woman of the *ton*. Mayhap he needed a wife from a similar background.

Granted, he didn't know Emily that well, and he'd vowed that if he ever took a wife he'd know more about her than her pedigree. Emily was keeping secrets about her past, and with some surprise Zach realized he wanted to know all of them. He wanted her to trust him enough to share the part of her that she kept hidden. He wanted to know why she'd thought she had to frighten him away.

Someday he might marry, but today he wanted to peel back the layers of the half-swooning spool of lace beside him and discover what made her laugh, what made her face light up with joy, and what else made her give that breathy little sigh she'd given when they'd kissed.

Emily backed away a step. "I am sure you will make some woman a lovely husband. However, that woman will not be me." She shook her head. "This whole topic is absurd. I never should have broached it. Please forgive me. The heat is addling my head."

"Why the getup, Emily?"

"I wanted to frighten you."

"I figured that. Why?"

She visibly struggled with the answer and he wondered if she would lie to him. "You kissed me," she said at last. "You kissed me and I cannot be involved with you."

"Because of your position as a governess?"

"No."

"Is it because of my beginnings?"

"Don't be daft."

"What, then?"

She fisted her hands in her gown and said, "Well to begin with, I am already married."

She'd well and truly managed to shock him. It would have been satisfying if it weren't also terribly wrenching. She was attracted to Zach's magnetism and humor, and despite her best intentions to cut him off, he'd continued to slip past her defenses.

And in those brief moments she'd let herself forget that she wasn't *really* a free woman.

Zach's voice was dangerously low when he said, "What?"

"I am technically married," she repeated.

Ice frosted his eyes. "To whom?"

"You do not know him."

"And does he know his wife is running about, kissing other men?" It was said with such cutting disdain that Emily flinched.

She pulled her spine straight and reflected his ice in her own tone. "He does not know where I am, and I do not officially know where he is."

"What else doesn't he know about you, Emily?"

"That is none of your concern, Mr. Denholm. If you will excuse me."

She spun, the full skirt of the gown whipping out like a fan. Before she'd made it a yard he'd caught up with her, his strides long in his fury.

"How does a married woman become a governess? And how does your husband not know where you are?"

"Life is full of mysteries," she snarled. She wished she hadn't said anything at all, wished she'd ignored his note and thrown the pasta in the bin. He'd called her bluff about wanting to marry him. Her entire plan to chase him off had failed, and now she'd done the worst thing possible: She'd further aroused his curiosity.

He strode silently beside her. She could almost hear his brain riffling through the puzzle pieces, turning and adjusting them, attempting to fit them together for a clearer picture.

Fear lanced through her heart. She could not, *would* not, let Zach discover her deepest shame.

"Stop that!" she shouted. "You keep trying to figure me out!

Well, let me save you the effort. I am married. My husband is wonderful. We have a home and three kids. He has taken ill recently and we needed money so I became a governess. I am sorry I kissed you. It was nothing but a dalliance. Although really, you are the one who kissed me and it was entirely inappropriate so this seems like a problem for which you have only yourself to blame."

"When were you married?"

"Two years ago."

"That is an awfully short amount of time to have three children."

Emily could have kicked herself. The heat was messing with her ability to think, and she was so parched she could have drained the Serpentine.

"Did I say two years? I meant ten. One of the children is from his previous marriage, and we had twins. That is three total. Do the numbers, Denholm."

When he smiled, Emily knew she was in trouble.

"I have done the numbers. You must have married extremely young. What I find strange is that you said your husband does not know where you are. Is he not in on this moneymaking scheme?"

"Well." She was forgetting her lies. It was exhausting trying to keep her stories straight in this blasted heat. "I have not told him where I am because I am afraid he will send someone to collect me. He did not want me to come to London, but we desperately need the funds."

"I see."

That was what she was afraid of. "Listen, Zach." She stopped and turned to him again, ignoring the carriage of curious faces that passed by. "My marriage is not fabricated."

He studied her with a single-minded intensity that left her feeling translucent. "But the rest is."

Emily bit her lip. "Noodles," she whispered. She tugged ineffectually at the neckline of the dress. Her ribs felt as if they were being pressed together by a vise.

The ice in Zach's eyes began to thaw. He stepped forward and cupped her elbow.

"Zach?" Emily gasped.

"Yes?"

"I am about to do something I have never done before."

"What is that?"

"Faint."

Her knees turned to marmalade, her eyes rolled into the back of her head, and she plunged into darkness.

Chapter 19

She was only passed out for a few moments, but it was long enough for Zach to hail one of the passing carriages and ask for himself and Emily to be conveyed to his own carriage half a mile off.

Fortunately Emily was unconscious for that part, and when she recovered she kept her eyes shut in case she opened them and saw she was in the carriage of a duke or someone else equally awful and then was obliged to die of humiliation.

Zach lifted her out of the carriage while Emily lay as limp as a rag.

"Lord, Emily, this dress is monstrous."

Without opening her eyes she said, "That sounded like a comment on my weight."

"I would not dare. Look, the carriage has rounded the bend. Do you think you can stand now?"

He let her feet drop to the ground and she popped her eyes

open. There was a small audience of onlookers out for an evening stroll.

"Thank you, good stranger," she said loudly to Zach as an older couple passed with a disapproving scowl. "We are not together," she called at their backs.

Zach was unimpressed. "Get in the carriage."

"No, but thank you for your kind assistance, GOOD SIR."

He bent down and spoke softly into her ear. "If you do not get into the goddamned carriage this minute, I am going to kiss you in front of all and sundry, husband or not."

She got into the carriage.

The curtains had already been pulled to block out the sunlight, but the temperature was still stifling. Emily felt as if she were a turkey that had just waddled into its own oven.

"This is not going to help. I am too hot, Zach. That is why I fainted."

"I know why you fainted. Now take that ridiculous gown off."

Emily's eyes rounded. "W-what?"

The carriage began moving beneath them. Zach sat across from her on a plush velvet seat, his knees touching the voluminous skirt of her gown. The interior smelled faintly of lemon and cinnamon, a tantalizing combination that was pure Zach.

"I have asked my driver to loop around and take his time. Now take that blanket off before you faint again."

"Not in this life."

"I am not trying to get under your skirts." He bared his teeth. "At the moment. You are overheated. If you do not cool down, you will lose consciousness."

"Drop me off at Eastmoreland House. I will disrobe in my

room, lie down, and drink some water." Even as she said it black spots danced in her vision. She wouldn't make it, she realized. Zach would have to carry her through the servants' entrance, and it would cause a mighty ruckus in the house.

"Oh, all right, fine," she grumbled, tearing off her hat. Pins clattered onto the floor but she couldn't see to pick them up. Not that she could have bent over even if she'd wanted to—the gown was cinched so tightly and the skirts were so thick that she was practically forced into an upright position.

Her vision was going. She leaned back against the seat, waiting for it to pass. The carriage shifted, and a moment later she felt Zach's large hand on her shoulder. He turned her to the side and nimbly unbuttoned the back of the gown.

"Disrobed many ladies?" she asked curiously.

"Some."

The front of the dress gaped, allowing cooler air to wash over her skin.

Zach didn't stop with the dress. When his hands yanked on the stays of her corset, the backs of his fingers brushing against the thin fabric of her chemise, Emily wasn't sure if she was aroused or humiliated.

Suddenly the restrictive boning of the corset collapsed and Emily sucked in air, her rib cage fully expanding. The spots in front of her eyes evaporated.

Now that the taste of freedom was so close, she couldn't help but go all the way. She wiggled out of the corset and the gown, letting it pool into a fluffy pile on the floor.

Dressed only in her thin chemise and stockings, Emily avoided Zach's eyes while she reveled in the ten-degree temperature drop.

When she finally worked up the nerve to look at him, she found that he'd returned to his side of the carriage and was politely keeping his gaze on her face.

"Better?"

"My options were to die of heat or of humiliation. Humiliation won."

Zach didn't smile. "No one has ever died of humiliation. You made the right choice."

"Says the fully clothed man."

"Do not worry, I'm not looking."

For some reason that didn't make her feel better.

"A woman disrobing in order to remain conscious doesn't do it for me. Now, if you were taking off your dress under other circumstances..."

Emily flushed as she shook her head. "Has the sun scrambled your memory?"

Her pulse tripped when his piercing blue gaze met hers. His hands were clasped together, his forearms leaning on his knees. He'd removed his cravat and unbuttoned the top buttons of his shirt, leaving the strong column of his throat bare. Emily found herself itching to touch her tongue to the hollow there, to taste his sweat.

"I've had time to think," he said.

"When?"

"Emily, where is your husband?"

Chapter 20

I told you, I am not sure."

He tapped a finger to his chin. "But you think you know."

"I see why you are a detective." And it was that tenacity and attention to the unsaid that made her shameful secret quiver with fear. "Yes, I think I know."

He leaned back in his seat and waited.

"I *think* he's at the bottom of the Indian Ocean. Or at least I hope he is," she muttered. "But since he was lost at sea, he cannot be declared legally dead until seven years have passed. By law, I am still married."

"Why not tell me outright? Why the lies and elaborate dress?" He waved one hand at the offending heap of satin. "Why the ludicrous story about three children?"

Emily jutted her chin. "My husband is presumed dead, and the world is better for it. Still, the law makes me wait seven years before it will release me from my bonds. In that time I am not a woman free to pursue other romantic engagements."

"So you thought to frighten me off because a relationship between us could not lead to marriage?"

"Perhaps I wished to end our association because I am a moral woman and did not want to break my marriage vows." Hardly, but it seemed like a nice thing to lie about.

Zach considered that. "Why was your husband crossing the Indian Ocean?"

"Money," Emily replied. "He was headed to Australia. He thought it was a fledgling colony ripe for the fleecing and rare on the law. He was going to establish roots and then send for me."

"Did you want to leave England?"

"No! I have never felt luckier than when I heard his ship went down."

Zach's lips pressed into a line. "I do not know you well yet, Emily, but I know human nature. What did he do to inspire such hatred?"

Emily's gaze shifted to the window. There were some things she hoped never to speak of. Those two, horrid years with Lionel were on the list.

Zach seemed to understand as only another survivor of traumatic experiences could. "Let me ask another way. Did he break his wedding vows to you?"

Emily tilted her head. "What do you mean?"

"Did he promise to love and cherish you?"

Slowly, "He did."

"Did he, Emily? Did he honor you, keep you safe, cherish you as if you were the only woman in the world? Love you? Make you feel comforted and valued?"

Emily's mouth felt as if she'd swallowed a cup of sand. She shook her head no.

"It sounds to me that he broke his vows to you. In my book, that releases you from yours."

"The law would not see it that way," she pointed out.

His eyes burned into hers. "Do you?"

The shameful truth was that she had never felt bound by her vows. She had been a prisoner of those words, forced into repeating them as if she were a puppet. She had not given her love freely. She had been sold like a hog on the market so that her mother could buy two weeks' worth of liquor.

She had hated Lionel with the same amount of passion she might have bestowed on a man she'd loved. He had been a common thief, much like herself, except where she had stolen to survive, he'd stolen as part of a crime syndicate.

He'd done more than steal.

Emily shuddered as she remembered the time he'd come home with blood splattered across his shirt. More blood than a simple fight could have explained. He'd peeled the shirt off and thrown it at her. "Wash it," he'd snarled.

She'd jumped back, not wanting the bloody material to hit her in the face. For some reason that had enraged him. She could still see the coarse hairs on his knuckles as he grabbed the shirt with one hand and her hair with the other. He'd ground the bloody shirt into her face until she'd thought he'd suffocate her.

Emily burned with the memory. No, she did not feel she had to honor her vows. She felt no particular fealty to the law, either.

The simple truth was that despite the feelings Zach awakened in her, she was still legally bound to the Pig, which meant she could only engage in an affair. All the bad parts of having to bear a man in bed and none of the good parts of being married, such as prestige and means? No thank you.

Then there was the not-so-small matter of her sinister past and her Big Secret. A secret that, should she have a weak moment and give in to her desire for Zach, could eventually surface.

She would not allow that to happen.

"I do not feel beholden to my wedding vows," she answered honestly.

Zach rubbed the back of his neck as if to relieve a tension headache. "Then why the attempt to drive me away? Is it because I cannot give you marriage? Or do you find me ogreish and wish I would simply disappear?"

Emily sucked on her bottom lip. This was her opportunity to tell him she thought he was ugly and boring and bothersome. Except she could not quite bring herself to speak the lies. "It is not that I wish for marriage, but the alternative is an affair, and the act of…" She paused, trying to think of how an upper-class lady might discuss intercourse before concluding one wouldn't. "The marital act is awful. I enjoy your company, Zach. I even like the way you kiss. But I am not sure I am willing to enter into something where the other person reaps all the pleasure, and I fear that is all that could come of our association."

Zach's mouth parted in what looked like horror before he quickly snapped his jaw shut. "Emily, it is not supposed to be that way. Both partners are supposed to find pleasure, not only the man."

She eyed him suspiciously. Men were very rarely honorable when it came to lifting a woman's skirt.

"Gentleman's honor," he said, as if he could read her thoughts.

"You are not a gentleman."

Zach's lips quirked. "Perhaps a true gentleman would play coy right now, but as you have pointed out, I am not a gentleman, so instead I will be frank: Since we have kissed I have thought of little else but the feel of your mouth under mine. I have gone to bed every night craving another taste, and I have woken every morning desperate to hear what outrageous thing you will say next."

Emily's heart faltered at the declaration. It was the single most romantic thing anyone had ever said to her.

"I won't pressure you, but I *will* make you a promise. If you decide you want more than friendship, I vow that whatever we have together will be nothing like what you experienced with your husband. I will treat you with respect and I will put your needs first." He leaned forward and said quietly, his breath hot on her cheek, "There are things a man can do to make a woman limp with pleasure, and it would be an honor to do those things with you."

Chapter 21

Emily couldn't wipe Zach's proposition from her mind. She thought of it while teaching the multiplication tables. By poetry, she had determined she would sever their acquaintance for good. Doubt niggled at the back of her brain during history. She blushed during music practice as she wondered what those *things that make a woman limp with pleasure* might be. By the end of the day's lessons she was no less confused than when she'd started.

Finally alone in her stuffy room, the heat wave having only grown worse, Emily withdrew her diary and charted a pros and cons list for having an affair with Zach.

Pros:
- *His sense of humor*
- *He calls me Noodles*
- *I am safe with him*
- *He is the most attractive man I have ever met*
- *He is kind*
- *The Pig is dead*

Cons:

- *I do not like the marital act*
- *My past thieving*
- *Cont. of point above: My Big Secret would destroy him*
- *He is a bobby*
- *I would be his dirty little secret*
- *I am legally still married, even though the Pig is dead*
- *The affair could never be anything but an affair (see above)*
- *When it ends, I might be left brokenhearted*
- *(If I have a heart anymore)*

Emily looked over the side-by-side lists and sighed. The cons clearly outweighed the pros. She knew what she had to do.

She rolled over on the bed, having stripped to her shift to find some relief from the heat, and opened the newspaper that East-moreland had read and discarded for the day. The headline added weight to the heaviness of her heart.

EVANGELIST STRIKES AGAIN:
POLICE NO CLOSER TO SOLVING

As the man in charge of investigating the murders, Zach must be beside himself. In addition to taking heat from the press, he was likely blaming himself for not stopping the most recent murder. She didn't question how she knew this after such a brief amount of time spent with him. She just did.

Emily imagined it would be difficult to do his job with all of society and the newspapers breathing down his neck. Although she felt sorry for him, she knew Zach had broad shoulders. He had that cool, stubborn disposition that fairly begged for people to unload their problems on him because they knew he could handle it.

Emily would not be one of those people. Zach may think he wanted to pursue a relationship with her, but that was because he didn't have all the facts. If her Big Secret were ever discovered and leaked to the press, it would destroy his career. That, she could not and would not tolerate.

Mind firmly made up, Emily found a piece of stationery in her desk drawer and scribbled out her note to Zach:

> *I have considered, and I have decided against furthering our relationship. Also, do not beat yourself up over the newest murder. You are not responsible for the actions of a madman.*
>
> —E

She would dispatch the note first thing tomorrow morning.

The next morning Zach read Emily's note and tossed it on his desk. He'd had a hellish night. After leaving Emily on her doorstep, half buttoned in her cupcake dress, he'd headed to Bethnal Green, where he met his men outside Red's Tavern. Despite their visible presence, a prostitute had been murdered anyway. This time, her breasts had been mutilated rather than simply exposed after death.

The Evangelist's behavior was degenerating.

Zach worried the mutilation was in retaliation for his presence.

Either that, or the Evangelist had laughed the entire time he'd stabbed the woman to death right under their noses and enjoyed himself the more because of it.

Wright had been sympathetic, offering to inflate Zach's resources and fend off the howls of outrage over the Metropolitan Police's ineptitude. Zach had declined, but had been reassured that he hadn't been chosen to lead the task force as a scapegoat.

As frustrating as the newspapers were, they were also annoyingly accurate. Zach's team truly was no closer to solving the murders than they had been at the start. Zach and his men had hunted down the beefy Italian or Greek man with the split lip that the prostitutes had told them about. His name was Raul. They'd locked him up for assault.

That had been before the murder.

Raul, although a criminal and a thug, was not their guy.

Zach scrubbed his hand over his face and realized he hadn't shaved in days. He needed sleep. He needed to clear his head.

He needed a breath of fresh air.

He picked up Emily's note again. If she'd simply told him to get lost, he might have just done it. But she'd added on the part about how the murder wasn't his fault, as if she'd known how much he would blame himself.

He'd told her he wouldn't pressure her for a relationship, but that didn't mean they had to stop seeing each other. He suspected something deeper and darker was holding Emily back from him, something that went beyond the fact that her husband had been selfish and abusive. Perhaps if he could gain her trust, she would share her worries with him. Zach had spent a lifetime helping other people solve their problems, and the first time he truly wanted to help carry someone else's burden, she wouldn't let him. Figured.

Zach scratched out a response, grinning as he handed it to his messenger.

Chapter 22

Emily broke the wax seal on Zach's letter and read it at the kitchen door.

Dearest Emily,

It is true that I am not responsible for a madman's actions, but I am responsible for stopping him. I have done a poor job of that so far. Any sage advice for this failing detective?

As for your answer to my proposal, I accept your decision, but I request that we remain friends. Surely you would not leave a detective high and dry at such a trying juncture in his life? Tell me how I might entice you into spending time with me. So far I have three ideas:

1. *I can rent out a modiste shop for the day and give helpful commentary as you try on as many hideous cupcake dresses as you desire.*

2. *We can visit Bethnal Green and count how many times*

you deflect pickpockets. (I eagerly await the day you share with me how you have come by this very unusual life skill.)

3. *You can let me take you to the opera. I do not understand a word of what they are singing, but people often cry so it must be very moving.*

—Z

Emily found herself smiling stupidly at the paper. As she'd suspected, the man was dogged in his determination. She'd never had someone make ridiculous suggestions or *play* with her the way Zach did. For a moment she let herself imagine what it would be like to visit the opera dressed in a gorgeous gown on the arm of a man like Zachariah Denholm. She, a girl who'd eaten potato peels to survive the winter. She, a girl who hadn't owned a pair of shoes for an entire year when she'd grown out of hers too quickly.

Then, regretfully, she let the fantasy dissolve. The *ton* would never stand for a governess in their midst.

Z—

My sage advice is to keep doing what you are doing. Will not a murderer eventually make a mistake? You will catch your man. In the meantime, I suggest you throw out your newspaper as soon as it is delivered.

I regret that I must decline your tempting offers. As humorous as it would be to watch you pretend to appreciate ugly gowns, it is clear you have no concept of how long it takes to wriggle into one of those things. We would be at the modiste for hours, and it seems to me the man hunting the Evangelist might find a better use for his time. As for my rumored pickpocket-deflecting skills, I think mayhap you had the moon in your eyes that evening, or at the very least an eyelash. Lastly, as much as I would enjoy trying to cry at the opera, you cannot be seen with a governess, nor I with you. It would be entirely inappropriate. Alas, I fear our friendship must consist of hastily written notes.

—E

P.S. Stop sending me noodles. Cook is beginning to think I am crazy.

Most Hilarious Emily,

Do not tell me Cook thought you were normal before the deliveries started! I would never believe it.

I see the problem, and I have found an elegant solution. I am pledged to attend a masquerade ball in three days' time. It is an end-of-the-season ball before the mass exodus of the gentry to the countryside for the summer. It would be the perfect opportunity for you and I to further our friendship in secret— no one would ever know you were in their midst. I think, as my hastily-written-note pal, you should do me this favor. I am feeling very low about my failures, and your presence would cheer me considerably.

—Z

....

Z,

What is low is how you are attempting to use your failures to guilt me.

—E

Most Un-Guiltable Emily,

Is it working? What do you say? Let me dance with you for one night. I will have a gown made and you can dress at my residence. We will keep it completely proper and on the up-and-up. All you have to do is say yes. (It is only three letters. Don't be stingy.)

—Z

Z,

I am never stingy, so I will give you four letters: Fine.

—E

She truly lacked common sense, Emily thought as soon as she dispatched her letter. What on earth had compelled her to agree to go to the ball with him? Aside from the fact that she'd always wanted to attend a ball, she would be completely hidden, and she'd have an entire night in Zach's arms without any repercussions, it was still a risky endeavor. A woman with more sense would have firmly told him to take a swim.

Emily tucked Zach's most recent letter into the bodice of her gown and tamped down a foolish smile. She was acting like Minnie at her first social event. The ball was still three days away, and she couldn't walk around mooning over it for the next seventy-two hours. She had a job to do.

Chapter 23

"Jonathan, for heaven's sake, please do not put ants in your pockets," Emily scolded, pulling the six-year-old to the side and discreetly attempting to empty his pockets. This was her penance for attempting to teach biology outside of a text, she thought.

Lady Eastmoreland had taken the girls to the modiste, leaving Emily with eight-year-old George, six-year-old Jonathan, and four-year-old Charlie. The heat in the house had been oppressive to the point where Emily could not bear it one moment longer, and she'd known her young charges were not absorbing a single word she said.

The three little boys had been thrilled when she'd announced they were going on a learning adventure to Hyde Park. They were going to study entomology, Emily had declared, stating it with such enthusiasm that the boys had squealed with delight. George had packed his magnifying glass, Charlie had brought his wooden butterfly net, and Jonathan—well, he'd brought his pockets.

"I want them as pets," Jonathan said. "Mother won't let me have a puppy."

"That is disappointing," Emily agreed, "but I am afraid the ants are best left out of doors where they belong. They would not be happy in a jar."

Jonathan sighed heavily and opened his breast pocket. "I suppose the slug wouldn't be happy, either," he said as he pulled the slimy insect from the fabric.

Emily stifled a smile. "I suppose not."

While Jonathan emptied his pockets of ants, slugs, and beetles, Emily watched Charlie run around waving his butterfly net, and even George, who was far too serious a boy when he wasn't causing trouble with his siblings, seemed to be at ease as he crawled on the ground and examined bits of nature with his magnifying glass.

The boys were on their best behavior and Emily didn't see any reason to rush their return to Eastmoreland House, so they walked a good distance, at last reaching the bridge that separated the Serpentine and the Long Water. The midmorning sun had grown hotter with each stride, the flies buzzing around her head more persistent. Emily was ready to turn back, but then Jonathan asked, "Can we walk to the other side of the bridge, Miss Leverton?"

"Well…"

Three little faces looked up at her with round, pleading eyes.

"All right, fine. But we must turn around at the end without argument. We have been gone far too long."

The boys crowed with victory, and before Emily could speak another word, they were dashing across the bridge.

What would it be like, Emily thought, to be a *normal* governess? One who could say no to longing little boys? One who didn't have to fear each moment that she would be discovered as a fraud?

One who did not report the rumors and gossip in her house to a woman who may or may not be who she claimed?

A governess like *that* one, Emily thought, as a young governess—identified by a drab gown very similar to her own—drew closer. The governess was holding the hand of a little boy, and she would occasionally stop and gaze into the distance before speaking with her young charge, likely dispensing rich educational material, as Emily should have been.

"Jonathan!"

Emily's eyes flew to George and Charlie, who were leaning over the railing of the bridge, screaming. Jonathan was...

Emily's heart stopped. Jonathan was nowhere to be seen.

"He fell over!" George shrieked.

Emily sprinted to the railing, ripping her hat from her head and throwing it to the ground. She was fumbling to climb the slats, cursing her gown, when she peered over and spotted Jonathan treading water and grinning up at her.

Oh! That rotter! Emily was so livid her hair curled from the steam.

"Don't be cross, Miss Leverton!" Jonathan called up. "'Twasn't my fault. I fell in! Ask George and Charlie."

"The odds are not in his favor," a matter-of-fact voice said at her shoulder.

Emily briefly closed her eyes before climbing down from the railing. She brushed off her gown, pasted a smile on her face, and turned to the governess who had joined them at the railing. The governess stood with her young charge at her side, watching Jonathan insolently backstroke. She was about Emily's age, with wheat-colored hair and striking blue eyes hidden behind a pair of truly hideous spectacles. Her nose was petite, her lips plush, her gown splattered in mud. Wisps of hair escaped an unfashionably simple chignon.

"Pardon me," Emily said, wishing with all her heart that she were back in the schoolroom, even if it meant melting into a puddle. "What did you say?"

"The odds are not in his favor," the governess repeated, using her index finger to push her spectacles up the bridge of her nose, "if one considers the high number of visits to Hyde Park each year. There are fifteen hundred peers, which, including their family members, equals about ten thousand total nobility, with roughly another two thousand governesses and nannies that might accompany said family members to the park. Then there are the tourists." The governess's eyes took on a faraway look. "Not everyone will visit Hyde Park—or cross the bridge—as some are ill, elderly, too young, or uninterested. Conversely, some will visit the park regularly during the Season. Once one estimates the number of total visits to the park annually, and then plugs that into a probability calculation, one finds that the chances of a visitor falling into the Serpentine are highly unlikely."

Emily gawked at her. What in heaven's name was she going on about? "My apologies, but who are you?"

"Miss Frances Turner, known mostly as Frankie, latest governess for the Willoughby family. For some reason they cannot seem to keep help on. Can you imagine? Porter is the most charming child."

The charming child smiled beatifically at them as he removed his shoe and tossed it over the railing into the Serpentine.

There was a splash, and then Jonathan's voice shouted from below, "Oi!"

"And you are?" Frankie asked, oblivious to Porter's antics.

"Miss Emily Leverton."

"Pleased to meet you, Miss Leverton. Who do you work for?"

"Lord Eastmoreland." Emily's eyes rounded with excitement. "Wait a moment, are you acquainted with…" She subtly pulsed her arms at her sides like a bird.

Frankie's charge tossed another shoe over the railing and danced about in his stocking feet for Charlie and George, who giggled in surprise.

"If someone throws ONE MORE SHOE AT ME!" Jonathan roared from below.

Frankie tilted her head and studied Emily's flapping arms. "Are you ill?"

Emily's cheeks burned with embarrassment. Before she could make up an excuse for her odd movements, Frankie gasped and clutched her arm. "Hold on a moment! You must understand that I have been a governess only a few weeks, but I have still heard rumors of a person named the Dove. Surely that is what you are alluding to? The chances of you flapping your arms otherwise are—"

"Let me guess, extremely low," Emily finished for her. Then she realized what Frankie had been saying about Jonathan. "Wait, are you telling me Jonathan *jumped*?"

Frankie gave a lopsided grin and swiped a strand of loose hair from her face. "As I said, the odds are not in his favor."

Emily scanned both entrances to the bridge. No one else was near, but there were figures drawing closer in the distance. She leaned over the railing and hissed loudly, "Jonathan, you'd best make your way up here right now or—or I will tell your father!"

Jonathan did a backward somersault.

Emily recalled her experience with the countess and knew

she'd threatened with the wrong parent. "I am afraid I shall have to inform your mother, then."

Jonathan's head popped up like a seal's. "No! I am coming, Miss Leverton!"

He hastily swam to the water's edge and climbed onto the embankment, his half trousers dripping and his hair plastered to his head. Ruefully, Emily thought he'd ended up much cooler than the rest of them.

She turned to speak further with Frankie, but the other governess had glanced down at Porter's feet with an expression of surprise. "Oh, drat! I did not see him do that."

Emily grimaced. She'd heard of the imposing and impossible-to-please Lady Willoughby, and the woman would *not* be happy when her son returned shoeless, having walked through Mayfair in his stocking feet.

"We must be going," Emily said, giving Jonathan a hard eye. "We will see if we can reach home before the gossip does."

Frankie righted her glasses on her nose again. "It was nice to meet you. I do not often have the chance to speak with other women of my station. The life of a governess can be lonely, can it not?"

Emily felt a pang of sympathy for the governess. She did know what it felt like to be alone in the world. "Perhaps we will see each other again."

"Unless I am dismissed." Frankie peered over the railing as one leather shoe floated away. "Oh, dear me."

Chapter 24

The next afternoon Emily did her best to linger about the house and make friends with the housemaids so she could drop into rooms she typically would have no business being in. Despite her efforts, all she discovered was that a housemaid and a footman were having an affair, and the dowager countess hadn't been out of her wing since the scandal with the prostitute.

Having accomplished very little, Emily set out with her parasol for Hookham's Circulating Library, which was located on Bond Street. Hookham's was a vast library with a reading room in which she could devour her books without imposing on the Eastmorelands' yearly subscription. Although the Eastmorelands had a library in their house, Emily always felt slightly uneasy using it. Where the abandoned Mottershead library had been a perfect escape, members of the Eastmoreland household often took advantage of their books so Emily never felt truly able to let down her guard enough to become immersed in another world.

When she'd discovered Hookham's her first week as a governess, she'd nearly swooned. During her days as an impoverished youth, a library such as Hookham's would have been as out of her reach as the moon.

The reading room at Hookham's wasn't popular only with Emily, but also with a large portion of the upper classes. It was a respectable place where both men and women could mingle, and in fact functioned as a daytime lounge. Women often visited Hookham's to see others and to be seen, so the prime spots in the reading room were near the entrances and the firesides. Emily, ever the invisible governess, had discovered that if she found a seat in the farthest corner of the reading room, she could remain virtually undisturbed and unnoticed for hours.

The murmur of voices in the reading room, along with the scents of tobacco, leather, ink, and women's perfume, lulled Emily's senses as she perused the shelves for novels and plays. Hookham's was careful to select texts that were in alignment with Victorian values, but they could—and did—occasionally miss what was written between the lines, and Emily would delight in stumbling across a story line more scandalous than Hookham's would have liked.

When Lady Rosigan elbowed her way beside Emily, shrilly declaring she could not *believe* the riffraff Hookham's was admitting these days, Emily gulped and slipped into the surgery section. Not for a moment did she entertain the worry that the baroness would remember spitting on her—why would the lady remember one dirty, starved-thin girl she'd harassed nearly seven years ago out of the hundreds of people she'd treated like rubbish over her lifetime? Still, Emily found it prudent to remove herself from the baroness's path. Rosigan was a troublemaker, and all Emily wanted was a little peace.

Safely several rows over, Emily heard a soft, feminine titter.

"Oh, Mr. Denholm. I declare, you are *too* ingenious!"

Emily peered around a shelf to find Zachariah Denholm, book in hand, literally cornered by a young woman and an older dame who was clearly her mother. The two women shared similar features: straight noses, high cheekbones, and darkly lashed eyes. They even had matching braided Tagesfrisur hairstyles, although the mother's hair included silver strands. The daughter was outfitted in the height of fashion: an open neckline that allowed an unfettered view of her smooth skin, a full skirt, and a yellow silk pelisse-robe. In short, she was stunning.

And she had one gloved hand on Zach's arm.

Zach shifted the book to his other hand, casually forcing the girl to drop her touch.

"Many of the *beau monde* would disagree with you, Miss Elizabeth," Zach said, taking a step back. His heel scraped the shelf. "I must confess that I am here on official business. Although it pains me to depart with your company, duty calls."

Emily grinned. Zach was a picture of courteous dismissal. His predicament reminded her all too much of their first encounter at the Exeter ball. Did this happen often to him? She had heard of single, wealthy men plagued by mothers with unmarried daughters, but she had not thought it was so literal.

Zach's face remained civil and unexpressive as the daughter, Miss Elizabeth, refused to take the hint. "Official business? How delightful! I imagine myself to be quite the sleuth, Detective Constable. I would find it a grand adventure to help with your work. I have a keen eye for spotting information in a text." She looked pointedly at the book in his hand. "I may even allow you to return the favor with a stroll in Hyde Park."

Wench!

The inner soldier in Zach must've sensed another presence, because at that moment he lifted his head and discreetly scanned the stacks, his gaze falling on Emily. She gave a cheeky finger wave.

The bland affect Zach had kept pasted on his face vanished, and he smiled directly at her. And when Zachariah Denholm smiled, it was breathtaking. Creases appeared in the corners of intensely blue eyes, that, when focused on her, made her thrill to the tips of her toes. His mouth quirked in that half-knowing way that hinted at a delicious secret only the two of them shared. It was a gorgeous, sinful smile. Emily's stomach did a slow flip.

Miss Elizabeth mistook the smile for her, and her jaw went slack. Her mother unconsciously lifted her fan to wave at her face.

"You must excuse me." Zach took advantage of their momentary stun to brush past them. He grabbed Emily's elbow and pulled her with him, ducking into a row over before the women could see her.

"Once again, laughing at my expense," Zach murmured in her ear. His warm breath sent chills racing up her arms.

"Once again flirting with the unmarried women of the *ton*?" Emily replied, letting him lead her deeper into the shelves of books.

"Ambushed," he corrected. "I was ambushed. I slipped in the side door in need of a specific text, but alas, I was spotted."

"Poor dear," Emily sighed. "Wealthy, handsome, and desired by all."

Zach stopped at the farthest corner of the library, the place where the oldest, dustiest, most out-of-date tomes went to die. He turned her to face him, his gloved hands cupping her upper arms. His eyes, although amused, simmered with a heat that made her corset suddenly feel tighter.

"I care only to be desired by one." His gaze fell to her mouth and Emily blushed at the remembrance of their last encounter— the feel of his hands nimbly unbuttoning her gown, the hunger in his eyes before he'd turned away so she could remove her stifling gown in privacy.

Emily licked her lips and fought against her impulses. They were in a public place that required the utmost decorum. It would be entirely scandalous, and frankly stupid, to act on the sudden and intense jealousy she'd felt when Lady Elizabeth had rested her hand on Zach's arm with such claim. Hadn't Emily decided it would be safest if she and Zach were friends and nothing more?

Take a step back, Emily silently instructed herself. *It is only a teeny-tiny step. You can do it. Do. Not. Give. In.*

Emily lunged for him. She wrapped her hand around the back of his neck and pulled his head down, pressing her lips to his. It was her first time initiating a kiss, and in his surprise Zach momentarily ceded control to her. Emily stroked his lips with her tongue, seeking the intimate contact she'd had with him in Bethnal Green. Zach acquiesced to her silent demand, opening his mouth and letting her explore. Just as during their first kiss, a curious heat pooled in Emily's core and her fingertips began to tingle. Acting entirely on instinct, she gently nipped his lower lip.

Zach pulled away and she caught her breath, suddenly afraid she had gone too far and antagonized him into anger. Then she remembered this was *Zach's* embrace she was in, not the Pig's.

Emily met his surprised glance and shivered when his eyes slowly turned dark and needy, as if the scrape of her teeth had loosened something primal and not-quite civilized inside him. Zach looped one arm around her waist and Emily squeaked when he swung her so that her back bumped into the shelf. Then he was on her again, devouring her, racing kisses down her jaw and then back up to her ear, where he sucked her lobe into his mouth.

Emily tugged him closer, desperate for further contact. Zach's large hand circled the base of her throat, just above the swell of her breasts, and he gently guided her mouth to his with electrifying ownership. At that moment a book behind Emily came loose and dropped to the ground with the crack of a gunshot.

They jumped apart guiltily and Emily pressed the back of her hand to her mouth. "Rake!"

Zach's lips parted. "Was it not *you* who kissed *me?*"

Emily sighed in despair. "I have terrible impulse control. It is truly a problem."

Zach readjusted his cuffs as a slow, wolfish grin spread across his face. "Noodles, you can lose control with me anytime."

During their moment of madness, Zach had shoved his book on one of the shelves. To give herself time to restore her rapidly beating heart to normal, Emily took the book down and read the title. "*Blair's Lectures on the Diseases of the Mind.* What is this for?"

Zach removed the book from her hand. "The Evangelist. It is possible he possesses a disease of the mind that makes him act the way he does. I thought to study the research and see if there is a profile that fits him."

"That is clever."

"I cannot take credit." Zach tucked the book under his arm as his gaze drifted over her gown. "The suggestion came from our anonymous source. Why is the neckline of the governess's gown so dastardly high?"

Emily's heart did a different kind of twist. "Anonymous source?"

"Yes. The Metropolitan Police enjoy the benefit of an irritatingly secretive, albeit shockingly accurate informant."

The Dove! Emily fought to keep her expression neutral. "You do not know his identity?"

Zach reached forward to tuck a tendril of hair behind her ear. "No, although not for lack of trying. One would think an entire police force could uncover his name, and yet we always seem to be one step behind him, and he two steps ahead of us. I do not know how he comes across the information he has. All I know is that he must hold a very powerful position in society."

Emily briefly nuzzled into the palm of his hand before she remembered herself and took a step back. If they were caught touching, it would be a scandal for the ages. "Really? Someone in the *ton*, you think? Has he helped the police solve crimes in the upper classes?"

Zach's eyes sharpened on her face. She had pushed it too far. "He has. Why the interest in our informant?"

"Oh, you know," she said, circling around until she was at the entrance to the abandoned book stacks. "Simple curiosity. Oh my! Did you hear the tower strike the time?"

"No."

"I must be going!" Emily cried over her shoulder. "I will see you tomorrow!"

She hurried past the other library patrons, her thoughts whizzing. So it was true! Without knowing it, Zach had vouched for the Dove's claims. If Emily helped the Dove, she would in essence be helping Zach, too. She could make a real difference.

When the Dove had first approached her, Emily had thought spying on the *ton* could be her chance for atonement; then she'd let her suspicions get in the way. With her conscience clear, Emily could now fully join the ranks of governesses who used their position to watch over those with less power.

She could begin to pay for the damage she had done all those years ago.

Chapter 25

To her horror, the next day Emily discovered that Lord and Lady Eastmoreland, along with Minnie, were to be in attendance at the masquerade ball. She nearly sent an emergency note to Zach to cancel, but then calmed herself down with the reminder that she would be completely unrecognizable in the domino mask. Besides, it wasn't as if her employers would ever expect their governess to be attending the same function. Emily had learned long ago that people saw what they expected to see.

After her duties for the day were completed, Emily slipped out of the house and walked to Zach's address. She didn't dare knock on the front door; it wouldn't do for someone to see her there. Instead, she made her way to the kitchen entrance and timidly tapped until the cook opened the door and stared, waiting for her to speak her piece.

"Ah, hello. I am Miss Leverton. I am expected."

The cook looked her up and down. "She doesn't dress like a maid, but the master makes up his own mind, he does. Never seen anything like it in all my years. Nice enough man, though. Well, you'd best come in. I'll fetch the head housekeeper. She's been interviewing girls for the position all day."

Cheeks flaming, Emily said, "Oh, no that is not why I am here. I am expected by Mr. Denholm."

Instead of shooing her away the cook simply said, "I don't know what to expect with that man anymore. Come in and have a spot of tea while I have the butler sort out what's what. Your name again?"

Emily almost ran out of the kitchen in shame. Instead she repeated her name and waited stiffly with a cup of tea in hand while the butler went off to fetch Zach.

Five minutes later Zach thundered into the kitchen, his brows drawn and his lips compressed. "What are you thinking, coming to the back door? You are my guest."

Emily's eyes darted to the cook and butler, who were watching with unabashed interest. "It is not proper," she said, secretly begging him to stop making a scene.

Zach must have read the embarrassment on her face because he reined himself in with visible effort. He straightened his cravat and said calmly to his butler, "Miss Leverton is my guest for the evening and shall be afforded the same status as any guest in this home. I will escort her to the formal parlor. Cook, we would like to eat at eight."

The butler and cook had been well trained, because neither of them so much as blinked when Zach took her arm and guided her out of the kitchen.

When they reached the hallway, Zach stopped, slid his palm into her hair, and brushed his lips against her temple.

Emily's breath caught in her lungs and a flare of lust sparked in her lower belly. She pushed at his chest. He stepped back easily, but his eyes devoured her like a starving man.

"Zach, you said it would all be proper."

"You are right."

"Kissing me is not proper. Looking at me like…like…"

"Like I want to pull you into my study and feast upon your mouth?"

Emily's cheeks, if possible, heated further, and her palms felt itchy. "Yes. Looking at me like that is not proper. You will start gossip if you do."

"My servants would not dare."

"I meant if you look at me like that at the ball. You promised me tonight would be respectable. That we would attend as *friends*. I made a mistake at the library, and I apologize for it. I did not think my actions through."

Zach scrubbed a palm over his face and increased the space between them. "No apology necessary, Em. I'll defer to your lead." He gave her a look that singed her brows. "We will remain friends while you work out what it is you want. Just know that all you have to do is ask for more, and you shall have it."

Emily nodded, the tightness in her chest loosening. It would be so easy to fall into his enchanting world, but men like Zach were not for women like Emily. There would always be something in the way, whether it was her station, her marital status, or a secret so shameful it kept her awake at night. At the library she had only made things more confusing between them and she could not allow it to happen again. If he had not already gone through the expense of commissioning a gown for her, she would have walked out right that moment. She was losing control to her impulses.

Losing her self-preservation to the relentless charm of the man standing before her. "I will not ask you."

He studied her face and then tapped her nose lightly. "Then friends we shall remain, Noodles."

Emily slipped her hand into the crook of his elbow and allowed him to lead her into the formal receiving room. It was a massive space, easily ten times the width of her narrow room at Eastmoreland House, but Emily suspected most parlors in Mayfair were. It had tall domed windows, a glittering chandelier, and a marble fireplace. Zach's parlor was oddly simple and spacious, without the fussy antiques and gold-plated scrollwork of the Eastmorelands'. It was a display of a different kind of wealth: discreet wealth. Emily found she vastly preferred it.

"I am going to call in my head housekeeper, Mrs. Figsby," Zach explained as he settled her on a settee of rich navy-blue upholstery. "She will act as your lady's maid today."

Emily blanched. "Zach! No! You cannot ask a woman of her position to assist a governess. It is a terrible insult."

Zach frowned, and Emily remembered he'd shot from poverty to extraordinary wealth and skipped the part where he learned about the intricate hierarchy and pride associated with servant positions.

"She will have to take it on the chin, then. I do not have a lady's maid lying around in my employ. I suppose I could ask one of the maids."

"I will dress myself," Emily said firmly. "I have been managing just fine all my life."

Zach pulled the chair out from the writing desk and sat down across from her. "There is a reason the gentry require assistance. They wear the most blasted clothing. You should see the buttons on your gown. Hundreds, I swear. You will have to do acrobatics to get into it."

"I will find a way. If I need help with the buttons, you can help."

His eyes darkened. "Maybe you have the right of it after all."

Emily fidgeted, uncomfortable with what she had to say next. Sure, she'd spent a good portion of her life as a thief, but she'd never taken charity. Mostly because there had been so little of it to go around and so much need. Still, in the Lewis household there had been unspoken pride in eking out a living, even if it was through thieving and prostitution. That meant it hurt to take the charity of an expensive gown from Zach. She'd known there was no way she could afford a gown suitable for the event that wouldn't embarrass him or peg her for what she was, so she'd accepted. Now she had to live with the humiliation of it.

Zach's eyes fell to her twisting fingers. "What's the matter?"

The detective in him would notice her body language, she thought ruefully. She cleared her throat and forced her hands into stillness. "Thank you for the gown." She knew color was rising in her tattletale cheeks, and that only embarrassed her further.

Zach rubbed the side of his neck. "The gown was part of the deal. If this were a normal courtship—if you were a free and interested woman—by now I would have spent a small fortune on flowers, sweets, and books of poetry. I would have dedicated hours of my time vying with other suitors for an ounce of your attention, begging you to accompany me on carriage rides, and staring down your fearsome female relatives in a stuffy parlor. But this is not a normal courtship, it is a friendship, and I have only stolen moments with you. Do not feel that you're getting more out of this than I am. Without you, I would have to attend tonight's ball with gritted teeth and a headache. You are doing me a great favor by going with me, and a gown is the very least I owe you in thanks."

He'd understood the source of her discomfort, Emily thought in some amazement. No noble-born man would have. She supposed it took living in poverty to comprehend the complicated feelings of shame and pride that were entwined with it.

Emily nearly jumped off the settee and threw her arms around his neck, but before she could act on her impulse, there came a soft rap at the door and a woman entered and curtsied. Mrs. Figsby, Emily presumed.

Zach smiled broadly. "Good afternoon, Figs."

Emily only shook her head.

"This is my guest, Miss Leverton. She will be attending this evening's masquerade ball with me and must dress before dinner. Please escort her to the guest chamber across from mine and see that the maids bring her everything she needs: perhaps a hot bath to start."

Eyes wide, Emily darted a look at Mrs. Figsby's face. She seemed unfazed by the request.

"Yes, sir. Will Miss Leverton require the assistance of the maids to dress?"

"No."

Mrs. Figsby was a tall, slender woman with broad shoulders that curved inward despite her near-perfect posture. She was younger than Emily had expected, perhaps in her thirties, and had pale-gold hair threaded with gray. Lines radiated from the corners of her eyes, and Emily understood why when the other woman turned and smiled warmly at her.

"That is a shame. The girls have been looking forward to helping Mr. Denholm's guest dress. They consider it practice. They are all aiming to someday be a lady's maid," she said confidentially, even though Zach could clearly hear her. "One of them has been practicing with the curling iron since the gown arrived."

Zach beamed at Mrs. Figsby. Then, turning to Emily, he said, "You cannot let them down, Miss Leverton. It would break their hearts."

Emily knew when she was being played, but the head house-keeper exuded such kind understanding, and it would look just as bad for her to decline and then come down buttoned when everyone knew only the master of the house could have done it. *Then* what would they think?

"All right, yes," Emily said. "Thank you."

Mrs. Figsby clapped her hands once and morphed from a picture of kindness and understanding to one of strict efficiency. "Excellent. I will have the maids draw the bath. We have a lot to do before dinner and not much time to do it."

Emily hustled as Mrs. Figsby ushered her out of the room. She glanced over her shoulder at Zach, but instead of the grin she'd expected to see, he was looking after her with a frown.

Chapter 26

Zach watched Emily leave the room while Mrs. Figsby delivered orders to the waiting maids, and he made a mental note to give the housekeeper a raise. Mrs. Figsby, although young to be a head housekeeper, had served as a maid in a duke's London residence for nearly a decade before Zach had poached her. She knew nobility in and out, and was no doubt aware that Emily's origins were lacking, yet she'd treated her as she might any other mistress. It was a good reminder of why he'd chosen her to manage his household. Above all else, Zach hired based on competency and loyalty. Mrs. Figsby had both.

Zach had several personal business matters to attend to before he dressed for dinner, but when he reached his study he found himself tossing a geode paperweight from hand to hand and contemplating his situation with Emily. He'd managed to badger her into dinner and dancing with him tonight, but no doubt the Eastmoreland family would soon pack up for their country estate and Emily would go with them. Zach, at least while leading the hunt for the Evangelist, was stuck in London. If Emily were in the city, he could manufacture ways to bump into her or entice her into other rendezvous with silly notes, but that would be impossible once she was in the country.

He could not abide the thought.

Zach was an honest man, and had the unfortunate habit of being honest with himself. He'd quickly realized his infatuation with Emily wasn't going to wear off. Each time she spoke he thought she was funnier than he remembered. Every time he saw her, he thought she'd grown more radiant.

He slammed the paperweight on the desk. Damn her dead-but-not-legally husband! It gnawed at him to know that by law she still belonged to that rotter. What had the bastard done to give her that battle-weary look in her eye that he'd seen in soldiers time and again? Emily was fierce and brave; she wouldn't have taken mistreatment with her head bowed.

He grimaced, knowing her spirit had likely made her marriage harder.

What had she said about her husband? He'd gone to Australia because "he thought it was a fledgling colony ripe for the fleecing and rare on the law." Emily didn't know how much that had revealed. She'd come a long way and disguised her past well, but with that comment Zach had recognized her as a fellow slum baby. Emily's husband had been a thief and a con man, at the minimum.

It explained so much: how she'd caught the pickpocket with honed reflexes, how she'd known to keep alert, how she'd taken her dagger and nearly sliced the manhood off one of the thugs.

Emily was more like him than she'd let on. He'd risen to the highest echelons of society, she to the position of a noble family's governess. Her feat was as extraordinary as his. He didn't know how she'd managed it, but he felt a warm burst of pride that she had.

If she wanted to keep her past a secret, he would continue to feign ignorance. He understood better than most the stigma of poverty. Eventually he would ease aside the barriers she'd constructed between them, but he was going to have to convince her to trust him, first.

That meant keeping his word about not touching her at the masquerade ball.

Zach groaned.

Although he'd be surrounded by debutants desperate to make a match at the end of the Season, the only woman he was interested in was the mouthy governess taking a bath upstairs.

The idea of her under *his* roof made Zach feel a visceral, primal possessiveness. He hadn't known how much he would like seeing her in his house, sitting on his furniture, chatting with his staff.

Was it irony, or simply Fate's cruel sense of humor, that the one woman who stirred feelings of protectiveness and lust in him was the one woman he couldn't have?

Tired of his brooding thoughts, Zach poured a rare amber Scotch into a cut-crystal glass and turned to his ledgers. He had a good hour before he had to dress for dinner, and he hoped the rows of numbers would take his mind off the fact that right that moment, Emily was sunk into a layer of bubbles without so much as a stitch to cover her.

He dropped his head in his hands. It was going to be a hell of an evening.

Emily groaned, sinking deeper into the copper bath and nearly slipping into a comatose state of pleasure. The soap was lilac-scented, the water warm and clean. Emily knew this was the only time in her life she would be able to soak in a bath while being waited on hand and foot, so she stayed in the water until it turned tepid, and then cold.

Finally, after the maids called in Mrs. Figsby to scold Emily for staying in the cool water for so long that she was bound to catch the sniffles, Emily reluctantly stepped out of the tub. Her skin was pink and wrinkled like a raisin, but the room was warm enough that she didn't shiver as she dried herself with a massive Turkish towel.

Emily quickly discovered that modesty had no place in a lady's dressing room. After she'd slathered on the cream a young maid had presented, she was helped into her underclothes. With the assistance of three maids under the supervision of Mrs. Figsby, Emily was tugged and tucked, her hair pulled and curled, her nails buffed and filed, until her entire body felt raw from the attentions. At last she was deemed perfect and allowed to view herself in the mirror.

The woman in the looking glass was not Emily, could not have been her. Governess Emily, with her freckles, stubborn hair, and simple dresses, was as far removed from this person as an orange seller from a queen.

Emily touched her cheek and stepped back, her gaze sweeping over what she'd been made into. Her naturally curly hair had been tamed with the iron, and one of the maids had expertly piled it on top of her head, leaving strategic curls dangling to soften the look. A thin, braided silver chain had been woven around the crown of her head, catching the light of the candles and flashing like sparks of sunlight on the ocean.

Her eyebrows had been plucked, and castor oil and charcoal

lightly smeared over her lids to create a dewy effect. The maids had powdered her nose in an attempt to conceal her unsightly freckles, but to no avail.

Although Emily herself had been bathed, buffed, and shined, it was the dress that was most stunning. Mrs. Figsby had confided that Zach had chosen it himself, even having the modiste visit so he could select the fabric and pattern. He'd had to guess at her measurements, but other than a slight amount of gaping, the dress fit like a dream.

He'd truly outdone himself.

The gown was sewn of midnight-navy silk of such fine quality that Emily was petrified of snagging it or even letting the hem brush the floor. The sleeves were tight to her elbow and edged with lace, the neckline low and off the shoulder. The bodice was formfitting and came to a point before it blossomed into a wide skirt that fell all the way to the floor. The entire gown was decorated with hundreds of tiny silver beads, strewn about as if they were stars on a night canvas. Every time Emily turned, the light caught the glass and she fairly shimmered.

Mrs. Figsby nodded in satisfaction, and a maid's eyes gleamed as she sniffed back tears.

The dinner gong rang, and Mrs. Figsby escorted Emily to the parlor where drinks were to be served before she and Zach ate.

Zach was already waiting, and when Emily entered his mouth opened in an astonishing imitation of a fish, while his fingers went so slack he nearly dropped his glass.

A wide smile on her face, Mrs. Figsby quietly exited.

Emily held out her arms and twirled. "Do you like it?"

Zach was suffocating. Or maybe it was the blasted cravat. No, it was definitely Emily responsible for his asphyxiation. He'd thought her beautiful in her governess gowns, but dressed in the latest fashion of the *ton* she was stunning.

He had the unwelcome realization that he might be fending off other men at the ball.

He stepped forward and fought the impulse to run a finger beneath his cravat. He was sweating like a schoolboy that had never been in the company of a beautiful woman before. Ridiculous.

"I…" His throat was dry. He took a gulp of Scotch and tried again. "You are stunning."

"It is the gown," she said practically. "It is the nicest thing I have ever worn."

"My butler in that gown would not look half as beautiful," he argued. "It is most certainly the woman wearing it. Would you care for a drink?"

"Yes." Emily stepped forward to survey the crystal decanters and pointed at one filled with clear liquid. "I will have gin."

Zach lifted the bottle. Gin was a poor man's drink. That was why he kept it on hand—it reminded him of his days as a soldier. "Know much about alcohol?"

"A little."

Zach would bet his fortune she knew quite a bit. He stashed that tidbit away, along with the fact that she was drinking gin at all—most young women would be aghast at the idea.

"I have a confession to make," she said, thanking him for the glass and taking a sip. Her face remained impassive; no gasping or watering eyes. This was not the first time she'd had liquor. "I am not a very good dancer. I learned at Perdita's, but I am afraid I might embarrass you. I should have told you before you agreed to take me."

"That is great news. I am not a good dancer, either. Now we can bumble about like buffoons together." He set his glass down and held up a finger. "I just remembered something." He walked to the small writing desk and returned with a rectangular blue velvet box. "Will you do me the honor of wearing this tonight?"

Emily hesitated only a moment before taking the box from his outstretched hand and lifting the lid. Nestled inside was an ocean-blue sapphire the size of a robin's egg, set in silver and strung on a braided silver chain.

She didn't speak for a full minute. The box trembled in her hand and her chest swelled over the gown. "Zach," she finally said, touching the stone reverently with the tip of her glove. "It is beautiful. I have never been entrusted with something so exquisite. How rich are you, anyway?"

He gave a bark of laughter and lifted the necklace from the jeweler's box. Emily turned her back to him and he clasped the chain around her throat, brushing his fingers against the soft curls at the nape of her neck. She smelled like warm lilac and soap, and his belly clenched with desire. He ached to feel how soft and warm she was in other places.

Emily spun and lifted her eyelashes. They stood nearly touching, her lips parted, the air between them heavy and tense. Then she shifted away and said, "Shall we eat?"

Chapter 27

Zach scowled across the ballroom as Lord Weeberly's hand drifted over Emily's back. Zach had introduced her to society as Miss Emily, his distant cousin from Kettering. He had hinted that a shipping magnate from Liverpool was pursuing her hand in marriage, thinking the lie would encourage the *ton*'s acceptance while discouraging suitors.

He hadn't counted on the opposite happening. The genteelly impoverished men who hadn't managed to snag an heiress during the Season figured that if a wealthy merchant were interested in Emily, then Zach must have bestowed quite a generous dowry on her indeed.

If Emily had been his cousin, they would have been right. But she wasn't. She was *his*, and he was about three seconds from knocking Weeberly flat on his arse.

"You look murderous."

Zach grunted at Wright's assessment without taking his eyes off Emily.

"Your cousin is beautiful. Where have you been hiding her all this time?"

Zach's frown intensified. "The country. Did you see that? Did you see the way he just moved his hand? She isn't a cat to be stroked."

"You are imagining things, Colonel."

At the address, Zach tore his gaze from Emily. "I am not your colonel anymore, Deputy Commissioner."

His friend sipped from a crystal glass, his dark mustache framing the rim as if giving it a hairstyle. "You have not made a report since you worked out the time frame the Evangelist operates within."

"Do not rub it in."

"What are your next steps?"

"I am going to play a game," Zach replied. At his friend's stony silence he grinned. "It will run in the newspaper tomorrow. I would tell you now, but frankly I am looking forward to your reaction. If I am correct, it will go something along the lines of 'Zachariah Denholm, what the hell were you thinking?' It should be great fun."

"Fun for whom?"

"Me, of course. You will be livid."

Wright sighed. "This is not inspiring confidence."

Zach's amusement faded into something quiet and still. "Do you lack confidence in me?"

Wright finished his drink and returned the solemn tone. "Never, Colonel."

Zach's lip lifted fractionally. "You remember that tomorrow morning when you are reading the paper. Oh God, is that Mrs.

Hill powering over here with her two dull daughters in tow? Save me."

Before Wright could respond, Zach shoved him forward and dashed behind another couple, sacrificing his friend while he escaped through the throng of bodies.

The musicians segued into a new song, but Lord Weeberly continued hogging Emily's attention. He was speaking earnestly while holding her gloved hand and trying to pull her into another dance. Emily stayed stubbornly rooted to the floor.

Zach appeared at Emily's elbow in time to hear the notorious rake propose to take her for a carriage ride the next day.

"No," Zach said.

Weeberly's surprise morphed into annoyance when he realized it was Zach who'd spoken. Lord Weeberly was considered a handsome man, with thick black hair, soft lips, and a delicate bone structure. The women of the *ton* called him a romantic, and it was usually said with a sigh. A pestilence was more like it. The man had gambled away a small fortune, drank heavily, and fornicated with anything that would have him. He'd tried more than once to weasel his way into Zach's pockets, offering investment opportunities that were nothing more than swindles. Zach despised him, and judging by Weeberly's scathing look, the feeling was mutual.

Zach slipped his arm around Emily's shoulders. Weeberly defiantly continued to hold her hand.

"With all due respect, *Mr.* Denholm, I believe your cousin can answer for herself."

"Lord Weeberly is right," Emily said, yanking her hand away from the dandy. "I *can* speak for myself, and my answer is no."

Zach smugly tucked Emily closer.

Lord Weeberly sneered. "It is for the best. I would not want to tarnish my image by continuing to consort with common company."

Before Zach could grab Weeberly's jacket and teach him some respect, Emily slapped her hand against Zach's chest and said firmly, "Please do not concern yourself with the words of this louse, cousin. He is simply bitter that you are filthy rich while the threads on his jacket are fraying."

Weeberly's cheeks flamed and Zach's eyes dropped to the man's cuffs. They were indeed frayed. The other man spun off in what was very close to a show of temper.

Several couples frowned at them for standing still on the dance floor, so Emily turned into Zach. He took her gloved hand in his and wrapped his arm around her waist, seamlessly pulling her into the spinning fray.

He had lied to her. He was an excellent dancer, good enough even to compensate for her missteps. Dancing had been one of the many skills he had determined to master before entering the world of the wealthy. Many nights he had stayed up well past the midnight hour, studying titles and address, learning which silverware to eat with and how to waltz, all for the sole purpose of impressing his business associates. It had been a strategic move that had allowed him to slip easily into high society. The gentry were more comfortable investing with a man who acted as they did.

"I wouldn't normally shame someone for lack of wealth," Emily said, unconsciously matching his movements. Despite her inexperience, Zach had never had a dance partner fit so perfectly in his arms, move so intuitively with his body. "Except he started it by drawing attention to your lack of title. And he was so smug the whole time we were dancing, treating me as if this were a grand adventure for the poor country mouse."

Zach's hand flexed on her waist. Maybe he *would* have a chat with Weeberly after all.

Emily suddenly seemed to realize they were dancing together again. "Isn't there a rule that you are not supposed to dance with the same partner twice in a night?"

"An arbitrary rule."

Her mouth curved into a smile. "There will be gossip."

Zach pulled her closer than propriety condoned. "Let them talk." His fingertips trailed up her back until they touched bare skin. Emily's expression shifted from playful to curious desire. Zach swallowed and closed the remaining distance, until their midriffs were touching. He wanted to run his tongue along the cord in her neck and nuzzle into the softness of her hair. He wanted to ravage her mouth until her pupils were dilated and she was gasping for more.

"Stop looking at me like that," she whispered.

"I cannot help it."

She licked her bottom lip.

Zach groaned. "You are killing me, Noodles."

Emily laughed. "I trust you will survive. How am I doing as your cousin?" She asked the question casually, as if she did not overly care about the answer, but Zach could feel the slight stiffening of her body. "Do you think anyone has guessed that I am a governess?"

"No one. You have every man in this room trying to finagle an introduction, and every woman hoping you do not appear next Season."

"I am the only person still wearing a domino. Everyone else took theirs off almost immediately."

"It only serves to make you more mysterious. You are doing beautifully."

Zach twirled her past Miss Hill, who was stomping her poor partner's feet into the floor. "Speaking of your position as governess..."

"No."

"No what?"

"No figuring me out tonight."

"I thought that was the whole purpose of tonight? We get to know each other and become inseparable friends." His fingers traced the skin of her shoulder blade and she shivered.

"Friends do not make one another feel...things."

Zach swayed with her in his arms, and for the first time in his life felt entirely comfortable on a ballroom floor. The light from the chandeliers above and the flames licking in the sconces on the walls reflected off the silver beads of her dress, making her appear to shimmer seductively with every movement. Her breasts swelled over the low neckline, and Zach could barely keep his gaze from the delicately freckled skin. Her dark hair curled in a riotous mass at the back of her head, held up by an army of pins; and her eyes, the color of the richest chocolate, sparkled with wit and humor. She was Penthesilea, the Amazonian queen from Greek mythology: both beautiful and fearless.

"What *things* am I making you feel?" Zach spotted the opened doors to the balcony and with each step maneuvered her closer. The room was stifling but, more important, crowded with watchful eyes. He wanted Emily to himself.

"I don't know how to explain it. I suppose you make me feel tingly."

Tingly was good. "We can expand on tingly."

"How so?" she asked curiously.

Zach continued to edge her to the doors and swiftly knocked back the icy rage that had materialized with the reminder of how Emily had been taken advantage of in her marriage. It was a man's duty to make sure his partner felt satisfaction, but there were far too many men who selfishly rutted like pigs. Clearly Emily's husband had been one of them.

He brought his mouth to her ear and lowered his voice so that no one else would hear him. "First, I would make your cheeks feel hot and your breath short. Your heart would race and your fingers and toes would tingle."

"You already do that."

He nearly nipped her ear. "Your breasts would tighten and all you would think about was how desperately you wanted my mouth on them, how you needed to feel my lips seal around your nipples and lavish them with my tongue. Just the thought of it would send a streak of heat to that place between your legs. You'd grow wet and slick, and you'd beg me to kiss my way down your body and—"

"Stop!" Emily gasped. Her eyes were round with shock and Zach was sure he'd crossed a line. What on earth had possessed him to talk to her like that?

"Zach," she said, drawing her shoulders back, "take me onto the balcony and kiss me."

Chapter 28

Emily was still flushed from Zach's dirty talk as he walked her onto the balcony. She should have been scandalized—certainly would have been if anyone else had spoken to her that way. But there was a realness to Zach that made her feel as if any topic, any taboo could be broached. It was so...*freeing.*

Well, almost any topic. The Big Secret wasn't one of them.

The balcony was crowded with attendees hoping to catch an errant breeze. Zach led her to the stairway and they descended into the courtyard garden, a haven of greenery complete with a miniature hedge maze.

They strolled past flowering roses and tulips and into the hedge maze, where Zach immediately and purposefully got them lost. The night sky was velvety, with a few bright stars penetrating the persistent smog. Torches had been lit along the garden path, but the maze had been left deliciously dark.

"We will not be the only ones in here," Zach murmured as he stripped off his gloves. He took her hand and tugged her close. "So we will have to be careful. Now say it again."

"Say what?" Emily asked, distracted. With her palms pressed to his chest, she could feel how firm and broad he was underneath the suit jacket.

"I told you I would not touch you tonight until you asked. So say it again. Ask me to kiss you."

Emily tilted her head, her stomach dipping with anticipation. "I will not join you in bed."

Zach's cobalt eyes drilled into her. "Understood. Now say it."

"You still want to kiss me, even if that is all we do?"

He caged her with his body, and she could feel the heat of him radiating through his coat. He lifted his hands and slowly untied the domino. Even though it was only a mask, when it dropped away it felt as if he'd taken a part of her resistance with him. "Emily, I could spend days doing nothing but kissing you."

"Why? Why me?" She waved her hand in the general direction of the ballroom. "There are leagues of high-society chits who would happily trip over one another to be with you."

"That is true enough. I have received more than one proposition tonight."

Emily's hand, still pressed against his chest, flexed painfully. *Who* exactly? She wanted a list.

"But," Zach continued, "there is a problem."

"What? Choosing which one?" she asked, annoyed she'd even brought up the topic.

Zach cuffed her upper arms and hauled her onto her toes. "They aren't you. Now bloody well tell me to kiss you, Emily, before I lose the last shreds of my dignity and beg."

She had given him fair warning. If he still wanted to kiss her, that was his problem. "Kiss me, Zachariah." She gave him her sauciest look and hoped it didn't appear that she was having a stroke. "Make it good, because it will be our last."

Zach growled at the challenge and crushed his mouth to hers. The first time they had kissed in Bethnal Green he had been gentle, coaxing. In the library he had been caught off guard. This kiss was nothing like either of those. It was as if Zach's inner restraints had snapped, releasing his primal beast. He kissed her as if he were marking her, owning her.

His mouth was hot and hard, his tongue skilled as it swept into her mouth and forced every rational thought into hiding. His hands slid down her arms to her back, lower and lower, until he was cupping her intimately against the rigid length of him.

Suddenly he released her lips with a nip, and Emily felt a wave of disappointment that it was so soon over. Then his teeth gently closed over her earlobe and he breathed something filthy that he wanted to do to her—she wasn't even sure she understood what it was—and began kissing a trail down the sensitive column of her neck.

Emily clung to his shoulders, her muscles having turned to the consistency of honey. The feel of his lips on such a sensitive, intimate place was shocking. The Pig had never kissed her, not even the back of her hand. But Zach, he was running his tongue over her as if her skin tasted of sugar.

He released her bottom, only to slide his fingers into the neckline of her gown, where he suddenly stilled. His searing eyes met hers and then he began to remove his hand.

Emily clamped down on his wrist to halt his withdrawal. "What are you doing?"

"Only kissing," he said, his voice guttural. "I promised you only kissing."

She knew she was flushing strawberry red when she said, "I wasn't specific about *where* I wanted you to kiss me, now was I?"

Zach froze. "Do you know what you are saying?"

"If I recall, you were fairly explicit in the ballroom about the places a woman could be kissed. And I have only experienced one of them."

Still he hesitated, and her heart tripped a little closer to an emotion she had no interest in exploring. She knew he wanted her—the look in his eye was enough to set her dress to flames, but he did not want to take advantage of her the way her husband had.

So Emily took matters into her owns hands. She pushed his wrist out of the way and slowly tugged the shoulders of the dress down, her breasts spilling free for the night air to caress.

She stunned herself with her wantonness, but the look of utter worship that crossed Zach's face made it worth it.

He cupped her breasts in his hands, and they fit perfectly in his palms. Chills raced up Emily's arms when his thumbs lightly brushed her nipples. They hardened instantly, and he dipped his head and took one into his mouth.

He had been right when he had spoken such scandalous words in her ear. His suckling sent a tug straight to her core, as if there were a string attached from her breasts to the junction of her thighs. She knew she was becoming damp *down there* and she might have been embarrassed, except Zach had talked about that, too, and when he had, it had sounded as if it *really* excited him.

He turned his attention to her other breast, the rasp of his cheek as intoxicating as the warmth of his tongue while he lavished her. When he pulled away, her nipples, still wet from his mouth, peaked stiffly in the night air.

Zach knelt, and Emily wasn't sure what he was doing, but she prayed it wasn't proposing.

"Emily," he said, his voice raspy, "you will have to let me know when you have had enough kissing."

Her knees were trembling and the hedges were jabbing into her back, but she didn't want him to stop, so she only nodded. If he would only stand up and kiss her again instead of talking at her from the ground as if he had to shine his boots!

Zach's hand, warm and callused, wrapped around her ankle, and her mouth popped open. What was he...oh! His hand slid up her stocking with agonizing slowness. He was touching her calf, her knee, and then he was at the top of her garter where the stockings gave way to silky smooth skin. The feel of his fingertips on such delicate flesh made Emily break out in chills.

"Zach?"

"Mmhmm?"

"What are you doing?"

His fingers continued trailing north, underneath the leg hole of her drawers. "Kissing."

Emily's heart was pounding so hard she thought even he could hear it. "This is not kissing."

"I'm getting there." His fingertips brushed the curls at the vee of her thighs and Emily, her pulse erratic and sweat sliding down her hairline, let him. In fact, she spread her legs farther.

"That's my girl." Zach murmured his approval as he moved ever closer to the center of her pleasure. "Is this still okay?"

"Yes. Yes!"

Then he was touching her there, rubbing his fingers through her wetness, circling the bud of pleasure she thought only she'd known existed.

"You know about that?" she gasped. Her former husband, the Pig, certainly hadn't.

Zach buried his face in her skirts, but not before she saw the smile. Suddenly self-conscious, she started to pull away. He stilled her with his hands and said quickly, "I am not laughing at you. I love that you know that about your body. It excites me."

Emily allowed herself to relax into his touch again, only to go rigid with disbelief when he shoved her skirts to her waist. Air whispered across her thighs, and it felt amazingly cool to be free from the layers of petticoats. Zach pulled the waistband of her drawers down, and before Emily could demand an explanation, he kissed her. Just as he'd said he would.

He was openmouthed, French-kissing her most intimate part. Emily had never heard of such a thing, and if she were a proper woman she would have been horrified. But she was common-born, so when her knees nearly collapsed from the pleasure, she told herself it was hardly her fault.

He ran his tongue over her, into her, and circled around the nub that had given her secret, sinful pleasure when she was alone. He kissed her as if he could not get enough of her, as if she tasted like ambrosia of the gods. His tongue was hot and thorough, and after he'd explored every inch of her he returned to that special bundle of nerves and there he stayed, focusing all of his attention on that exquisite spot. It didn't take long before Emily was lifted higher and higher, and then she shattered into a thousand pieces, pleasure soaring through her veins like a drug. She cried out in ecstasy, neither cognizant nor caring of who might be near to hear. When she went boneless, Zach caught her, quickly easing up her drawers and replacing her skirts.

They sat together, he leaning against the hedges with his legs outstretched, she cradled in his lap. His arms were draped loosely around her as she relaxed languidly in his embrace.

For the first time in her life, Emily knew what it was to feel pure contentment.

Chapter 29

Zach's breeches were painfully tight against his erection, and having Emily's gorgeous bottom resting against him wasn't helping. Neither was the fact that he'd just had the most erotic experience of his life. Zach was hardly new to sex. He'd been with his share of women, yet he'd never before felt this mixture of possessiveness, lust, and tenderness. Like a beast, he wanted to rip Emily's dress off and plunge into her, feel the sweetness of her closing tightly around him, hear that cry of ecstasy cling to her lips as he drove her to climax again. And then he wanted to hold her, just like this, only skin-to-skin.

Then he wanted to do it all over again. For days.

What was happening to him? When he pursued a woman, it was usually a simple, straightforward verbal contract. Sex, some baubles, and then it ended after a few months. No cuddling. No declarations of love. No hassles. When the women of his affairs moved on to other lovers, he was always immensely relieved. Whereas the idea of another man touching Emily made him want to commit hot-blooded murder.

"You are tense," Emily murmured sleepily. "I am sorry you did not get to, you know."

Of course she would know about the male orgasm. She had been married. That was the crux of the problem, wasn't it? Zach *hated* that she was still legally bound to another man, no matter how dead. Amusing, brave, enticing Emily was his to protect and cherish now, and he didn't give a bloody damn whether or not she'd taken those vows with someone else.

"Trust me, I am satisfied."

She stirred in his arms just as a branch snapped and someone giggled. Emily heard it as well and vaulted to her feet. Zach joined her and then tugged on her hand, pulling her deeper into the maze.

They ran together, down one path and up another, and by the time they'd reached a dead end Emily was laughing so hard she couldn't breathe. Zach grinned, charmed by her playful attitude toward their near disaster.

When she stood straight again, Zach brushed a curl behind her ear and said, "Get a divorce."

The joy drained from Emily's face. "I cannot divorce a dead man."

"Why not? If the law makes you wait seven years to declare his death, I do not see why you cannot divorce him in the meantime."

Her expression grew thoughtful. "I never thought of that, although I admit for good reason. You know how this world works. Only men can file for divorce, and only on grounds of adultery. It is very expensive."

"Excellent. You are committing adultery with me, and I have lots of money. It looks like you meet two of the requirements."

She lifted one hand, palm-up. "You jest, but I would not even know where to begin."

"I will consult with my solicitor," he said, dropping the teasing tone. "I presume there were witnesses to your marriage that could testify on your behalf. Your mother?"

Her face went white. "No."

"I would pay her."

"That is the problem." Emily's lashes swept across her cheeks as she looked down at the gravel. She toed a pebble with her slipper, and when her gaze lifted her eyes were solemn. "You do not know my mother."

"Would she take offense?"

Emily gave a most unladylike snort. "The opposite, Zach." She sighed deeply. "I suppose you will learn about my past sooner or later. You are a detective; I am afraid curiosity is in your blood. I might as well be the one to divulge my shame. Here is my great secret: I was raised a dirt-poor thief."

Chapter 30

It wasn't the Big Secret, but perhaps it was enough of the truth to quell his curiosity over her circumstances.

Zach didn't turn his back on her, flinch, or really show any signs of surprise at all. Instead he seemed to take it in stride, saying, "That makes sense."

Emily was horrified. "How?"

"Your ease at Bethnal Green, how you knew who to watch, the knife. The pickpocket."

"Yes, well, perhaps the moon wasn't in your eyes after all. It takes a pickpocket to know a pickpocket."

His expression was sympathetic when he turned her to face him. "You did what you had to in order to survive."

She shrugged. "I suppose you could say the same about my mother when she arranged my marriage to Lionel. Not only was he willing to take me without a dowry, he paid *her*. Besides, I was cramping her style. It was a win-win for everyone but me."

"How were you cramping her style?"

Well, here went nothing. If he still wanted to have an affair after hearing about the filth she came from, then she was Queen Victoria.

"When I was a child, we moved from town to town. My mother and the man I called my father treated my younger sister and me like their personal props for their swindles. Father was very good at it, actually, and for a while we always had food to eat. My mother would even buy new gowns and lord it over the other women. Then Father stole from the wrong man. He was caught and sent to prison, where they hanged him.

"After his death, my mother took on what laundering work she could, except her fingers were too sticky for honest work. Eventually word got around and no one would hire her, so we moved to the city. By that time she'd begun sleeping with men for money. Sometimes her johns would get violent. Fortunately they were almost always drunk as well, so I was able to run them off. My younger sister began whoring but I refused. That is why my mother sold me to Lionel, because I wasn't 'pulling my weight,' even though I brought home just as much with odd jobs and thieving as either of them did on their backs."

To Emily's astonishment, she began to feel lighter as she spilled her sordid history. Although the lies and half-truths had kept her safe, they had also kept her chained, slowly eating at her from the inside out. This was the real Emily, as ugly as it was. This was the past from which she had come. She couldn't change that, just as she couldn't change what had happened when, as a girl of fourteen, she had met her true father after they'd moved to London.

For a split moment the echo of his voice rang in her ears, as cutting and cruel as the day her mother had ambushed the marquess outside his club, clawing and cringing as she demanded funds.

"You left me with your bastard child!" Emily's mother had screeched.

Emily may have been young, but she'd been aware enough to be ashamed of her mother's behavior.

The marquess had barely given her dirty, barefooted figure a glance. "You have no proof. And even if she were, what makes you think I give a single damn about a by-blow?"

On the heels of that humiliating memory crowded another, this one of Emily two years later, standing at the servants' door to her father's kitchen, passing a note to the cook and receiving a mealy apple and a half loaf of bread in return.

"Can I see him?" Emily had asked. "He's my da. He reached out to me. Mayhap he would see me now..."

But by the pity in the cook's eyes, Emily had known it was useless. Her father had sought her out after he'd come across her selling flowers in Mayfair. When he'd walked past her on the street corner, blooms wilting in her arms, she'd known by the burning in his eyes that he recognized her from the altercation with her mother two years prior. Yet he'd strolled by her as if she were nothing more than a shadow. So she'd been more than a little surprised when, later that night, she'd found him waiting for her as she wearily trudged home with her unsold flowers, knowing that if she wanted to help pay the rent she'd need to lift a few purses.

He'd asked her to collect information for him: gossip, rumors, and the daily grievances of the *ton* that she overheard while selling flowers. He'd assured her it was harmless, that it simply gave him a competitive edge in his business, and she'd been too naive to the world of the aristocracy to know any better. In return for her help, Emily's father had promised to recognize her as his bastard child and fund her dowry. At sixteen, Emily had known marriage was on the horizon, and a dowry and an honorable name could mean the difference between a lifetime bound to a distant, if respectable, partner and one chained to one of the more violent men who populated her life. For two years Emily had dutifully upheld her end of the bargain, desperately hoping each time she knocked on the marquess's kitchen door that *this* would be the time her father honored his end. That this would be the time she was lifted out of poverty.

It never was.

And after the scandal that ensued when she turned eighteen, Emily could not have been more grateful for her anonymity.

Now it was six years later and she still carried the guilt of that deal with her father like a second shadow. It took residence in her soul, ate at her conscience.

If Zach ever found out what she'd done...

Emily shook off the thought. For tonight she would forget about the final chapter of her past. She would share herself with Zach, even if she couldn't share her deepest shame.

Zach's jawline could have been chiseled from stone. "Did she know? Did your mother know what Lionel was?"

Emily's hands fisted. "She knew. My marriage was the age-old story. I was sold off to the highest bidder. The same happens here," she said, jutting her chin toward the house, "the gentry just dress it up prettier. Lionel was a monster from the start. He never showed me any love or compassion. The only time he touched me outside of the marital bed was to hurt me. One day he hit me so hard I couldn't hear out of my left ear for a week. I don't remember why. Something to do with his dinner, I think."

Zach's eyes visibly frosted and even though the air was oppressive, Emily shivered.

"When he boarded that ship, I wished with all my heart that it would go under, Zach. And when it did, I didn't feel guilty. I felt pure, unadulterated relief, as if I had been granted this precious gift of a new life. In that moment I decided I wasn't going to waste it thieving anymore. I had the inspiration to become a governess and support myself far away from my family.

"*That* is why you cannot pay my mother to testify against Lionel. If she knew about your interest in the divorce, she would find a way to bleed you dry. She is a greedy, selfish woman. Blackmail would only be the beginning. Soon she'd be showing up on your doorstep, threatening to go to the gossip rags and demanding more and more."

Emily straightened her shoulders and met his eye. "That's my history, Zach. I'm not an upper-class or middle-class governess. I don't even speak like this—it's all an act. My education is painfully lacking and Perdita's could only do so much to fill in the holes. I'm married to a dead pig, and I might be one of the best thieves you've ever run across." She lifted her hand, his billfold dangling between her fingers.

Zach's jaw dropped. "Unbelievable," he said, taking the fold from her.

Emily breathed deeply, the pain of losing him before ever properly having him already raw. She hadn't even wanted this—whatever *this* was—with him, and now it was all she could think of. "Thank you for tonight. I am sorry I let it go so far before telling you the truth. All I ask is that you not reveal my past to my employers. I assure you I am no longer a thief and I pose no threat to them. I just want to live a quiet life. A safe life."

When Zach didn't say anything, Emily's throat tightened. She would *not* cry in front of him. Even as she made herself the promise, her vision blurred. Terrified he would see, she shoved past him and began to run.

She didn't get far before Zach caught her wrist.

"Where are you going?" he demanded.

"What, do you want to arrest me?" A tear leaked from her eye and slipped down her cheek. *Stop it!* Emily scolded herself. *Have some pride!*

"How dare you," Zach snarled. "Look up at me."

Emily choked on a sob. "No."

"Emily Leverton, if that's even your real name, look at me." Zach's hand tilted her chin, forcing her to face him through her tears. In that moment she hated him for making her reveal her weakness. "I am sorry you had an unhappy childhood. So did I, as a matter of fact. If you have not forgotten, I grew up in the slums as the son of a butcher who could not afford to feed his family the food he sold in his shop. Like any other starving kid, I did my fair share of thieving, although I am not as impressive as you are."

The tears continued to roll, but only because Emily was so emotionally wrought from all that had transpired that night. Did he, a policeman, just admit to being a thief?

"I swear to God, queen, and country, I don't care if you were born in a literal sewer and your street identity is Sadie Sticky-fingers. I want *you*, the real you, and only you. How dare you insult me by suggesting that your impoverished past would frighten me off? How dare you think I would judge a child for doing anything she could to survive? Do you really think me such a morally superior prig?"

Emily didn't know what to think anymore. Her heart was sore from all the flip-flopping it had done the past few hours, and she was sure if she lay down and rested her eyes she could sleep for a week.

Zach wiped the silent tears from her cheeks and kissed her softly on the mouth. "I have not told you about the time I stole a chicken and was spanked by a ninety-year-old woman."

Emily smiled through her tears. "Are you making that up?"

"No, unfortunately. I was six or seven at the time, and as my father was a butcher you would think I would have chosen something more novel to steal. But I was at the market and this old woman was selling chickens. I was so hungry—we'd had cabbage soup for six nights and we had run out of bread a few days prior. I saw those chickens and I swear I began to salivate, you know the kind where it actually hurts?"

"I do."

"There were ten chickens and this little old lady to watch all of them. Sometimes one would wander away and come back, and it seemed as if the woman was not paying any attention. She kept talking to customers and looking toward the sky. I was confident I could grab one of those chickens and run before she ever knew one was missing.

"When one of the chickens wandered close enough, I finally worked up the nerve. I scooped it up in my hands and sprinted. I had not counted on the fact that the chicken might not want to be held. It began pecking furiously at my arms until I yelped and dropped it. By that time the woman, who was freakishly spritely for her age, had caught up to me. She bent me over her knee, spanked me until my bottom burned, and sent me on my way."

"Oh, Zach." Emily was covering her mouth with her hand, not sure if she was amused or horrified for him. She knew all too well what it was like to live with such desperation and humiliation.

"The moral of the story, Noodles, is that for every shameful memory you have of your past, I can tell one worse. Poverty doesn't inherently make a man or woman any less worthy than someone born to money. Your past does not define you. Your decisions now, those are what make you who you are."

Emily peered into his face. The moonlight glanced off the dark blond of his hair and laid white shadows across his shoulders. His jaw was relaxed, but his stance was wary. His military past, she thought. He wore it on him still; even at ease, he was prepared to act.

When she met his eyes, it was the intensity and purity of passion she saw in them that were her undoing. This man was unlike anyone she had ever met, and she finally admitted to herself that she wanted him as badly as he wanted her.

What about your Big Secret? a little voice whispered in her head.

Her secret was only dangerous to Zach if it was discovered. But if they conducted an affair in private, it was doubtful anyone would take enough interest in her to figure it out. Zach would be safe.

Emily lifted her hand and ran her fingers through his hair. Her decision made, she felt deliciously nervous. "How do you feel about being more than friends?"

Chapter 31

Zach felt as if he had been handed a precious gift, and not only because Emily wanted to continue their foray into *kissing*, but because she had trusted him enough to share her troubled past. He tugged her close and took her lips tenderly. He wanted to linger, to take his time earning her sighs and gasps of ecstasy, but there was the quiet chatter of voices a few rows of hedges over, so he reluctantly pulled back and tucked her hand in the crook of his elbow.

"In case my response was not answer enough for you, I am very invested in this more-than-friends idea, Emily Noodles Leverton. I look forward to kissing you from morning until night."

Emily shifted her eyes heavenward. "I work morning until night, and so do you."

Zach pressed his hand to his heart. "I can do better. I shall romance you with my words. How about: Your eyes are as brown as chocolate, your hair as rich as...er...a black cat, your mouth sweet like two sugar plums."

"Just stop."

"Grand idea."

"I have conditions, Zach."

"Whatever you want, the answer is probably yes." He felt light-hearted and boyish in a way he rarely had, even as a child.

"Don't you want to hear them?"

"Yes of course. I was just letting you know where I stand," he said. They reached a divider hedge and Emily led them to the right. "Do you know where you are going?"

"I have a decent sense of direction. Most city thieves do."

It was true, he thought wryly. He had seen his share of officers chase a thief into the slums only to lose him in the unintelligible maze of streets and dead ends that was London.

"First," she said, "our association must remain completely secret. No one is to know about us, not even your staff. I know you trust them, but gossip is rife and I fear it could reach Eastmoreland House."

That could be arranged. It would be annoying, but possible. He could sneak Emily in and out of his house without any of the servants being the wiser. Even if they knew he was entertaining a lady, they would not be able to definitively identify her.

Emily held up a second gloved finger. "No more outings together. Your cousin, Miss Emily, is going to marry her fiancé in Liverpool and the *ton* will not see her again. No running into each other on the street. No walks or carriage rides. If you see me in public, you will ignore me."

Zach scowled. He could manage without the operas and dances, Lord knew, but he did not like the idea of publicly turning his back on the woman he was secretly undressing at night. It seemed wrong, as if he were ashamed of her, when the opposite was true. He rather felt like shouting about her from the rooftops.

"Third, if for any reason I suspect my family has discovered my whereabouts or that I am in a relationship with you, we will end our association immediately and there will be no further contact between us."

Zach stopped and Emily took another step before her arm in his pulled her back. "What?" she asked.

"No."

"No what?"

"No to your third condition."

"Zach, you do not want those people in your life. They would make it hell. You must remember that you have no legal claim over me or this relationship," she said quietly.

Zach's skin turned icy. "You will not disappear without a word. You will extend me the courtesy of telling me first."

In which case he would promptly talk her out of it. Emily believed her family capable of destroying him. She did not know with whom she dealt.

Emily nodded reluctantly, and he wasn't sure he believed her.

"Fourth," she continued as they began walking again. She took a left path and then a quick right.

"Geez, Emily, how long is this list?"

"Do you want to be more than friends or not?"

"By all means," he grumbled, "continue."

"Either one of us is able to end this at any time for any reason. No cages. No commitments. No promises. No hurt feelings."

"So you are not going to fall in love with me?"

"Certainly not," she said stiffly.

If Zach were a less confident man, she might have wounded his ego. "I accept your challenge."

"That is not a challenge, Zachariah! I'm an impoverished,

legally married woman. There is no happy ending to be found here. This is temporary. We will enjoy each other while it lasts, and then we shall part ways amicably."

"I will think on it," he said. When she frowned, he shrugged. "I'm only being honest."

"I suppose I will have to accept that." She didn't look happy about it.

"Are you ready for my conditions?"

She seemed surprised that he had any, and then wary. "What are they?"

"While you are with me, you are with me *only*. I do not care if your husband shows up from a watery grave waving about your marriage contract. I'm terrible at sharing. Ask anyone who knows me."

"But the Eastmorelands just took on a very handsome footman..."

Zach pinched her arm teasingly and she laughed.

"By the same token, I will have no lovers other than you."

"Will this upset many women?"

"None, currently. It has been a rather slow spring."

"Good," she said fiercely, and he liked her possessiveness.

"Second, you will allow me to buy you gifts from time to time simply because I want to and will enjoy it."

"*Small* gifts."

"Fine. Small gifts." *Small* was a relative word, wasn't it? "Lastly, you will be honest with me. If you like something, by all means shout it at the top of your lungs. If you hate something, tell me. If you are worried or uncomfortable, share with me. I will not be angry unless I discover you are holding back and I have unknowingly upset or hurt you."

They arrived at the entrance of the maze and Emily removed her hand from his arm. "I will share with you if you share with me."

"I think I can manage that."

"Then we have a deal, Zachariah Denholm."

"There is just one more problem," Zach said as they continued across the grassy strip separating the hedge maze and the flower garden. "When are the Eastmorelands leaving for the country?"

Emily gave a small gasp of dismay. "I forgot all about that! The maids are packing luggage as we speak. They plan to depart to Brixton Hall within the week."

Zach rubbed his thumb over his lip as he thought. There was no way he was willing to let her go, and yet he could not leave the city—at least not permanently and not while he was on the hunt for a killer.

The obvious solution struck him: He would buy a summer manor close to the Eastmorelands and spend a week there at a time, alternating with weeks in the city. The travel would be tedious, but Zach was willing to do it if it meant seeing Emily.

Requesting the time off from the Metropolitan Police would not be a problem—he made his own hours, and it was not as if he drew a salary.

Pleased, Zach dropped his hand from his mouth and Emily asked, "What are you grinning about?"

"I'm going to buy a place near Brixton Hall."

"Just like that? You're going to snap up a country house."

"Yes. We can call it our love nest."

"Do not be absurd."

"Darling, life is too serious for it not to be absurd."

Emily peeled off her glove and trailed her fingertips over the velvety rose petals in the garden. It was an unconsciously sensuous act, and Zach's lower belly tightened as he watched her fondle the plants in the dancing torchlight.

Really, now *that* was absurd, being excited by a woman touching flowers!

They reached the stairs to the balcony and a soft cacophony of voices and notes of music could be heard overheard.

She turned to him. "You are serious. You're going to buy a house in Cheshire. And what about when we end things and you are left with an expensive property?"

He straightened his cravat. "I have been thinking about buying a country estate for some while now. The timing was never right before. Now it is."

"You could do it then, you could buy an estate?"

He studied her quizzically. "Yes. You seem surprised. I told you I possessed a fortune."

"You did. Only…it seems so surreal."

"I am one of the richest men in England." If he had been born upper class, the words never would have passed his lips, and even *he* knew it was crass to brag, but it was also the truth. "My wealth is the only reason I am welcome at a place like this. Even the *ton* can relax their standards when enough money is involved."

She caught his hand and brought his fingers to her lips. The tenderness of the act struck him like a knife in the heart. "They are idiots if they cannot see you for what you are."

He began to reach for her when a figure appeared at the top of the stairs. Emily quickly dropped his hand and put a respectable amount of distance between them.

"Let's go back in," she said once the gentleman had passed. She retied her domino and tugged her glove on while he did the same. "We have been gone too long."

Zach didn't give a damn what anyone thought about their disappearance, but Emily seemed to, so he followed her back into the crowded, stuffy ballroom.

"Speaking of flowers," he whispered in her ear, pleased when she shivered, "what is your favorite type of bloom?"

"We were not speaking of flowers."

"We are now."

Emily snorted at his logic. "My—"

"Why, Mr. Denholm! What a pleasure to see you here!"

Zach turned, irritated with the interruption, and found himself face-to-face with Lord Eastmoreland.

Chapter 32

*W*ell, *that was the shortest affair in the history of affairs*, Emily thought. One illicit tryst in a miniature hedge maze and their secret was already dangling on the precipice of exposure.

She stared horrified at her employer as he talked business with Zach, Eastmoreland's eyes occasionally darting in her direction until Zach, rather ungraciously she thought, introduced her as his cousin.

Emily curtsied and the earl took her hand. "You have stolen the hearts of the *ton*, Miss Emily. I can see why Mr. Denholm kept you a secret for the entirety of the Season: You are a jewel that I am sure many gentlemen here would wish to abscond with."

Emily forced a giggle, and in a voice pitched higher than her own said, "You do flatter me, my lord. I am sure no one has noticed me among the many beautiful women here tonight, including your own wife and daughter."

Lord Eastmoreland shook his head in amazement. "Your accent! Why, you do not sound like a poor country girl at all. It is remarkable."

Emily giggled again, purposely glossing over the rude comment. Her one goal was to end this transaction and put as much distance between herself and the earl as possible. Zach was not so forgiving.

"That is because she is hardly a *poor* country girl," he said icily.

Eastmoreland seemed to realize he had given insult because his colorless cheeks took on a crimson stain. Emily was quickly learning how reluctant most of the *ton* was to antagonize Zach—at least to his face.

Eastmoreland was in his mid-sixties—nearly two decades older than his wife—with a thick head of gray hair, a drooping mustache, and a sagging belly. His skin was doughy and pale, as if the blood had been leached from beneath his skin, and his cheeks and fingers were sallow from tobacco use. In comparison, the countess was a sleek beauty. A year ago Emily would have been surprised to see such a pair, but she had learned since that the *ton*'s marriage matches had nothing to do with attraction and everything to do with purses. Attraction was left for affairs.

The earl dipped his head over Emily's hand, his gray coat and moss-green cravat straining so that the skin at his neck bulged like a bullfrog's. "My deepest apologies. I meant no offense. Might I make amends by offering the next dance?"

Emily's heart stuttered. "My dance card is already—"

"Surely," he said with a surfeit of confidence, "the young gentleman on your card can find a more suitable partner. Unless, of course, you have promised the next dance to the marquess?" He laughed, his belly rippling in a wave from top to bottom.

The only peer in attendance with a higher title than Eastmoreland was the Marquess Barthel, who was nearly eighty with arthritic knees, and attended balls with the sole purpose of sitting in a chair and scowling with disapproval at the immorality of waltzes.

Emily swallowed what felt like a walnut in her throat and widened her eyes frantically at Zach. Zach opened his mouth to protest, but at that moment the quartet struck up the music, and before Zach could step in to save her Eastmoreland tugged her onto the dance floor.

Within moments they were consumed by a kaleidoscope of straight-backed men and pastel dresses swirling elegantly across the gleaming wood floor. A showroom of precious-gem necklaces and diamond hairpieces refracted light from the chandeliers; the joyous crash of voices rose with the late hour and the consumption of punch and stiffer beverages.

Lord Eastmoreland was close enough that Emily could smell the stomach-turning scents of tobacco and meat on his breath. He stomped on her foot and she winced. When she'd danced with Zach, even though she was a novice, they had glided together as if they had been partners for a lifetime. The same magic was not happening with the earl, who jerked her this way and that as if she were a puppet.

Emily sucked herself closer to the earl in the nick of time, avoiding careening into another couple. The earl must have seen this as an invitation because he kept her there, gripping her with surprising strength.

"Do tell me, Miss Emily, how you are finding our lovely town?"

Oh, splendid. I have endured eight of your daughter's poems about ponies, watched a maid slap a footman, and was nearly let go by your wife.

"It is very hot," she said. At the house she had glimpsed the earl only in passing, and was now grateful she hadn't had to endure his odious attentions before. He was very much a product of his position and wealth: indulgent and self-centered.

"Oh, it is not so bad." Sweat beaded above his lip. "Although I admit I will rejoice in relocating to the country for a spot of hunting and a bit of breeze."

"That sounds refreshing. How is your eldest daughter? Lady Minnie, I believe?"

"Eh? Oh, she is dear. Simply lovely. Say, how long do you plan to visit with your cousin? He is certainly an enigma. Think, only a decade ago he was off fighting on the Continent and now he is a majority shareholder in one of the largest railroads in the country *and* tasked with discovering the identity of the Evangelist."

"Yes. We are very proud of him."

Bushy eyebrows drew together. "Who is 'we'?"

"My fiancé and I," Emily lied.

"Right, right. You must be very *close* to your cousin if he is willing to bring you out to London for a stay."

Emily stiffened at the words. Was he insinuating that she and Zach were more than cousins? "We know each other well enough," she said coolly.

The earl didn't seem to pick up on her tone, clearly prepared to blaze ahead with his agenda, whatever that was.

"Say, does he have any leads on the Evangelist? The newsies have been shouting day and night about it, but there is no real substance in the papers." The earl cleared his throat and gave a dry chuckle. "I am just fascinated by the whole story, you see. It is such a *bizarre* situation. On one hand we have a murderer running loose among the slums of the city, but on the other hand he is killing women who are a scourge to society: women who lead men astray from their godly and pure obligations to their wives.

It is a moral dilemma of the highest order. Does one support his vigilantism? Surely not. Yet is he ridding our society of filth? Indubitably."

Emily's lips parted. She knew she shouldn't tell the earl that he was an insufferable ass, and yet how could she be expected to listen to him espouse such drivel as if men were not given free will? As if men did not have all the power in the world while women were second-class citizens without rights?

She decided to take a page out of the *ton*'s handbook and cut with sugar.

"The women hardly peddle their wares in Mayfair," she said sweetly. "If the men didn't wish to be led astray from their godly duties, perhaps they should not go looking to do so."

The earl's meaty fingers flexed with disapproval. "The men are led there out of temptation, which only exists because of the women. A woman of solid breeding would agree."

A not-so-subtle dig at her common roots. Emily realized that no matter what she said, the earl was not going to change his mind on the topic. He wasn't looking for a lively intellectual debate; he wanted a simpering show of agreement and gossip on the investigation. Anything she said to the contrary would be chalked up to her ill breeding. It would do neither her nor Zach any favors to taunt him. It was time to shut her mouth.

"The God-fearing men and women of solid breeding should know they have the power to prevent such temptation," Emily said archly. So much for shutting her mouth. "They could donate funds to the poor, or pass laws that benefited the lower classes instead of oppressing them, and then the women of ill repute would have no need to seek clientele in order to feed themselves and their children. Problem solved."

The earl looked down his nose at her, scorn clear in the pinch of his brow. "Pardon me, I should never have brought up so intellectual a topic. The minds of young ladies are not equipped to handle this type of political scope and consequence. Perhaps we should talk about the newest opera, or fashion?"

Emily ground her teeth together and stepped on the earl's foot. He flinched and she gasped, "Pardon me!"

"Not to worry. Accidents happen—ow!"

"Oh goodness, I am so embarrassed. I seem to have acquired two left feet tonight. I cannot seem to keep the steps straight in my simple mind."

The sarcasm swooped over the earl's head and he again assured her she was forgiven. Emily took the lead and barged them toward the center of the room, spinning with dizzying disregard for other dancers and knocking the earl into a baron. While the earl blustered an apology to the stunned dancer, Emily looked over in time to see the second Hill daughter, Miss Jane, who was not so sweetly dumb as her older sister, give her a malicious glare.

The music came to a halt and Emily batted her eyelashes. "It was a pleasure, my lord."

The earl was sweating profusely, his monocle askew and his hair ruffled. To Emily's bafflement, he grinned like a young boy and said, "I have not danced like that in ages. What a take-charge young lady you are. I would not expect anything less from Mr. Denholm's relative."

Emily could only gape as Zach appeared at her side and ushered her away. When she looked over her shoulder, Eastmoreland was gazing after her with the longing of a puppy.

Zach steered her toward the door, his face twitching oddly. "What?" Emily snapped.

A small laugh escaped his lips, and then another. He walked faster. By the time he handed her into his carriage, he was in hysterics. Emily couldn't help but grin herself. Zach was laughing so hard he had doubled over. It was joyous, unrestrained laughter that she had never heard from him, but now that she had, she wanted nothing more than to hear it again.

When his mirth had subsided, Zach, still suffering the occasional convulsion, took her hand in his and pressed his still-smiling lips to her palm. "I thought you were going to railroad him into every couple on the dance floor."

"You should have heard the man! Insufferable to say the least. I got so angry, and he kept excusing me for stepping on his feet, so I may have lost control a bit."

Zach pressed her hand to his heart. "Darling, the man is a known submissive. All of his mistresses could have been war generals."

Emily scrunched up her face. "I did *not* want to know that about my employer."

"I fear he is smitten with you now."

"Good thing your cousin does not exist."

"Good thing indeed. Now, about tonight…" His eyes turned from amused to darkly passionate and Emily felt an answering tug in her belly at the predatory shift.

"I need some time before we… kiss more."

Zach stretched an arm over the seat and relaxed into the cushions. Dark night air rushed into the carriage, and for the first time in days, Emily felt a welcome chill. "Take all the time you need, Noodles. I'm not going anywhere."

Chapter 33

The following morning Mrs. Hill was perched on her settee, her thoughts deeply troubled. There were no suitors clamoring to visit her daughters after the masquerade ball the night before. There were no flowers in the sitting room. No invitations in the mail. Her brother, Lord Moore, was a baron who had inherited a crumbling estate in the country that barely generated enough income to cover his gambling debts, much less outfit his nieces with proper dowries. Their father had died ten years prior, leaving Mrs. Hill with two big-boned daughters and debt collectors at the door.

When Olivia had entered the Marriage Mart two years ago, Mrs. Hill had been hopeful that her daughter would make an advantageous match. Not many knew how destitute the Hills had become, as they had bought the Season's gowns on credit to continue appearances. Olivia, while somewhat vapid, had wide childbearing hips and would be eager to please her husband. Mrs. Hill had been *sure* she would be snatched up within a few dances.

She had not been.

So this year when Jane had made her debut, Mrs. Hill's hopes had fallen on her. Although Jane wasn't as pretty as her sister, with her limp dishwater hair and thin lips, she was decidedly more intelligent. The problem with Jane was that she was ambitious without ambition and would settle for nothing less than the richest man on the market.

To that end Jane had turned down two marriage proposals, much to Mrs. Hill's dismay. The first had been a gentleman who was rather old and indebted himself, so Mrs. Hill hadn't minded terribly. The second marriage proposal had come from Jane's second cousin who had returned from America missing an arm but having gained a fortune. Jane had turned him down because she did not like his teeth.

Mrs. Hill had wept angrily. She had threatened, even slapped the girl, but Jane had only become more mulish. Certain she was going to be saddled with two aging spinsters while they slowly starved to death, Mrs. Hill had felt she had been handed a gift from above when Mr. Denholm, an upstart who seldom attended *ton* events, had made an appearance at the Exeter ball. Mrs. Hill may have once turned up her nose at someone like Mr. Denholm, but he was rich and times were changing. She was willing to change with them.

Mrs. Hill had forced her brother to make introductions. When Mr. Denholm had shown no interest in Olivia, Jane had been perversely delighted. The next morning Jane had grandly announced that *she* was going to become Mrs. Denholm. She'd flounced about the house, describing to her older sister in great detail all the gowns she would own once she snagged his purse.

"And what if he does not want you, either?" Olivia had snapped, still feeling the sting of rejection.

"Why would he not? *I* am the blood relation of nobility, and everyone knows it is a commoner's dream to marry into the aristocracy. Besides, I have a better favorite book than the Bible."

That had devolved into hair pulling.

Jane had remained determined and confident until the masquerade ball. They had all been horrified when Mr. Denholm had arrived with his cousin and danced and laughed with her as if no one else in the room existed. It had been so...so *common*! He had flaunted the little wench as if she had every right to be in the same room as nobility. It hadn't helped that the men had been clamoring to meet the mysterious woman who so rudely refused to dispense with her domino.

Mrs. Hill scowled at the empty silver tray that should have been heaped with calling cards. She didn't know what was happening to the world. In years past someone like Mr. Denholm, no matter how wealthy, would not have dared show his face at such an event. She supposed it was a circumstance of the times. The noble class's finances were dwindling and those who refused to change with the world were finding their purse strings drawn tighter and tighter each year.

Jane entered the room still in a poor temper from the night before. She snatched up a porcelain vase and smashed it into the fireplace. Mrs. Hill was used to Jane's vicious moods, but this display of petulance only ignited her own. She stood and slapped Jane smartly across the cheek.

"Ow!" Jane howled, clutching her face. "What was that for?"

"For breaking the vase, you ingrate. And for failing to secure a dance with Mr. Denholm last night."

Jane's lip poked out. "How could I? He hardly left that bitch's side."

The language was uncouth, but accurate. "Do you know how impoverished we are, Jane? The debt collectors are nearly breaking down our door, and unless you or your sister make a wealthy match soon, we will be ruined. There will be no more Seasons. No more dresses. Do you understand?"

"What am *I* supposed to do about it?"

"You said you were going to marry Mr. Denholm."

Jane's already sickly pallor turned ashen. "Do not rub it in my face."

"How easily you capitulate," Mrs. Hill snarled. "Has an engagement been announced in the papers? Have the banns been read? We do not even know for sure that he is courting his cousin. They did say she was to marry a shipping magnate in Liverpool."

"It hardly matters. He has shown no interest in me."

"That is your own fault."

"How so? Why are you not blaming Olivia? She is the one who bungled the first introduction."

Mrs. Hill turned her back on her daughter and paced to the window, where a stagnant breeze struggled into the room. "You have to *make* him notice you. Lower your neckline, do your hair differently. Add subtle rouge and makeup. Entrap him in the garden. Do something!"

"It will not matter if he has eyes only for *her.*"

"Yes," Mrs. Hill mused. "We will need to knock his little cousin from her pedestal." She turned to her daughter, who had crept forward with interest gleaming in pale eyes that were too close together. Her father's eyes, Mrs. Hill thought with annoyance.

"How do we do that, Mother?"

Mrs. Hill did not know, but a plan was beginning to form. She lifted the newspaper and tapped the front page. "Did you read this?"

Jane sniffed. "I have better things to do."

"Not anymore, you do not. From this moment forward you will devote yourself to learning everything you can about Mr. Denholm. You will read the gossip columns and the paper. You will discover who his friends are, what books he reads, how he likes his tea. You will run into him whenever he is in public so that he has no choice but to think of you."

"How am I expected to know where he will be?"

"We will have to engage the help of your dear uncle, of course. He has a network of acquaintances that will be useful."

"And what will you be doing all this time?" Jane asked sourly. "Why do I have to do all the work while you and Olivia get a free ride?"

Mrs. Hill considered slapping her again and decided against it. She needed the girl on board, not angry. "I am going to discover the identity of his cousin and discredit her in front of the world. Once I do, Mr. Denholm will have no choice but to disown her, and you will be right there waiting to comfort him." She waggled the paper in front of Jane. "Pack your bags. We are going to Cheshire."

Chapter 34

Deputy Commissioner Wright Davies set the newspaper down, not caring that it was spread over his breakfast. A dot of preserves soaked through the paper in a greasy smudge. He dragged a sweating palm over his face, closed his eyes, and briefly wished he were dead.

No, it would be far better to kill Denholm. Infinitely more satisfying. His butler entered the room balancing a silver tray, a tented note in the center. Wright accepted the note with a sense of foreboding about its author. When he saw the handwriting, he knew his intuition had been right. It was from the police commissioner, who in no uncertain terms wanted to know what the *hell* was going on.

Wright would like to know that, too. Before he met with the commissioner, he needed to speak with Denholm.

Goddamned Zach.

"Deputy Commissioner Davies to see you, sir."

"Send him out," Zach replied, wiping his rolled sleeve across his forehead. The heat wave still hadn't broken, and everything outdoors seemed brittle and bleached by the sun. The small courtyard in his town house hadn't seen a gardener in ages, and the bushes and wild weeds had long since taken over. Zach had a hundred other tasks demanding his attention, but he'd needed the physical labor and hadn't felt like attending one of the clubs to fight. The rosebushes had been the next best thing.

Zach yanked on a dead bush until the roots upended. He threw it on top of a burgeoning brush pile. The scents of dusty earth and plant decay clung to his boots and shirt along with the dirt. A bird trilled and flies buzzed around his head. Zach swatted one away and was taking a swig of water from a glass when Wright stepped into the courtyard.

"Don't you have enough money to hire a gardener?" Wright asked.

"I keep forgetting."

"It is blasted hot out here. Let us talk somewhere cool. Maybe over a drink. Or two."

"Grab a shovel."

Wright grumbled and moaned. Finally loosening his cravat, he tossed it aside and rolled up his sleeves.

"What does this weather remind you of?" Zach asked, gesturing toward a plant that needed to be dug out.

"Burma." Wright jammed his boot into the spade, and it bit into the dusty earth.

"I keep getting goose pimples and expecting to hear shots fired."

"That is not the war that gives me chills," Wright said grimly.

Zach knew what he meant. They'd both witnessed horrific tragedies in the Portuguese Civil War. Sometimes it was hard for his subconscious to choose which war to give him nightmares about. None of it had been pleasant. He wasn't even sure it had been *right*.

They worked together in silence with nothing but the sounds of spades hitting the earth, the occasional grunt, and the feel of sweat sliding down their backs.

At last the final rosebush had been tugged free and Wright leaned against his spade, panting. Zach handed him a drink and they both swallowed deeply.

"Zach," Wright finally said, setting the glass down on the brick with a clink. "You know why I am here."

"I sure do."

"I need an explanation. The commissioner wants answers and I will admit I am confounded. What are you playing at?" He pulled the article that had run in the papers that morning from his pocket and unfolded it. "How about I start reading, and you tell me what I am missing."

Zach leaned against the brick wall and crossed his ankles. Wright was sweating profusely; too many drinks and not enough manual labor. Zach would have had nothing but contempt for any other man who'd come by his rank through connections, but Wright was a good person and fit for the job. He'd given Zach free rein to conduct the investigation how he pleased. Zach supposed now it was Wright's neck on the line, and he owed him answers.

Wright snapped open the paper, popped his monocle in his eye, and cleared his throat. "Headline reads: EVANGELIST GETS SLOPPY." He stared at Zach. Zach stared back. Wright continued.

"The Metropolitan Police have had a major breakthrough in the case involving the murderer known as the Evangelist. According to an officer assigned to the task force led by Detective Constable Zachariah Denholm, the team has discovered key evidence that points to the identity of the madman. When this publication contacted Detective Constable Denholm, he said: 'The Evangelist is not as smart as everyone seems to believe. Mistakes have been made recently. Sloppy mistakes. We are closing in on the murderer. I am not at liberty to give the press details. All I can say is that I will soon be retiring to my country home in Cheshire with the killer behind bars.'

"A policeman on the task force confirmed that key evidence had been processed. He did not comment whether an arrest was forthcoming."

Wright let his hand drop. "Last I checked, you did not have a single clue who the killer was."

"That is correct."

Wright looked pained. "I was hoping you would not say that. Why, Zach? Why lie to the public? Has the pressure been too much? Has it addled your brain?"

Zach snorted. "That article was not for the public, it was for *him*."

Wright opened his mouth, closed it. He opened it again, and once again snapped it shut. A gleam appeared in his eye.

Nodding, Zach said, "Exactly. I want to rattle him. I want to make him doubt himself. My guess is that he has loved the attention. It makes him feel smart and powerful for outwitting the police under the watchful eye of all of London. The article called him sloppy and stupid. It has rubbed some of the polish off his reputation. We want him to think he messed up last time, that he left evidence behind that can help us identify him. The more shaken he is, the more likely he is to make an actual mistake. He will retaliate, but he would have killed again anyway. This way, I have hopefully angered him enough that he will reveal something about himself with what he does next."

"What if he does not do anything differently?"

"Ah! Then I can only assume he is of the lower class, or perhaps the middle class and cannot read. If he does, then I will know he is educated enough to read the newspaper. We may be dealing with another killer from the *ton*."

Wright groaned and mopped at his forehead. "That is the last thing we need. Lord, what a political mire."

Zach shrugged. "That is why you have me, mate. I can weather any political damage because I do not give two figs."

"I wish you would have warned me in advance about what you were doing."

"No," Zach said instantly. "You would have told me not to do it."

Wright looked sheepish.

"Plead ignorance to the commissioner and tell him it is entirely on my shoulders. If he has any questions, he can ask them of me."

"That is not how rank works and you know it."

Zach pushed off the wall and slapped his friend on the shoulder. "Then tell him to take a swim."

"What about when the Evangelist strikes again and you do not catch him? Then *you* will look like the fool to the public. And before you tell me you do not care, it reflects poorly on the entire organization."

Zach had considered that, but the benefits of rattling the killer had outweighed the risk of looking like an idiot. "We will cross that bridge when we come to it. Now I believe you have a meeting with the commissioner, and I have business to attend to."

Wright shook his head as he retied his cravat and placed his hat atop his balding head. "I hope you know what you are doing, Colonel."

"I do not," Zach said sincerely. "I am making it up as I go like everyone else."

Chapter 35

Dearest Not-My-Cousin,

Will you join me at my house tonight, say around 8 o'clock? Do not worry, we will have a private dinner and no one will know that I have the most beautiful governess in all of London in residence.

—Z

Dear Flattering Sir,

Flattery will get you everywhere, except in this instance. Unfortunately, I have a prior commitment this evening. Might I suggest you celebrate your big break in the Evangelist case instead?

—E

....

Dear I-Have-A-Prior-Commitment,

Here is a secret: The article was a lie meant to anger the Evangelist and encourage a misstep. In fact I have nothing to celebrate, especially now that you have other plans. Should you decide your plans would be enhanced with the inclusion of a detective constable, I will be at your service.

—Z

Emily chewed on her fingernail. After her awkward dance with the earl at the masquerade ball, Emily had mentioned the man's curiosity over the murders in her report to the Dove. The Dove had promptly asked her to follow the earl and document his activities. The earl was expected to attend his club that night, and even though Emily suspected spying on him would consist of nothing more than a rip-roaring good time of sitting outside his club while waiting for him to stumble out at 2:00 a.m., she had a job to do.

That job did not include Zach. Although it hadn't been explicitly stated, it had been implied that her work for the Dove would be kept secret.

Dearest Liar,

If you make me dinner tomorrow, I will tell you a joke I once overheard at an outdoor gambling game. It is very filthy, and I suspect you will love it.

My favorite flowers are tulips.

—E

···········

Dearest Tulip,

I suppose I shall have to resign myself to working the case tonight. Tomorrow I will feed you the most delicious Cornish hen you've ever tasted in exchange for one filthy joke.

—Z

After Emily had sent her message to Zach, she looked down at the other piece of correspondence that had arrived in the post, addressed only to Miss Leverton, Eastmoreland House. She broke the wax seal uneasily. The handwriting did not belong to the Dove, and other than Zach, who would write to her here?

Dear Miss Leverton,

You may not remember me, so I shall first attempt to jog your memory: We met at the Serpentine one afternoon not long ago (when a certain boy and a certain pair of shoes took a swim). You told me you were situated with Lord Eastmoreland's family, and I pray this is still true so this missive may find you. Actually, perhaps it would be best if it were not still true.

I must beg a meeting with you at once. It is imperative that we speak at your earliest convenience. Write to me at the address enclosed to make arrangements.

Ever yours,
Frankie Turner

Emily frowned and set the note on her chiffonier. What could Frankie, the mathematician and governess she'd met briefly in the park, possibly have to speak to her so urgently about? Since their initial meeting, they had not crossed paths again.

More than a bit curious, Emily pulled a fresh sheet of paper from her stationery box, glanced at the time, and immediately dropped it again. She was going to be late!

She hurriedly dressed in her newly modified outfit, completely forgetting about Frankie's letter.

Chapter 36

Emily had briefly considered renting a hansom cab to follow Eastmoreland, but in the end she had not been willing to part with such a large sum of money. Instead she would follow the earl by foot. She hoped it would not be too difficult to keep up with his carriage: Usually the streets were choked with traffic at this time of night, so she thought she would be able to keep pace well enough.

She knew Eastmoreland's valet was dressing the earl because she'd discreetly inquired about the earl's plans for the evening. Apparently he had an early dinner engagement before the club, which meant he would be leaving any moment.

Emily slipped out of the house and removed the small book she'd stowed in her pocket. Standing in the elongating strip of shade offered by a lamppost as the sun slowly sank behind the buildings, she pretended to read while she waited for the earl to emerge.

Half an hour later the earl appeared. He was dressed with the casual elegance of his class: tight fawn-colored trousers, a forest-green waistcoat that flared about his hips and added unfortunate volume to his already portly frame, and a matching green silk top hat. From a distance Emily observed the footman bow and open the carriage door. This courtesy was no more noticed by the earl than a baker would notice flour on his clothes—it was so ingrained, so a part of his life, that he wasn't even aware of the privilege anymore, if he ever had been.

"Do you think he waxes his mustache?" Emily whispered to herself, stroking her bare upper lip.

"He might, although it is rather droopy."

Emily squealed and spun around, her eyes meeting Zach's in shock. Happiness flushed over her, but it was entwined with annoyance at having her plans crashed. "What are you doing here?" she hissed.

Zach gestured to a rather shabby carriage parked farther down the street. "I'm off to spend an inconspicuous evening in Bethnal Green, and I thought I'd drop my letter to you on the way. I did not intend to interrupt your night; I was going to leave the note with the butler. But alas, here you are, reading a book on the street and talking to yourself about men's mustaches. I admit that I am offended you found such plans more enticing than dinner at my house."

"It is certain that mustaches are—oh, he is about to leave! Quickly, can we take your carriage?"

Zach gave her an odd look but kept stride with her as she took his silence for acquiescence and hurried to his unmarked carriage. She wrenched open the door and hopped in before the driver could even get down from the box. Zach followed her inside.

"Do you own this carriage?" Emily asked. She was dressed in a sedate blue gown with a scooped neckline and cap sleeves in deference to the heat. She'd spent the past four hours modifying the dress to include a discreet slit up the side, and underneath she wore a pair of dark, fitted breeches. It was completely scandalous, but if Emily had to run she wanted to be able to *move*.

Zach didn't answer. Instead he dove his hand into her hair, mussing her pins, and dragged her mouth to his. He kissed her greedily, nipping and lapping until Emily was dizzy with desire. Unsated, he pressed her into the threadbare cushion of her seat and slid a hand down her thigh. She knew the moment he discovered the slit in her gown because he stopped kissing her and pulled back to look at it. He peeled it open, revealing the breeches.

"Emily?"

"Yes?"

He lifted eyes dark with passion. "I think you have just given me new feelings for breeches."

She laughed, but before he could pounce again she pressed her hand to his chest. "I need to focus, and I cannot do that when your hand is under my skirt."

Zach groaned and sat back. "What is going on, Emily?"

Emily chewed on her bottom lip. "I am following the earl to his dinner arrangement."

"Why?"

She could not tell him the truth, and so with guilt nearly choking her, she lied. "The countess is punishing me, I think. She has asked me to spy on the earl and report back to her where he goes."

Zach stared at her, and she was almost certain he could see through her fib as easily as he had all the others. She held her breath, but before he could say anything the earl's coach rattled past the window.

"There he goes! Are you pledged to visit Bethnal Green, or can you make a change of plans?"

"Oh, I am far too intrigued now. You would have to pry me away from you."

"Then quickly, tell the driver to follow at a sedate distance."

Zach did as she ordered with an amused look in her direction.

"What?"

"You seem rather excited by this cloak-and-dagger game."

The carriage lurched forward and Emily grabbed onto the first thing she could reach to restore her balance. It just so happened to be Zach's thigh. His hard thigh encased in smooth navy trousers. Emily should have jerked her hand away, but she left it there, stroking a small circle on the fabric. A wanton sense of possession overcame her. She was stroking the thigh of a man who was not her husband, a man who'd put his mouth on her in the most intimate of places and catapulted her to dizzying heights of pleasure. It was unreal, all of it. It had to be. And yet—he wasn't pushing her hand away. In fact, his callused palm laid over hers and slowly moved her hand upward.

Emily's breath quickened. She'd never actually *touched* a man's member. She'd had intercourse, but she'd never *played* or had fun. She was fairly certain it was wicked to do so. Sex was supposed to be for procreation, not pleasure. That was what the vicar had said.

Zach closed her hand around him and she was surprised by how hard and thick he was. She could practically feel him pulsing, straining against the fabric of his trousers. Experimentally she rubbed her palm over his length and was rewarded when he groaned. After a moment his hand tightened over hers, stilling the motion.

"Does that hurt?" she whispered, although there was no one else to hear her.

Sounding strangled Zach said, "No. It feels good. Too good.

I'm about three seconds from jumping on you and peeling off those ridiculously attractive breeches."

Emily squeezed her thighs together at the sound of raw lust in his voice.

"Are you actually considering it?" Zach asked huskily when she didn't remove her hand.

"That thing you did to me in the hedge garden," Emily said, "is that something women do to men as well? Put their mouths *there*." She studied his strained face in the meager light.

"Some women do."

"Well, do you like it?"

Air hissed between his teeth. "Yes."

She bit her lip in concentration and nimbly went to work releasing the buttons on his trousers. His erection sprang free and she gazed at his imposing length for a moment before gently stroking the satin-smooth skin.

In the gray light Zach's eyes were the darkest shade of cobalt, his expression tense and focused. Tentatively, Emily dipped her head and touched the tip of her tongue to him, tasting the salty fluid that leaked from the tip. She licked him as he had her, swirling her tongue over the head of his erection, her stomach clenching when he let out a low, husky growl. She gradually grew bolder with her motions until she took him fully into her mouth. Zach's hands rested lightly on her shoulders, his thighs taut beneath her palms. When she looked up at him, his jaw tightened and his eyes went hot and possessive.

The carriage suddenly ground to a halt and Emily shot up, letting him slide out of her mouth with a wet sucking noise.

Zach tucked himself into his trousers just as the carriage

shifted with the driver's descent from his seat. He pulled her in for a searing kiss and said, "My place. Tonight."

"Tonight," Emily agreed. There was something powerful in the ability to give him such pleasure. It made her feel as if she were an equal in the relationship.

The door swung open, but Zach shook his head and instructed the driver to mount the box again. Emily peered through the curtains. Their carriage had parked across the street from a tall, narrow residence that was neither shabby nor opulent. Eastmoreland knocked on a black lacquered door and was immediately admitted entrance by a butler.

"Did he say where he was having dinner?" Zach asked, having joined her at the window.

"Lord Cornwell's."

Zach clucked his tongue. "This is not the baron's residence. In fact, he left the city last week. I know because he and Wright are good friends."

Emily's brows arched. "Well then whose house is this?"

"I do not know, but there is one way to find out." Zach leapt from the carriage and spoke with the driver. A moment later the man lumbered across the road and knocked on the same door. The butler answered again and they had a brief exchange before the driver tilted his hat and returned to the carriage.

When Zach opened the door, the driver grunted, "Lady Artice," and returned to the front of the carriage.

"Well now, isn't *that* interesting," Zach said on a low whistle.

"Why? Who is she?"

"Behind her back she is called the Black Widow. Not because she kills her husbands, mind you, but because she is a widow and her heart is charred. She knows more about the *ton*'s affairs than the *ton* knows itself, and she uses that information to ruthlessly blackmail anyone she can. It is a wonder she has not been murdered yet. Then again, she is a smart old witch. She likely has fail-safes in place in the event of her death."

That *was* interesting, Emily thought. She studied the unassuming door of the house with curiosity. What secrets were hidden within? What information did the Black Widow hold over Lord Eastmoreland?

"I would bet my hat she is blackmailing him over his visits to Mistress Victoria."

"You know the name of his mistress?"

Zach cleared his throat. "Victoria runs the establishment Eastmoreland is rumored to frequent. It is said to cater to, ah, specific needs."

"What *specific* needs? I swear you are blushing. Do not dance around the topic. I am not fashioned of glass, Zach. I will not splinter when you tell me."

Zach slipped a finger under his collar as if it were too tight. He was uncomfortable, but she didn't think he would deny her. That was one of the things she liked best about him: He treated her as an equal, which quite frankly was not something afforded to many women of any class. "Well, men—and women—are at times excited by things that are not considered the norm."

"Such as what?"

"Such as what, she wants to know," Zach muttered. Then he shrugged and said, "If you can think of it, it is someone's preference. There are men who are excited by feet, being strangled during the act, spanked, kicked in their parts, or being watched having relations. They may be especially attracted to large women, skinny women, short women, tall women, or men. Some men like to watch women eat food. Others like to watch women with other women, or with more than one man at a time."

Emily knew her cheeks were turning scarlet. The illicit things he so casually discussed were strangely intoxicating. It was as if there was a whole world of secret pleasure out there that she'd never even known existed.

Zach edged closer, his eyes drifting to her rapidly rising and falling chest. "Some men have a fetish for a woman's breasts. Others love her bottom or her legs."

Emily met his eyes. "What excites you? Do you have a, what did you call it? A fetish?"

"Mmmm...I do. But it would be cheating if I told you, Noodles. You will have to discover it for yourself."

Emily was suddenly desperate to know just what it was that made Zach tick. She arched her brows and said, "And *you* will have to discover *mine*."

The air thickened between them, as if someone had stirred flour into the humidity. Zach said quietly, "You have a fetish, Emily?"

She didn't actually, but a little mystery never killed anyone.

Lord Eastmoreland exited the house, no doubt with lighter pockets. Zach thought the Black Widow was blackmailing the earl over his sexual proclivities, but what if the Black Widow—Lady Artice, the driver had said—knew something darker about him? What if the blackmail had something to do with the Evangelist? What if Lord Eastmoreland was somehow involved?

It was a ludicrous idea, and yet Emily was sure it was something the Dove would consider after Emily made her report.

Emily twitched the curtain aside and poked her nose out the window. "Follow that man!" she hissed.

The driver grumbled, "Yeah, yeah, I get it," and the carriage rumbled forward.

"Have you found a property in Cheshire?" Emily asked, shifting away from conversation topics that might end with consummating their relationship in a carriage.

"My manager has found two for private sale. He is there now examining the properties. He knows what I am looking for, and if he is pleased, he will make an offer. Both are within ten miles of Brixton Hall."

Emily tangled her fingers together. It appalled her that he was willing to spend such an extraordinary sum in order to be near her. Appalled her—and flattered her. The Pig couldn't be bothered to buy her a pastry on their anniversary. Even if they'd been flush with money, he still wouldn't have spent half a farthing on her.

The residences crawled past and Emily soon realized Eastmoreland was headed toward his club on Pall Mall. The driver of their carriage rolled past the club, circled the horses, and parked farther down the street so Emily and Zach had a clear view of the club entrance. Eastmoreland descended from his carriage and started toward the stone steps. Outside he met with another gentleman and they stood chatting for a few moments before they both entered the exclusive club.

And there he stayed for the next two hours.

By the time ten thirty rolled around Emily was hungry, thirsty, cramped, and she had to relieve herself.

"This is bollocks," she muttered.

Zach shifted uncomfortably in the carriage. "Indeed. Stakeouts have never been my favorite part of the job. Perhaps you would like to share with me why we are really here?"

"As I said, I am spying on Eastmoreland."

"And how did that come about again?"

Emily was perspiring so much that her gown was soaked through under the arms. As charming as the look was, she'd had enough. She had just opened her mouth to call off the stakeout while blatantly ignoring his question when the club door opened and out stepped Lord Eastmoreland, rather unsteady on his feet. Before Emily could snap instructions to the driver, Zach clamped onto her forearm and hissed, "Wait a moment."

Emily wasn't sure what she was supposed to be waiting for. The lamplighters had been around an hour earlier setting the streetlamps aflame, and as their lights flickered against the darkening summer's eve, the street bustled with the same steady tenor it had kept the entire night: clopping horse hooves, the creak of carriage wheels, voices and shouts, pops and hisses of machinery. Emily had not noticed a single thing out of order.

"There," Zach said, pointing to a curricle that pulled quickly into the road and traveled a sedate ten yards behind Lord Eastmoreland, who was weaving along the sidewalk in defiance of the lushly upholstered family carriage waiting for him. "That curricle arrived an hour ago and parked where it had a clear view of the club door, but the driver has not exited the vehicle and no one has joined him."

"Did you see the driver's features?"

"No, he parked in shadow and the hood is pulled on the curricle."

"He was waiting for Eastmoreland and now he's following him!" Emily exclaimed. "The *nerve*. How dare he encroach on our territory?"

"Yes, how dare he," Zach repeated.

"Let us find out who is trailing Eastmoreland." Although she wanted to charge up to the curricle and shine a lamp in the man's face, Emily instructed the driver to keep a good distance behind the person pursuing the person *they* were pursuing.

It was a curious train, should anyone have been observing them. Lord Eastmoreland weaved along the road, bumping into gentlemen and likely slurring his apologies, while the curricle crawled behind him so obviously that only a drunk would miss it, and behind that, the carriage she and Zach rode in.

Emily's curiosity about the identity of the man in the curricle was inflamed, but she fought her impulsive side. There was a time to act and a time to observe. This was the latter.

Lord Eastmoreland turned onto a poorly lit street and the curricle lurched forward, the horse thundering beside the earl and coming to a quick stop. The driver tossed his reins aside and leapt to the ground. With a swift blow he struck the back of Eastmoreland's head and the earl dropped like a sack of potatoes.

Emily jumped out of the slowly moving carriage and shouted, "Stop!"

The earl's attacker spun around just as a roll of summer thunder boomed overhead. His horse screamed in panic and bolted, the curricle veering wildly down the road.

Emily started across the street. As soon as the man realized she was coming toward him, he took off.

"Oh I do not think so," Emily said, hitching up her skirts.

Chapter 37

Lord, she was fast. Zach considered himself a fit man, but Emily was setting a pace that put even him to the test. He doubted she was aware of the physical exertion, so caught up in the pursuit she was.

He'd been there before. He'd also been burned by the chase before.

Emily's breeches and boots were coming in handy as she twisted down a narrow alleyway, her instinct for the maze of the city innate, her reflexes sharp as she hurtled over a heap of bricks and, to his surprise, veered to the left instead of following the man to the right.

Zach made his choice in a split second, peeling to the right to follow the man who'd assaulted the earl. Emily, master thief and con woman, could take care of herself, but she'd never forgive him if he went after her instead of their target. Of *that* Zach was certain.

He slowly gained ground as the perpetrator crossed into another alley. Zach had the man ten yards in his sight when something jumped from the ledge overhead and crashed into the man, dropping him as surely as he'd felled the earl.

That something was Emily.

Zach's face split into a grin. Clever little minx. She would have made a good constable—her instincts were spot-on.

The man cussed up a storm as he rolled around, wrestling with Emily. At last, feeling as if he'd stood by long enough, Zach waded into the fight and hauled the perpetrator off Emily just as she was about to take a big chunk out of his shoulder with her teeth.

"Remind me never to land on your bad side," Zach muttered, throwing the man into a brick wall.

Emily stood and brushed off her overskirt. "Indeed, Detective."

The man made a lunge for the alley exit, but Zach hauled him back and pressed his forearm into the assailant's throat. There wasn't enough light to see the man's face clearly, but Zach estimated his height at five foot ten, his build medium with just enough flesh on him to classify him as middle class.

"Wait a minute." A strike, a hiss, and then a lit stub of candle appeared in front of Zach.

She was a most extraordinary woman, Zach thought. What other female of his acquaintance wore breeches, could fell a full-grown man, and carried a candle in her pocket? He wondered what else she had on her person.

The flame of the candle glinted in eyes that were glazed and watering from the pressure of Zach's arm. He eased off a bit and Emily lifted the candle high and low, illuminating the perpetrator's face in its entirety.

"Who are you?" Emily demanded. Wisps of dark hair had

fallen from her pins to frame her freckled and determined face. "Why did you strike Lord Eastmoreland?"

"I will not answer to a dollymop," the man wheezed, eyeing Emily with disgust.

Zach smacked him across the face hard enough that he spit blood. "You talk to her like that again, you won't speak for a month."

Instead of shrieking or fainting at the violence, Emily beamed brilliantly up at him.

Zach knew in that instant he would fight a thousand men to keep that smile on her face. Was this how every man felt about the woman he was falling in love with? Zach didn't know, as he'd never been in love. He'd thought himself in love a few times, mostly as a young man, but he had never known it to be as true and potent as the feeling he had when Emily smiled up at him in gratitude that he had defended her honor.

She returned her gaze to the perpetrator, her smile fading. "Speak," she commanded.

The man mumbled his name. "Mr. Jonathan Brown."

The lack of title along with the fraying disrepair of the man's clothes told Zach that although Mr. Brown was middle class, he'd lost any wealth he'd once had. Judging by the puffiness of his face, the bloodshot eyes, and his twitching eyelid, he was now simply a drunk.

"Who hired you?" Zach asked, his tone calm and flat. "Or were you bug hunting?"

Emily tilted her head. "Bug hunting?"

"When one spends the night hunting for drunks to attack and rob."

"No, I wasn't doing that," the man said, poking out his lower lip. "I don't know who hired me. 'Twas in the pub. I couldn't pay for my tab and a figure in a green cloak approached me. He paid my bill, and it wasn't small change. He said all I had to do in return was clock the earl over the head. He even rented the curricle and told me where to find him. Said I should wait outside the club tonight."

The story rang true, but incomplete. Zach had heard enough half-truths in his lifetime to spot them as easily as a lie. "What else?"

The man's face turned mulish. "Nothing."

Zach studied him, replaying the assault in his head. Brown had struck the earl but had not run away after, at least not until Emily had shouted at him. Zach spotted his error straightaway: Brown hadn't been hired to simply knock the earl unconscious. He'd been hired to do more, and Emily had interrupted him.

Without asking permission, Zach yanked open the man's coat and felt around in his pockets. Something smooth brushed against his fingers and he pulled out a scrap of dirty, cheap pink satin. Zach's heart leapt into his throat before slamming back into his chest.

He recognized that fabric.

The first prostitute the Evangelist had murdered had been wearing a dress of that very type and color. But why had the coroner not discovered the missing snippet? Excitement and anger warred in his chest.

Zach held the satin in front of Mr. Brown's face. "Tell me the rest. You weren't only hired to knock out the earl, were you?"

The man didn't reply. Zach pressed again with his forearm.

"All right!" he gasped. Zach eased up. "He asked me to put this piece of fabric in the old man's coat. I don't know why, I swear!"

A drop of rain splattered from overhead.

"You are coming to the station with me," Zach said. He felt as if his blood were rushing through his veins at double time. "I need a thorough description of the man who approached you." He would drill Mr. Brown until the drunk gave up information he wasn't even aware he knew. By the end of the night Zach would have a description of the green-cloaked man's gait, his voice, and the time and place he approached Mr. Brown.

It seemed Zach's baiting had worked: He'd succeeded in rattling the Evangelist enough that the killer had hired Mr. Brown to disable the earl and plant evidence on him. It would have worked, too, if Emily hadn't interrupted Mr. Brown before he could complete his task. There was no doubt in Zach's mind an anonymous tip implicating Eastmoreland would have been placed with the police and the gossip rags the next morning. If both the police and the press believed Eastmoreland to be the killer, it would take attention off the real murderer. Not to mention it would make Zach look like an incompetent fool when the Evangelist struck again.

The Evangelist had just made it personal.

Unease niggled at the base of Zach's skull. Why had the killer targeted Eastmoreland? Was it mere coincidence that he was Emily's employer?

There was something off about the entire picture, and Zach wasn't going to rest easy until he discovered what it was.

Chapter 38

Emily dispatched her message to the Dove and returned to the kitchen to snitch an apple. She hadn't heard from Zach since they'd parted ways last night.

In the morning she had pretended to be as surprised and horrified as the rest of the staff when a detective escorted the earl home. A bandage over the earl's left eye was the only evidence the assailant had left behind. Eastmoreland had assured the countess he had searched his pockets and found nothing missing, so the police considered the attack a random act of violence.

Emily knew better.

It made her shiver to think how they'd blundered into Zach's first real lead, and what would have happened if they hadn't.

Why Eastmoreland? Emily took a bite out of the apple and crunched as she thought. Well, why not? With his well-known penchant for dominant prostitutes, he made a plausible suspect for the Evangelist to frame.

Which would mean the Evangelist either knew the earl in person, or knew *of* the earl.

"Shame, isn't it?" Cook asked as she mixed a bowl of flour, her powerful forearm plowing the wooden spoon through the forming dough. "It's getting so a decent man can't even walk down the street at night without being attacked."

"Mmm," Emily said through a full mouth. Cook was so focused on her grievance that she didn't notice the apple in Emily's hand. Once Emily had swallowed she asked, "How is the dowager doing? Is she well? I have not seen her about the house lately."

"Fit as a fiddle if her food intake is any indication," Cook said, then caught herself gossiping and turned her ire to the apple in Emily's hand. "Is this your kitchen or mine, missy?"

"Sorry!" Emily called, her back already sailing through the doorway.

Emily was crossing the great hall to fetch a charcoal drawing one of the children had left in the parlor when there was a knock at the door. The footman was nowhere in sight so Emily shrugged and swung it open.

"Eastmoreland—" she began, and stopped short. Zach stood tall in his navy police uniform, his broad shoulders blocking out the sun. His golden-blond hair caught the glint of afternoon light, making him appear strangely angelic. When her eyes met his, however, it wasn't an angel looking back at her. Zach's gaze was hot and secretive, as if he had already seen her undressed and was looking through her clothes at her naked body.

Emily's whole body flushed, and it was a full fifteen seconds before she even realized there was another man standing beside Zach. He was a tall, lanky constable with a cap of sandy-brown hair and an odd, tilted way of holding his chin that reminded her of a bird.

"Good afternoon," Zach said, his lips twitching. "Is your employer, Lord Eastmoreland, in residence?"

"He is resting."

"I am afraid we will have to disturb his sleep," Zach said. It was a command that even the haughtiest of butlers would have found difficult to ignore.

"Come into the parlor." Emily opened the door farther. "Straight ahead to the right. I will fetch the butler."

Zach gestured for his companion to enter first. Emily shut the door, and when she turned around Zach grabbed her around the waist and gave her a quick, breathless kiss before releasing her and following the constable.

Emily touched her lips and glanced around, but no one had witnessed the scandalous kiss. Zach was playing with fire. If anyone had seen such improper behavior, she would have been in a real pickle.

She hurried off to find the butler, who told her in no uncertain terms she had no place opening the door and the police had no right to disturb his lordship's rest.

"Then you had best tell that to the police," Emily huffed.

The butler stomped off to the parlor and reappeared a moment later, snapping at one of the footmen to wake the earl. Emily suppressed a smile. She was beginning to realize how hard it was to say no to Detective Constable Denholm.

How she wished she could be a fly on the wall!

The head housekeeper passed at that moment and gave her a stern look, so Emily reluctantly headed for the courtyard. The house was bustling with servants preparing and packing for the move to the country, and with her lessons over for the day, Emily was simply in the way.

She dodged a maid dashing past with a stack of linens and found her way into the sun-bleached garden. The heat wave was so intense that even the gardener appeared to have given up on watering the thirsty plants; they were fragile and yellow, as if they'd all been placed in the oven and left to crisp.

Emily perspired as she paced the garden, her thoughts whizzing. Why was Zach there? Had they discovered further evidence? What was so important that he had need to rouse the earl from his rest?

She'd worn a path in the yellowing grass by the time she heard the front door open and close. Taking a risk she slipped underneath the cool stone overpass, into the larder, and out onto the street. Zach's young colleague was mounting a horse. He saluted Zach and took off, leaving Zach standing beside his dappled stallion.

Emily hurried to catch him before he left. He must've heard her coming, because he turned as she approached. His smile blossomed and then inexplicably dimmed. Emily glanced over her shoulder and saw, to her dismay, the Hill carriage bearing down on them.

She walked briskly by instead.

"Meet me at the Wellington Arch, nine o'clock," he murmured as she passed.

Emily nodded once, rounded the building, and then turned to peer from the corner at the unfolding scene.

The Hill carriage had stopped at Zach's side and Mrs. Hill was poking her head out the window, her puglike nose flushed red with the heat. Her voice was so shrill Emily could hear her at a distance.

"Mr. Denholm! What a surprise! I see you are on duty. You are no doubt calling on Lord Eastmorcland. What a shame he was attacked! It has been in all the papers today. Have you come to let him know you have caught his assailant?"

Zach's voice was low, however, and Emily was not able to hear his response.

"Nonetheless, I am sure your department is working tirelessly on his behalf," Mrs. Hill responded. She fluttered the fan rapidly in front of her face. "We are on our way to the country to escape this intolerable heat. We have a lovely place in Cheshire. Will you be leaving the city as well?"

Zach replied again and Mrs. Hill's face glowed.

"What a wonderful coincidence! I do hope we will run into one another. Jane has been voraciously reading about the Anglo-Burmese War. She is delightfully interested in all military history. I swear I do not know who she inherited her intelligence from." Mrs. Hill tittered. "I am confident you two would have *so* much to discuss."

Emily imagined Zach giving the requisite response.

"Whatever happened to that charming cousin of yours? Will she be joining you in Cheshire? Oh, what a tragedy she has returned to her Liverpool fiancé. What was her surname again? I believe we have distant cousins from the same parts."

Zach turned his profile enough that Emily could read the stony expression ten yards off. He was not pleased with Mrs. Hill, and even Emily knew the old bat was fishing for gossip.

He must have given his excuses, because he swung up on his horse, touched the brim of his hat, and trotted off. Emily would have followed him with her eyes but they were glued on Mrs. Hill, whose mask had slipped the moment Zach had turned his back. The cheerfulness faded, her mouth drooping into something sour, her eyes slitted with malice. Emily felt a surge of protectiveness over Zach. She suspected she already knew Mrs. Hill's plot: ensnare Zach in a compromising situation with one of her dull-witted daughters. She would be damned if she let a sniveling, bitter Hill trap him in marriage. He was *hers* now.

She would have to keep an eye on those Hills.

Chapter 39

"What is a pretty woman like you doing alone in the park?"
Emily had her blade at his throat before Zach finished
the sentence. She gasped when she recognized him, sheathed the
dagger, and gave him a little shove. "You frightened me!"

No, Zach had never met another woman like her. "Sorry, Noodles. You seem nervous tonight."

Emily caught her bottom lip between her teeth. "I thought—
no, never mind."

Anyone else and Zach might have chalked her anxiety up to
being alone in the park after dark, but Emily had chased a man
into an alley and tackled him from a rooftop—if she was worried
about something, Zach trusted her instincts.

"Tell me," he insisted.

"I thought I was being followed on the way here." She shook her
head. "But every time I stopped or doubled back, no one was there."

The tingling feeling one felt when being watched by another
was almost unmistakable. If Emily had felt it, then someone *had*
been watching her.

Zach expanded his senses, waiting for the familiar whisper of danger to shimmy along the edges of his periphery. Nothing.

"Be careful, Emily," he said. He loved that she was so self-sufficient and he hated it at the same time. The thought of her doubling back on a possible thief made him break out in a sweat. "Although this is Mayfair, no place is entirely safe from scoundrels and thieves."

Emily gave his hand a placating pat. "Do not worry, Zach, I am always watching my back." She nodded at the curricle. "No carriage?"

He wanted her to take his warning seriously, but there was no point in lecturing her. Whether he liked it or not, Emily was entirely capable of "watching her back," as she'd put it. "I thought you might enjoy the breeze. It is nine o'clock at night and I will wager still in the nineties."

"Bless you!" she exclaimed, and hurried to the side of the vehicle. She nimbly climbed aboard despite her cumbersome navy skirts, and Zach took up the reins to the pair of ebony mares.

"Normally this would violate our contract," Emily said, arranging her skirts, "but it is so dark I doubt anyone will recognize me."

Zach lifted a brow. "Our contract?"

"Yes, our relationship contract."

"Is that what we are calling it?"

"Do you have a better name?"

Zach bit his tongue. It made their...whatever this was, sound boring and stuffy, like a loveless marriage.

"Are we going to Stanford House?" Emily asked. The wind whipped delightfully at their faces, and she lifted her arms over her head and tilted her chin back, letting the breeze play over her body. It was unintentionally sensuous; Zach knew she had no idea how much of a nature goddess she looked in the moment, worshipping the wind.

He replied with a question. "Do you want to go to my house?"

"Yes. I want to get this over with, and then we can talk about why you were at Lord Eastmoreland's house today."

Get this over with. Although he should have been insulted, he knew her reaction stemmed from her previous experiences with her husband. So far she had been pleased with their explorations of each other, but he could not judge her for being hesitant about engaging in an act that had once been an expression of ownership rather than pleasure.

"Let's not do anything more than kiss, Noodles. Not tonight."

"Nonsense. Then it would not be a proper affair, would it?"

"We will wait until you are ready," he said firmly.

Emily faced him, her expression determined. "I am ready."

It was how she approached life, he realized. When Emily settled her mind on something, she went for it, no matter how much it frightened her or how challenging the obstacles. What other woman of her class and circumstance would have *dared* impersonate a governess, even going so far as to forge a letter of introduction from a peer? What woman would resist her mother's life of prostitution despite the pressures to provide for the family on her back?

"Stop trying to figure me out."

"I am not. I have already figured you out."

She scowled. "You have not."

"And tonight," Zach continued, lowering his voice, "I am going to discover every little pleasure point on your body until you forget you ever had a husband before me."

He left the curricle with his stable master and snuck Emily in through the servants' entrance and up the stairs to the east wing. It irritated him to treat her like a dirty secret, but she had made it plain she wouldn't be seen and judged by his staff. He would have destroyed the first of his staff to make her feel less than, but he wasn't oblivious to reality. Just because he wanted his staff to keep their mouths closed, it didn't mean they would.

In his chamber Zach lit candles until the room was ablaze with light and shadow. Emily stood in the center, proper and straight in her governess gown, and surveyed her surroundings. For a moment Zach felt nervous about her approval.

Finally she faced him and said, "I like it. It's very much you."

"How so?"

"Clean. Simple. Sophisticated without being showy."

"So you think you have me figured out?"

"I know I do."

He grinned, crossing his arms and leaning against the door. "Are you hungry? Shall I send for a tray?"

"No. Help me take my gown off."

"Emily, why don't we ease into—"

"No," she interrupted. "We have talked enough." She gave him a half smile that was both shy and inviting. "You have made a lot of promises. Let us see if you live up to them."

His mouth went dry. She couldn't have been more arousing if she were an experienced courtesan. He pushed off the door and walked toward her until he towered over her. Slowly, one by one, he removed the pins from her hair until her chestnut locks tumbled over her shoulders and down her back. Her breath hitched, her lips parted slightly, and her eyes widened.

"Why do you always want my hair down?"

"I love your hair. I have been dying to run my hands through it." Which he did, reveling in the way the strands slipped through his fingers like silk. "I want to see it spread over your creamy breasts."

"Is that your fetish? Hair?"

Zach smiled.

Chapter 40

Emily was like a fox sighted by a hunter, so intense was Zach's concentration on her. His fingers, rough and warm, traced gently over her cheekbones to her mouth, where he pressed on her lower lip with his thumb and leaned forward to kiss her.

Her knees weakened, but she was determined to keep up appearances. So far she had enjoyed what she and Zach had done, but she assumed that was because she had not shared such sinfully pleasurable things with Lionel the Pig. However, she *had* experienced sex, and she was confident she would not like it, even with Zach. That said, she was willing to give it a try if it meant spending time in Zach's company and possibly doing more of that delightful "kissing." She would simply have to hope he wouldn't want to lie with her often.

Zach's mouth traveled to her ear, where he blew softly, sending chills down her spine. He kissed her neck, his hands tracing lightly over her back, to her bottom, and then up to her shoulder blades again.

Emily squirmed against him. "Take my dress off."

She didn't need to tell him a third time. Zach's hands deftly helped her shed her simple gown until she was left standing in her stockings and a very thin chemise, worn fragile from use rather than from the sheer nature of the material.

Zach's gaze burned into her, his eyes traveling over her breasts and down to her legs. Her cheeks flaming, Emily unrolled her socks and dropped her shift until she stood in front of him entirely nude.

Her fingers were tingling, her heart pounding. She knew she was shapely enough in a gown, but what if he wasn't pleased with her nude body? Her breasts were slightly uneven, and she wasn't as plump as fashion dictated.

After Zach didn't speak Emily crossed her arms under her breasts and said crossly, "What? You do not like what you see?"

Zach swallowed hard and said hoarsely, "You cannot be serious. You have the most beautiful body I have ever seen."

Mollified, Emily let her hands drop. She stepped forward, reaching for his cravat. "I want to see yours."

Choking on a laugh, Zach helped her shuck his clothes. Society men's clothes were rather complicated, she discovered, but finally he stood before her as nude as she.

Emily was surprised. He didn't look as she'd expected. She'd seen statues, of course, but in books the most interesting parts were always carefully concealed. Lionel had been squat and bullish with hair on his arms, knuckles, belly, thighs, and really every part of him. And his member had been ... Emily bit her lip. Well it had been far smaller than what she was looking at right now. Zach was nicely muscled, with a dusting of dark blond hair across his chest that tapered into a line leading to the thatch of hair from which his member protruded, longer and thicker than she'd realized in the carriage.

"This is not going to work," she said, eyes on his groin.

Zach laughed, pulled her close, and kissed her until she was breathless. Then he continued kissing her, using his tongue to make love to her mouth. At the same time he backed her up until her knees hit the bed and they both fell onto the soft covering.

The coverlet was cool on her back as Zach's hands traveled to her breasts. He cupped each one and rubbed his thumbs over her nipples until they were hard. He tore his mouth from hers long enough to suckle one of her breasts, nipping and tugging until Emily mindlessly lifted off the mattress, seeking closer contact.

Heeding her silent plea, Zach slid a hand between their bodies and found her, already wet, and slowly inserted a finger. Emily thought she saw stars, but that was just the beginning. He moved his finger in and out of her before gently stretching her with a second, the pad of his thumb pressing on her nub to circle and tease until hot, liquid desire pooled in her belly and she was squirming with impatience.

"Do it now," she breathed.

"Are you sure you're ready? We can—"

"Yes!"

Zach's mouth fell to her neck as he moved over her and grasped the base of his penis, stroking the head against her opening until it glistened with her own moisture. He slowly began to push inside her, his skin taut over his cheekbones as if it were painful for him rather than pleasurable.

Whenever Emily thought he surely must be seated, he kept going, until at last he was fully inside her, stretching her to a limit she hadn't thought possible. He stayed still, not moving, his jaw and arms tense.

"Are you all right?" he rasped.

"I think so."

He shifted slightly, and a sunburst of sensation shot through Emily's core. At her gasp of surprise, he repeated the motion, rotating his hips so that he ground against her most sensitive flesh. Then he slowly withdrew and returned, the action familiar and yet unlike anything she had felt before. It was as if every inch of him were rubbing against exposed pleasure nerves, filling her, stroking her, dragging her to heights she had not known existed. Zach continued the rhythm, slowly increasing speed until Emily was panting and moaning. He kissed her again, and she wrapped her legs around his waist and met his eyes as he moved deep inside of her, rocking her hips in time with his.

Some indefinable feeling tugged hard at her heart. For a wild, crazy moment, she felt as if she and this man belonged to each other.

Before either of them could climax, he withdrew. Emily sat up in dismay. "What is the matter?"

"Turn over."

"What?" she gasped. "That is not how proper—"

"Fuck being proper."

"I thought we were already doing that."

He gently smacked her bottom, grinning. "Naughty girl. Now turn over."

Emily rolled onto all fours, knowing what he was asking for and both humiliated and excited by the request. She was embarrassed knowing what his view must look like and thrilled to be doing something so outrageously sinful.

When Zach entered her from behind, she suddenly understood all of the promises he'd made. She'd thought she'd already experienced the pinnacle of pleasure one could reach from joining with another, but this was a sensation she couldn't even describe. As he drove into her she moaned into the pillow, pushing back against him. His hands squeezed her butt cheeks as the full length of him slid in and out until she was gasping and wiggling, her face flushing and her skin covered in chills as she ached for release.

Emily wasn't sure she could take any more when Zach shallowed his thrusts, hitting a spot inside of her that made her eyes fly open. "Zach, that...don't stop that!"

He didn't. He continued at the same pace, relentlessly driving her to a place where she came undone, screaming his name into the pillow. Before she collapsed she felt him go rigid and pull out, falling beside her on the mattress. Their ragged breaths filled the silence of the room.

When she finally regained her senses, Emily made the great effort of moving closer to lay her head on his chest. He stroked her upper arm, his other hand propped behind his head. He was sporting a smug smile.

"Well?" he asked.

"Looking for compliments?"

"Was it what you expected?"

No. No, it hadn't been. It had been exciting and pleasurable and delicious in every way that mattered. In short, it had been the opposite of anything she'd had with Lionel.

Zach slid down her body to kiss her belly, his hand drifting between her thighs, his cobalt gaze already heating again.

"Why did you...?" She waved her hand, too embarrassed to ask why he'd pulled out at the end. Lionel never had.

"You are not my wife."

Her smile faltered.

"You know how babies are made, right, Em?"

"Well, I...I suppose so," she stammered, although it had not once occurred to her while she was considering sleeping with him that it could happen to *them*. It had not happened with Lionel, and so she had assumed she was barren. The flaw in her reasoning was instantly obvious, and she was enormously grateful Zach had possessed the foresight she had lacked. She could not, *would* not bring a bastard child into the world. She knew all too well the humiliation a bastard child bore. And what of her position? She would be let go at once if she were discovered to be with child.

"You've gone pale," Zach said.

Emily launched herself off the bed and pulled on her chemise. "I cannot believe how dull-witted I was not to have considered the consequences. Such a thing cannot happen, Zach."

Zach's features chilled. "Would it be so terrible to have a child with me?"

Emily looked sympathetically at him. "You dear, stupid man. It does not matter if you sire a *hundred* illegitimate children: Society and the law will treat you no differently. I am a woman. A legally *married* woman. It would be devastating for me."

Zach didn't thaw. "You are aware I would insist on marriage should that happen."

"Alas, polyandry is not yet an approved way of life in England."

Zach raked a hand through his hair and growled. "Then divorce your dead husband."

She didn't say anything. She didn't tell him the legality of her marriage wasn't the only reason they could never be together.

Zach approached her, his expression guarded and intense. "Would you marry me if you were free to do so?"

Emily sensed this was a very important hypothetical to him, so she thought hard about it. If she were free to do so, it would mean Lionel was legally declared dead and she did not bear the burden of her Big Secret. Would she marry him under those circumstances?

Zach was handsome, kind, and funny. He didn't try to make her feel like less of a woman because she wore breeches or carried a dagger; in fact, he seemed to enjoy that about her. He knew almost everything about her past and it hadn't made a difference to him. Despite her best efforts to shake him off, he had continued to pursue her, to send her gifts. He had even struck the man who had called her a whore—and it had been the first time in her entire life someone had defended her honor. Would she want to spend the rest of her life with a man like that, if she could?

Yes. She'd be a bloody fool if she didn't.

Should she admit as much to him? She didn't see the harm. It was a hypothetical. She was still legally married for another six years, and there was nothing either of them could do about it.

"Yes," she said, "I think I would."

Zach's eyes lit as if she'd just accepted a proper proposal from him and he kissed her, warming her from the inside out. "Then we will continue to make love without making a baby." He lifted her off her feet, causing her to shriek as he tossed her on the bed. "Let's practice until our marriage is official."

"Zach—"

"Too late," he said, peeling off the chemise she had just put on. "You accepted my marriage proposal."

Emily laughed and swatted at him. "Come on."

"You think I am jesting, but I am not." Suddenly Emily was afraid he really was serious, because his gaze was solemn and determined. "We are getting you that divorce, Emily, and when we do, you will be mine."

Chapter 41

They made love three more times that night. Emily was beautiful, sensuous, and they moved together in such synchronicity that it was as if they'd been forged by the same celestial blacksmith to complement one another. Zach loved every inch of her body, the way her skin tasted salty of sweat, the little half-moon of moles underneath her left breast, the way she bit her lip and covered her eyes when she was coming. She was a goddess.

And he'd discovered the last time they joined, looking into each other's eyes and moving dreamily in the early hours of dawn, that he was desperately in love with her.

She didn't think he was serious about marriage, but Zach had never been more serious about anything in his life. First thing in the morning he would engage his solicitor to discuss a petition to Parliament. He did not see why it should cause any great controversy: Emily was already a widow. Why not grant the divorce from a dead man? If a few palms needed to be greased, a few promises made, Zach was happy to do so. There was no way he was waiting six years to make her his wife.

"You look fierce," Emily said, stirring beside him. She propped her head on her hand, her hair tumbling wildly over her bare shoulder. The sun streamed through the window and cast her skin in tones of gold. Zach's heart squeezed at the image she made in his bed.

"Just thinking."

"You never told me why you were at Eastmoreland's," Emily said, naturally assuming he was thinking about the case.

Zach stacked his hands behind his head. "Lord Eastmoreland was chosen as a scapegoat for a reason; the Evangelist is too careful and methodical to pick someone at random. The Evangelist either knows him personally, or knows of his reputation for seeking out prostitutes. We had some delicate questions to ask Eastmoreland about his friendships, where he has been, and who knows about his affairs."

Emily's eyes widened. "He admitted to the affairs?"

"He did." At first the earl had blustered, threatened police harassment, and raged that he would have their heads on a platter by the time the night was out. Zach had calmly told him no such thing would happen, and warned that if the earl wasn't careful, he could wind up charged with the murders. That had sobered the man quickly.

"You are good. Did you learn anything?"

Zach lifted a shoulder. "I'm not sure. Right now we are collecting facts. Think of the murderer as a puzzle. Each fact we gather is a puzzle piece, and the more pieces we have, the clearer the picture that eventually emerges."

Emily reached over to trail her fingers through his chest hair. Even though they had made love more times that night than Zach had had sex that entire year, his body began to stir. If he had access to her every day, he wondered if they'd ever leave the bedroom. He smothered a smile. Of course they would. He had a plethora of rooms in which he could lift her skirts, furniture that he could bend her over, walls he could press her against.

Leaving the *house*, now, that was the question.

Great, now he was hard again.

"What about Mr. Brown's statement?"

"Full of holes. He was drunk the night the Evangelist approached him. He remembers him as being deep in shadow, wearing a green cloak, and he thought he was rather tall and thin. Even so, it is the best—no—it is the *only* description we have of the man."

"Why do you suppose the Evangelist chose now to frame Eastmoreland? Do you think your claim in the newspaper rattled him?"

Zach sat up and stretched, for once wishing he didn't have his police job to interfere with his personal life. "I suspect so, but it could also be a natural escalation. I have seen killers in the past become so bloated with their successes that their confidence led to mistakes. This was the Evangelist's first mistake, but I am convinced there are more to come."

She shivered, and he bent and softly kissed her lips. "I need your husband's full name."

"Why?"

"I am getting you a divorce."

Emily shot out of bed, snatched her chemise off the floor, and pressed it to her chest. Her eyes were wild as they darted about looking for her clothes. She appeared…frantic. Terrified, even.

"Why are you so upset?" Zach asked as she continued pulling on her clothes, missing buttons in her hurry.

"A divorce is expensive. You will be made a laughingstock, paying for a governess to divorce her dead husband." Emily shook her head in disgust.

"After a decade of war, I think I can face the scorn of a few snotty noblemen."

"That is not all you have to worry about," she muttered.

"What was that?" Zach climbed out of the bed and casually pulled on his trousers, but the fine hairs on the back of his neck were standing straight, his intuition softly stirring at her words.

"Nothing." She gave him a bright, cheerful smile that was as fake as a paste diamond. "May I take your unmarked carriage back to Eastmoreland House?"

Zach buttoned his shirt. "Of course. When are you leaving for the country?"

"The majority of servants depart this afternoon, and I am scheduled to ride in one of their carriages. The Eastmorelands leave tomorrow after breakfast. Have you heard from your manager about the properties?"

"I received a message early yesterday. He made an offer on one of the residences and with any luck I will be moving to the country in the next few days."

"What if the owners do not accept your offer?"

"They will."

"You seem awfully confident." She deftly pinned her hair atop her head and shook her finger at him when she caught the gleam in his eye. "I know that look, Mr. Denholm. It is already near morning and I have children to teach."

"I love your hair."

"Hair fetishist," she said, a half smirk on her lips. "Now tell me why you are so confident the owner will sell?"

"I had my solicitor look into his finances. The owner is nearly destitute, and my offer is more than generous. He would be an idiot to refuse. Besides, aside from a skeleton staff, the estate is sitting empty. It is nothing but a burden on the man, and I plan to relieve him of it."

"So chivalrous," she said, and pecked him on the cheek.

By the time he secured her in the shabby, unmarked carriage and waved her off it was nearly nine and Emily was fretting that she really would be late.

It would be another hour before Zach realized she had never given him her husband's name.

Emily asked the driver to drop her off at the end of the street, and she walked the remainder of the way to Eastmoreland House. She was disheveled, having dressed in a hurry once Zach had started talking about divorce, and prayed the good eyes of the *ton* were still tightly shut in sleep.

Emily was relieved the Eastmorelands were headed for the country. The heat wave had sucked the life out of London, and even the most optimistic souls were flagging. Surely one could only stand so much humidity before melting? It wasn't even nine o'clock in the morning and the front of her gown was already damp with perspiration.

When she reached Eastmoreland House, Emily thought she saw a curtain flutter in a second-floor window, but when she stopped and looked upward no one was there. It had probably been an errant breeze, even though there seemed to be very little of it at the moment.

Emily bustled past Cook, commenting loudly on how lovely her morning walk had been, and hurried to her room, where she quickly washed and prepared to dress for the day.

She paused as she pulled off her gown, studying her slender frame in the small mirror propped atop the chiffonier. She didn't look any different, and yet she felt like an entirely new woman. She had been *loved*: truly, thoroughly loved. It turned out that when one's partner wasn't a selfish ass, sex could be an extraordinary act.

A secret smile tugged at Emily's lips. She'd never felt so relaxed or content. If she were a cat, she'd stretch and curl up for a nap in the sunshine. But she was not a cat, she was a governess who was late for her work. She hurriedly pulled on a fresh dress, and despite her resolve to focus on her duties for the day, her thoughts returned to Zach's bullheaded insistence on buying her a divorce.

She had lied to him. Although she truly did believe divorcing a dead man would be one for the scandal sheets, that was not what had frightened her enough to make her skin go cold.

She had agreed to their relationship comfortable in the knowledge that she would not be a free woman for six years. Zach would be tired of her long before then, so there had been no real danger to him so long as no one discovered who she was. He was safe from her past.

She had not counted on a marriage proposal.

For one brief moment she allowed herself to imagine what it would be like to be Mrs. Denholm. In the summers she and Zach would holiday in their country house in Cheshire, sip sweet lemonades, swim in their pond, and make lazy love all afternoon. She would have her very own library. After a year of wedded bliss she would fall pregnant, and instead of being terrified, she and Zach would be overjoyed.

Her heart blipped at the memory of Zach's words: *Would it be so terrible to have a child with me?* No, it wouldn't. In another life she would have loved it.

Emily banished the fantasy. She would never agree to file for divorce. As much as she dreamed of being entirely free of the Pig, it would not be at the expense of Zach.

He could not marry her. Her past would ruin his career, his reputation, and the social standing he'd begun to attain.

She would not let that happen.

Chapter 42

W ell?" Mrs. Hill questioned the investigator standing in her fraying Cheshire receiving room. The rented estate was crumbling and in dire need of repairs and updates, but all that mattered was that the Hills were in one of the fashionable country seats for the summer and Mr. Denholm would arrive any day.

The investigator's appearance made Mrs. Hill uneasy. He had rounded shoulders, slicked hair beneath his hat, and eyes that were so flat and black they were almost reptilian. That must have been how the man had earned his reputation as the most ruthless purveyor of information in London. He was unscrupulous in gathering intelligence for his clients and he was no stranger to using blackmail or threats in order to get what he wanted.

In return, his clients paid handsomely.

Mrs. Hill had nagged her brother, Lord Moore, until he'd agreed to finance the investigator's fee. It had turned out to be an extraordinary sum, and her brother had complained ceaselessly since. Even Mrs. Hill had begun to doubt her rash decision. If the investigator, known only as Craven, had returned empty-handed, it would be a colossal waste of funds. However, if he'd succeeded, it could be instrumental in securing their future.

"He's clean."

Mrs. Hill wanted to scream. Instead her face closed into a solid mask of ice. "Are you certain?"

"Mr. Denholm's financial dealings are all aboveboard. He's thorough about investigating the companies he invests in, and he funds several charities. Man dun't even cheat at card games. Clean as a whistle."

"Then what did we pay you for?" she hissed. "You were supposed to dig up dirt on the man, not sing his praises."

Craven appeared unaffected. "I named my terms before your brother paid. You also asked me to look into Mr. Denholm's family connections. He has very few: his mother, who lives in Hastings in Essex, and his father, who passed away five years ago. No brothers, sisters, aunts, or uncles I could find. His grandparents are long gone, and both his parents were only children."

Mrs. Hill's rage intensified. "You useless cur! That is no help at all. That is—wait, you said no aunts or uncles?"

"None."

Her anger slowly ebbed and was replaced with wicked satisfaction. No aunts and uncles, no family connections. That meant Mr. Denholm's cousin, the lovely Miss Emily whom he'd been so infatuated with at the ball, was not a blood relation at all. A mistress, perhaps? A married woman? What other reason would he have for concealing her identity?

Mrs. Hill's teeth poked over her lip in a rusty smile. It looked as if she had been dealt an ace after all.

She dismissed Craven and howled to Jane to come to the parlor.

When the girl arrived, sullen and bored, Mrs. Hill snapped at her to get dressed.

"Whatever for?" Jane complained. "We have no invitations. No one cares that we are here."

"Do not sulk. We are headed to the dressmaker."

Jane arched her brow. "We have the funds for that?"

"Of course not. We will have to purchase on your uncle's credit."

"Uncle will be cross."

"Not when he realizes it has resulted in your engagement to Mr. Denholm."

"You are delusional, Mother! He is not interested in me. He is infatuated with that stupid little cousin of his. You saw him at the ball. It was disgusting."

Mrs. Hill couldn't stop smiling. "Ready yourself, dear girl. You are going to swoon when you hear what I have to tell you."

Chapter 43

The children were so excited to be leaving for the country that they struggled to pay attention to their lessons. The heat in the third-floor schoolroom was insufferable; even Emily found her mind wandering. The little girls wilted in their dresses, and the boys longingly gazed out the window.

"Miss Leverton," Charlie asked, sweat sticking his hair to his brow, "can we go to the park again? We learned so much about eto ento etomolgy."

"Yes, please!" the other children begged.

"I like bugs," Georgiana lied. It was true desperation when Georgiana was willing to look for insects.

"After what happened last time?" Emily exclaimed. It had been pure luck that the heat had dried Jonathan's clothes by the time they'd returned to the house after his swim in the Serpentine.

"I promise I will be on my best behavior," Jonathan pleaded. "I shall burn my model ship if I am not."

"I'll help watch the little ones," Minnie offered, slipping into the schoolroom.

Ignoring her better sense, Emily capitulated. It was their last morning in the city; why not take a jaunt and say their goodbyes? She was willing to try anything to alleviate the terrible humidity of the schoolroom.

Emily and the six Eastmoreland children set off for Hyde Park, the stench of the steaming London streets enough to curdle the strongest stomach.

Along the way, Emily again had the uneasy sensation of being watched. Prickles raced up the backs of her arms and she paused as if to arrange her gown, then turned her head sharply to the left. She could have sworn she saw a shadow vanish around the bend, but by the time she reached the corner of the street no one was there but a crossing sweeper twirling his broom.

She frowned. Zach was right: Her nerves were on edge. Perhaps it was from so much change in such a short amount of time.

"I cannot wait for the countryside," Minnie declared once they'd reached the carriage road where the shaded greenery offered a whisper of relief

Emily mopped at her forehead with her handkerchief and fantasized about swimming in a cool Cheshire pond.

She and the children dawdled along the lane. The younger ones raced into the grass and around tree trunks and Emily didn't have the heart to scold them. Most of the gentry had already left the city, and it was too early in the morning for those that hadn't. Emily spotted a few nannies with the same idea of cooling off in the park.

The children had run ahead to gather a bundle of wildflowers when a gloved hand slipped around Emily's arm and spun her around.

"What...*Frankie?*"

Frankie looked almost exactly as Emily remembered her:

dirty-blond hair falling out of a chignon, urgent blue eyes, gigantic spectacles. She was breathing heavily, as if she had just run a great distance.

"It *is* you!" Frankie shouted, then lowered her voice. "You *do* still work for the Eastmoreland family. When you did not reply to my letter, I thought you had found a new situation. But then I spotted you across the park. Poor Porter is still trying to catch up." She waved encouragingly at Porter, who raced along the carriage road with war whoops.

Emily gave her a wary smile. "My apologies. I intended to respond but I suppose I got distracted."

Frankie stood a few inches lower than Emily, but her gaze was level and earnest when she said, "You must leave your situation."

"Pardon me?"

"I have been following the trajectory of the Evangelist murders. The math points toward Eastmoreland as the killer."

Emily yanked her arm away. "You are insane. You expect me to believe you figured out who the murderer is with mathematics?"

Frankie frowned. "Math can tell you anything."

"How did you do it, then?" Emily challenged. She didn't know a lot about mathematics beyond the basics, as the boys would receive separate and more intensive tutoring in the subject when they were older and the girls were deemed to have no use for it beyond the ability to calculate basic sums, but she did know a lot about cons. She'd grown up under the tutelage of a con artist and was therefore well versed in suspicion.

"I have a goodly amount of spare time," Frankie admitted. "I began by using the gossip rags to make a list of all peers present at balls, soirees, operas, and other public functions during the nights of the murders, careful to exclude any venues that would have permitted one to leave halfway through unnoticed. I also excluded those who were too infirm to travel or physically overpower the women. Then I cross-referenced the names with *Burke's Peerage*, plotted the data from the murders onto graphs, and completed probability calculations. Eastmoreland came out as the most likely culprit, followed by Lord Weeberly."

Emily gaped at her, unsure what to make of her outrageous claims. Was it possible that Eastmoreland had planned the assault on *himself* to throw off suspicion? He *had* been pumping her for information at the masquerade ball. He was also a known prostitute enthusiast who simultaneously thought very poorly of the women he visited. On top of it all, he had a fetish for the rougher side of the bedroom.

Then there was Lord Weeberly, the *ton*'s most darling poet and wastrel, and the man who'd insulted Zach's lack of title at the ball when Emily had refused his advances. He'd given her the impression of a man so spoiled by his wealth and title that he had become embittered by his ennui. Had he decided to liven things up by murdering women from a class for which he held so much scorn?

Could this bespeckled, dirt-splattered slip of a governess be right?

"Have you spoken with the police?" Emily asked.

Frankie shook her head no. "A newer, more pressing situation has come to my attention. My sister has recently run off, and it is imperative I find her at once." She snatched the hand of her young charge, who had caught up with her and was about to dash in front of a lone horse and rider. "I must be going," she said over her shoulder as the boy surged ahead, pulling her with him. "Be careful!"

Emily watched her leave, a shadow of foreboding creeping over her.

Chapter 44

Once they returned to the house, the children had their noon meal while Emily begged Cook to allow her to stand in the cool wine cellar. Cook said she would need the butler's permission since only he had the key, and Emily knew the old curmudgeon would never permit it.

Afternoon lessons were canceled to allow Emily time to pack her few possessions, and during the hottest part of the day she piled into a carriage with three young maids. Even with the curtains open the body heat was suffocating. Emily wasn't sure she would survive two days of travel.

When she and the children had returned to the house, she'd thought about dispatching a note to Zach and the Dove about what Frankie had told her, but everyone in London had a theory about who the Evangelist was, and Frankie Turner was no different. The woman was nearly a complete stranger, and Emily had no way of knowing if she was sane or not. She'd certainly been one of the oddest people to cross Emily's path since moving to London. That said, what Frankie claimed to have accomplished with her graphs and math was interesting. Emily didn't see any urgency in alerting Zach and the Dove by messenger, but the next time she saw them she would mention Frankie's theory.

And in the meantime, she would keep a sharp eye on Lord Eastmoreland.

Having slept very little the night before, Emily promptly drifted asleep and stayed that way for most of the afternoon journey. When at last they arrived at the inn in Northampton, she gloried in stretching her legs.

The three maids had giggled and gossiped the entire trip and appeared to be the best of friends. They were nice enough to Emily, but she was clearly an outsider, as was evident when the three of them hooked arms and bustled into the inn to have dinner, leaving Emily behind.

It was eight o'clock and Emily's stomach was rumbling, but the dropping sun had cooled the evening by a few degrees, and the fresh air after months of London's smog was too tantalizing to resist. Emily decided she would prowl the streets of the town and enjoy her liberty for an hour or so before she took her repast.

Emily delighted in the quaint village. Although the shops were closed, candles were lit in the windows of the modest houses she passed, and the town was clean and readied for the influx of travelers. After a while, Emily discovered a grassy bank on the Nene River and sat, tucking her knees under her chin to watch the slow-moving barges traverse the sunset-spattered waters.

She'd been gazing at the water for nearly an hour, the stars slowly emerging on the horizon, when the creeping sensation of being watched returned a moment before an oily male voice startled her.

"'Ello, doll. It's been a while."

Cold dread formed a pit in Emily's stomach. *No.* It couldn't be.

She jumped to her feet and spun around, her hand sliding into her pocket to close around the hilt of her dagger.

Before her leered a burly man with a thick neck and greasy black hair.

"Lionel," she whispered.

⚬❧⚬

Zach spent the morning catching up on correspondence, reviewing accounts, and reading reports from his solicitors and fund managers, and all the while Emily's refusal to reveal her husband's name continued to nag at his subconscious. At last he sat back, steepled his fingers, and gave in to the urge to examine their parting interactions.

Why had she been so afraid to share her husband's full name? What could have possibly put that look of terror on her face?

Without having come to a conclusion, Zach rang for Charles and told the butler he was leaving for the country.

"Sir, you are not packed. Your estate purchase has not been finalized. Where will you stay?"

"There are plenty of inns." Now that Zach had made the decision, he felt an inexplicable sense of urgency to catch up with Emily. He couldn't rationalize it, couldn't explain it, but he'd learned long ago that his gut was more accurate than his brain. In the military, trusting his instincts had often meant the difference between life and death. And at this moment his gut was telling him to find Emily. Immediately.

He stopped into the police station to let Wright and his team know he was leaving town, and when he returned to his house his bags had been packed and his horse saddled.

"No carriage?" Charles asked, paling slightly.

"Horseback is faster."

Zach eyed the setting sun. He was several hours behind Emily, assuming her carriage had left on time. He'd already studied the map and chosen the most likely route the carriage would have taken, feeling as if he were strategizing at war again. The Eastmoreland servants would have to find lodging for the night, and he would bet a good deal of his fortune they'd stop in Northampton, as it was roughly halfway to Brixton Hall and had an abundance of lodging.

Urgency pressed at the back of his skull as he mounted his gelding and took off, the smoggy heat of London clinging to his coat.

Chapter 45

Lionel had not changed in the year he was presumed dead. His heavily muscled shoulders bulged uncomfortably in a dirty waist-shirt, and mended trousers clung to his squat legs. Long greasy hair was tied in a queue down his back, and his beard was of the same coarse black hair that covered his fore-arms and knuckles. Blue eyes squinted from between swollen lids, and when he smiled, she noticed he was missing another tooth, from either fighting or rot.

The wind gusted behind him, and Emily smelled the all-too-familiar reek of alcohol and sour sweat. She schooled her expression, voiding her face of emotion. She would not give him the satisfaction of seeing her horror and dismay.

"Why are ye standing there, yer face hard as stone? That's not a nice way to greet yer husband."

"You are not my husband. He is dead."

Lionel lifted his arms. "Yet here I am, in the flesh."

"Your ship went down."

He nodded. "Yer right. 'Cept I so happened to miss that ship.

I was lying with a whore and didn't hear the whistle. I was angry at first and stayed in port thieving from passengers to pay for the next passage. When I heard the ship sank, I realized I'd been saved. I thought, why waste a perfectly good opportunity to die? No more debts, no more calls fer my arrest. I'd have a new life."

"Then why are you here?" she asked coldly.

He squinted and spat a stream of liquid on the ground. "Still ain't respectful of your place, I see. Yer lookin' mighty fancy, Esther, or should I say *Emily*. Got yerself all dressed up like a proper woman and got yerself a respectable job. I wonder what yer employer would think if he knew ye was nothin' but a thief an' a liar?"

Emily shoved her fear deep inside and concentrated on keeping her face emotionless. Lionel's ability to read human emotion and prey on it was uncanny; it was part of what made him such an excellent con man. He'd somehow discovered her position with the Eastmorelands, but did he know about Zach? If not, she had to do everything in her power to make sure he never found out.

"How did you find me?" Emily asked. She would not cede control of the conversation. One of Lionel's most reliable personality traits was his love of boasting, especially if he thought his exploits made him sound brave or clever. She would use that against him to get answers.

"Word gets 'round, Esther. London is a small town after all. Mary Lou's cousin is a scullery maid and swore up and down she saw ye parading about town with some toff's children in tow."

Mary Lou—one of Lionel's many admirers and, at one point, his mistress.

Emily raised a brow. "Mary Lou knew you were alive?"

"I sought her out an' told her. Thought she'd be tickled by my death."

Of course, Emily thought with disgust. It was not enough for Lionel to shirk his responsibilities by faking his death; he needed *praise* for how clever he was.

"When she told me I thought, what is that little bitch up to? 'Tweren't hard to find out if it was true or not. A couple days of skulking about and I saw ye walkin' down the street wit' a little 'un, all stiff and proud as if ye belonged wit' those fine folks. I followed ye to that earl's house but I couldn't find a way to talk to ye, so I waited and sawed they was packin' up and I followed behind."

"What do you want with me?"

Lionel's dirty face split into a wide grin. "I know what ye've done, ye lyin' whore. I know ye've spread yer legs for that policeman."

Emily's heart sank and her hand went clammy around the hilt of the dagger. *Please, no!*

"First I thought mebbe I'd blackmail ye wit' yer little secret, but then I said to meself, Lionel, don't ye know that policeman's face? And surely I did. You clever li'l girl, runnin' the biggest con in London on the richest man in London. Surely ye did not think ye would cut yer husband out of the profits?"

It's not like that! she wanted to scream, but Lionel wouldn't understand and she wouldn't give him the satisfaction of knowing she cared for Zach.

"I think ye know where this is goin', my love. Yer comin' wit' me, and we're goin' to send a little note to yer lover." His piggy eyes danced with glee. "I'm goin' to be a rich man soon. How much do ye think yer worth to him?"

Emily shrugged. "He is one of the wealthiest men in London,

how much do *you* think he cares for the lowly governess he bedded?"

Lionel took a menacing step forward, his fist clenched. "Don't matter. If he don't come, ye'll still do nicely fer a lay. Me an' Mary Lou got ourselves a boomin' business set up at the port. There's plenty o' demand for a clean snatch."

Emily was shaking with rage. "You cannot make me prostitute myself."

"The hell I can't. Yer my wife. I *own* you. Yer my *property* by law."

"You cannot have it both ways, Lionel. Either you are dead and I am a widow, or you are alive and I am your wife."

Lionel scowled, working out what she meant. Then he lifted a shoulder, unconcerned. "Once yer used a bit, it won't matter what ye are." He looked her up and down, a leer twisting his lips. "Esther, I swear ye got prettier while I was gone. Think I'll take advantage of my husbandly rights before I rent ye out."

She *hated* him. Rage and loathing boiled in her soul. If she were stronger, she would kill him right then and there, but he was as solid as a block of granite and skilled in a fight. If she rushed him, he'd relieve her of her dagger and she'd be entirely defenseless.

She would have to bide her time, wait until he was off his guard, and then strike. She would not let him send that letter to Zach, and she would not ever let him touch her again.

"We can do this one of two ways: Ye can come quietly wit' me, or I can strike ye until ye drop cold and carry ye over me horse."

Even though the words tasted bitter in her mouth she said, "I'll come with you."

"Never were stupid. Now give me my dagger."

"I do not know what you are talking about."

"Dagger in yer pocket, bitch, or we take the second way."

Fuming, Emily slowly removed the dagger. She contemplated lunging for him anyway but he must've seen the murderous glint in her eye because he moved with unexpected speed and snatched her wrist in a crushing grip.

Emily cried out when he squeezed and the dagger fell from her hand. Lionel picked it up off the ground and turned it over in the fading light. "I missed ye, old friend."

He led her to where he'd tied his rented mount and hefted himself over the horse. Emily slapped his hand away when he tried to help her up, and when he went to strike her in the face she dodged the blow.

"You lay a hand on me and I will scream," she said. "We are in the center of town now."

"Ain't no one interferin' wit' a marital dispute."

"Who said you are my husband?" she challenged. "Do you have the marriage certificate? Who will believe someone like *you* is married to someone like *me*?"

She had a point and he knew it, because he said nothing as she mounted behind him, doing her best to keep her skirts from brushing against him.

She would have screamed anyway except Lionel knew her Big Secret. If she exposed him, he would expose her in turn and ruin Zach.

They took off, and the gait of the horse nudged her closer to him. He cupped his crotch and said, "Miss this, my treasure?"

His ego was astounding. "Like I would miss maggots in my stew." If she still had the dagger, she'd wedge it in his kidneys.

He chuckled. "Come now, don't show yer disappointment so plainly."

She couldn't help taunting him. Lionel's pride in his manliness was his Achilles' heel. "Truly, before Mr. Denholm, I did not know any man could be that good in bed, or that *big*."

Lionel grabbed her thigh in a punishing grip that Emily knew would leave bruises. "Ye need to be taught a lesson, ye loud bitch."

"And you're the man to do it?" she asked sweetly. She'd never spoken to him like that when they were married, instead preferring to avoid him as much as possible. But she knew who she was now and what life was like from underneath his thumb. She knew what it was to love, and she was never going back to the way it had been.

Love. Oh God, no. Surely that had been a slip of the mind. She didn't love Zach, did she? Care about him? Sure. Want to spend every waking moment with him? Absolutely. Willing to do anything for him? Of course. But love? Did she love him?

Yes.

The realization struck her harder than any of Lionel's hits ever had. She was in love with Zachariah Denholm, her handsome, funny, shrewd Zach, and she would do anything to make sure her tainted past never touched him, even if it meant making him hate her.

Slowly, a plan began to form in her mind.

"Ye've got a mouth on ye. Ye think yer better than me now that ye've lived in that big, fancy house?" Lionel's grip on the reins was so tight his knuckles were white.

"Lionel, I've *always* been better than you, even when I was dirt-poor and thieving."

"Brave words from a murderer."

Emily's veins iced. "I am not a murderer."

"What's the word? An accomplice, then."

She went silent. He had not forgotten her Big Secret.

"Not so mouthy now."

"Where are we going?"

"The Wilmcote ruins."

She wrinkled her nose. The Wilmcote ruins was a fifteenth-century castle that had long since been abandoned. Once glorious and proud, it was now a crumbling stone façade choked with weeds and wildlife. Saplings sprouted from within the walls, and the roof was almost entirely caved in. There were tales of it being haunted by its last owners, who supposedly perished in a tragic fire. The local children of Wilmcote routinely dared one another to creep into the ruins in the middle of the night. It was a rite of passage and marked the bravest of the lot.

Wilmcote had been one of the many towns her family had lived in before they'd been run out. Lionel knew of Wilmcote and the ruins because they had been married in the town. Wilmcote's priest had been one of her mother's earliest johns, so the man had been willing to marry them quickly and without fuss despite Emily's resistance, lest her mother rat him out.

"Why there?" Emily asked.

"Because yer my golden goose, and I ain't goin' to let ye near anyone till yer lover shows."

"He won't."

"Then it's a quiet place where no one will hear ye scream."

Chapter 46

W hat do you mean she's not here?" Zach roared. The three maids exchanged stunned glances with one another.

"She . . . she was right behind us and then she was gone!" one of the girls exclaimed, wringing her hands together. "We went in for dinner and were entertained by some soldiers and we lost track of time. We haven't seen her since we arrived."

Zach reined in his fury. He'd pushed his horse hard and fast, the feeling that something was wrong intensifying with every hoofbeat. Now he'd arrived at the inn only to discover Emily had disembarked in Northampton and disappeared, leaving her belongings behind.

If Emily had planned to abandon the Eastmorelands, she would have taken her bag with her. The fact that she had not meant something was wrong indeed.

Perhaps she had taken a walk and twisted her ankle, he thought as he slammed out of the inn. He would canvass the town and see if he could find anyone who'd spotted a raven-haired governess wandering the streets.

At the stables he traded his horse for a fresh one and mounted again, taking off for the main street in town. The dark horizon was to his disadvantage, hindering his range of visibility. The only good news was that at this time of night the local tavern was stuffed to spilling.

He went inside, stopping at each table and asking if anyone had seen Emily earlier. He was about to give up when a man with a russet-colored beard damp with ale foam said he'd been on his way to the tavern when he'd spotted a woman matching Emily's description mount a horse behind another man. He described the man as being burly and ugly with dark hair.

"Did she appear to be in distress?" Zach asked.

The laborer shrugged and swallowed the last of his ale. Zach paid for another mug, and the man suddenly remembered that the woman had appeared unhappy and hesitant.

She hadn't gone willingly then.

Fear, true fear of the kind he hadn't felt since war, wrapped itself around his lungs and squeezed. If Emily's abductor harmed a single hair on her head, he would kill the bastard in cold blood.

Some of Zach's murderous intent must have shown in his eyes, because the man mumbled apologies for not knowing more.

"How long ago was this?"

"An hour or 'round about there," the man replied.

"In what direction did they leave?"

"Quarry Road, methinks. It's the only road northwest out of town."

Zach exited the tavern and remounted his horse. Emily's abductor had an hour lead and could have stopped or turned off at any point. Zach felt like howling with impotent rage. She was within his grasp, and yet every moment he wasted pursuing the wrong lead meant she slid farther and farther from his reach.

Think. Think. He was supposed to be a master of strategy, wasn't he? He'd been promoted to colonel at far too young an age, had coldly bet his life at the tables, and then made a fortune rolling the dice on a risky venture. He was letting his emotions stymie his process. The icy cool he'd become legendary for seemed to have disappeared when it came to Emily.

Start from the beginning, Zach told himself. Who had taken Emily? Had it been a criminal jumping at an opportunity when he saw her alone? Had the person known her? The man Red Beard had described was clearly not from the village, since no one in the tavern had recognized him. What was the abductor's intent? To sell her? Molest her? Ransom her?

A sliver of impossibility occurred to Zach. Had she been taken hostage by someone who knew she was having an affair with him?

No, that was absurd. No one knew of their relationship, and even if they did, they would not have known where Emily was unless they'd followed her from Eastmoreland House.

And yet chills crept up his spine and made the hair on the back of his neck stand straight.

Emily's abductor had left town with her, but he would not get far on the road at this hour with thieves afoot during the high travel season. He would not stop at another inn; Zach would bet his life Emily would scream the house down if he tried. If it were Zach, he would take her somewhere remote until dawn, where no one would happen across them and Emily couldn't escape or run.

If this *was* a blackmail scheme, the perpetrator would also need access to the post to mail his blackmail letter.

If it was not a blackmail scheme and the man was planning on selling Emily, he could already have a crime syndicate in mind and—no. Zach wouldn't go there. *Couldn't* go there.

He vowed right then he would do whatever was needed to find Emily, no matter the expense or how long it took.

For her sake, and his, he hoped he found her fast.

Keeping his criteria in mind, Zach set off on Quarry Road, praying harder than he had in a long, long time.

⊙⥁⊙

When they dismounted at the ruins, the sky was full black and glittering with an ocean of stars, as if a giant hand had flung gold paint droplets across the night canvas. The wind and open fields dissipated some of the day's sun, unlike the crowded stone structures of London that seemed to hold on to the heat with an iron grip.

Emily inhaled deeply, glorying in the scent of sun-sweet grass. Crickets chirped in an unbroken chorus of sound, and an owl hooted in a nearby tree. Emily wondered what night creatures were taking refuge in the cool shade of the Wilmcote ruins. She shuddered at the thought.

"Cold?" Lionel asked. As if he cared.

"No." She stroked the horse's flank. It was not the beast's fault he'd been loaned to a monster.

Lionel unbridled the gelding and let him roam. "Alone at last," he said.

Emily could not see his face well in the dark, but she could easily imagine how it looked. He would be bloated with his own sense of cleverness, and with that would come the twin follies of overconfidence and plain meanness. He'd always been the most violent after he'd pulled off a con or robbed someone wealthy.

The grass rustled beneath his boots, but before he reached her Emily said sharply, "In the very unlikely event Mr. Denholm shows up, if you so much as lay a finger on me now, I shall tell him you are my husband and he will never pay you. He is a snob and he likes his women untouched. He has told me so himself. It was why I pretended to be a virgin when I met him."

Lionel paused. She'd said the words with conviction, and it was so dim he could not read truth or lies in her face. It was a plausible story; there was no shortage of cads who enjoyed untouched women because they were clean and could not pass them the pox.

Laughing softly Lionel said, "Then I'll gag ye."

"You could, but I guarantee he will not pay you until he has spoken with me and heard that I have been treated well. No man wants to shell out large sums of money for damaged goods."

It sickened her to talk about herself as if she were simply a cow to be sold at auction, but she had to speak in terms Lionel would understand.

She knew she'd won when she heard his teeth grind together. It was a sign of his irritation, but his greed was stronger than his need to inflict pain.

He spat on the ground. "Fine. But if he doesn't show, I'm goin' to give ye a lengthy welcome-back present, *wife*."

From the saddlebags at his feet Lionel withdrew a lantern and lit it. Oblong windows of light sprayed in a circle across the grass as he hefted the saddlebags over his shoulder and grunted, "Follow me."

The ruins were in worse disrepair than Emily remembered. They were so crumbled and exposed to the elements that sleeping outside would have offered the same level of shelter.

Lionel found a corner of a stone room and tossed her a worn wool blanket. "Get comfortable. Yer goin' to be here awhile."

"I'm hungry."

"I don't got any food."

"Water, then."

He pulled out a canteen and drank long and hard before licking his lips and passing it to her. If she wasn't so thirsty, she would have thrown it in his face. Instead she pressed her lips to the rim and tried not to gag at the knowledge that her mouth was touching the same place his had.

She laid the blanket on the ground and sat, swatting off mosquitoes. "You know, Lionel, this does not sound like a well-thought-out plan. No food? How fast do you think the post will deliver your letter in the mail? We will be here for days. Really, you have planned better cons than this. I'm disappointed. I believe you have lost your touch."

"Don't ye worry. Lionel hasn't lost his touch. Now shut yer mouth, bitch, or I'll shut it for you."

Emily wrapped the blanket around her and curled into a ball, aware that Lionel's piggy eyes were on her as she pretended to fall asleep. After a long, long time, she finally did.

Chapter 47

Emily was woken by Lionel roughly dragging her off the ground and slamming her against the unsteady stone wall.

"What?" Emily managed to squeak before he stuffed a filthy handkerchief in her mouth. He tied another handkerchief around her head to keep it in place and withdrew a length of rope.

"Hope ye had a good sleep, angel," he said as he wound the rope around her hands. "'Cause I didn't, and that's got me in a bad temper."

Her hands tightly trussed, Lionel proceeded to thread another rope between her wrists and lash them to a sapling that had invaded the castle ruins. With an eight-inch trunk diameter, Emily would have to have superhuman strength to free herself.

"I'm headin' to town to mail a letter, and mebbe even fetch a few supplies. If yer quiet I'll feed you. Then again, mebbe I won't." His sick excitement about the absolute authority he held over her most basic needs turned her stomach.

When she was fully bound, he stroked his dirty paw over her head and let his eyes travel over her breasts.

Emily was afraid he would forget the reason he'd decided to leave her untouched, but he whistled for the horse and lifted the saddlebags off the ground as he exited the ruins.

Alone, Emily allowed the tears she'd been holding back to leak from her eyes. She was in a terrible predicament. As soon as Zach received Lionel's letter he would come, and she knew he would pay whatever outrageous sum Lionel demanded. She also knew the extortion wouldn't end with her release. Lionel would continue to find ways to dip into Zach's pockets. He would be a lifelong scourge. He might even be wise enough to grant her a divorce, only to threaten to expose her secret if she didn't pay him a monthly stipend. They would never be free of him. Emily didn't think she could bear a lifetime squirming under Lionel's thumb, and she knew she couldn't bear the thought of Zach doing the same.

She'd been a fool to get involved with Zach. She'd *known* she bore a secret that could destroy his reputation should her association with him be discovered, and yet she'd forged ahead anyway because she'd craved him, because she couldn't stop thinking about him, because she'd wanted to bask in the sunshine of his personality. She'd wanted a tiny slice of happiness, and now Zach was the one who would pay.

Selfish, that's what she was. She'd done what was best for her, not for Zach.

The tears came faster, blurring her vision and wetting the handkerchief binding her mouth. She was cramped from sleeping on the hard ground, half bitten to death by mosquitoes, thirsty, and hungry. On top of her worry and fear for Zach, she was feeling sorry for herself. She'd had a good thing going with the Eastmorelands and her side job with the Dove, but life had once again found it prudent to knock her down a few rungs. She wasn't meant to leave the slums.

Sniffling, she blinked rapidly to clear her eyes. Just because she'd failed in her venture as a governess it didn't mean she had to live a life of prostitution with Lionel. She would save Zach even though it would break her heart to leave him, and then she *would* find a way to escape Lionel. She would disappear entirely, maybe even leave the country. Emily Leverton would not be bested by the likes of Lionel the Pig.

She heard horse hooves approaching and cursed herself for crying. Lionel would be thrilled to see her display of weakness. He adored making her cry. For some reason it made him feel powerful, perhaps because he was too stupid to understand that real power was found in making a woman smile.

A moment later footsteps approached and a form appeared at one of the many crumbled entrances. It was a man, scanning the ruins with a sense of desperation and urgency.

Not just any man. *Her* man. Her glorious, tall, cobalt-eyed man, his face lined with fatigue and worry.

Emily screamed into the gag and Zach's head whipped around. As soon as he saw her he broke into a run. He fell onto his knees in the grass before her and pulled a knife from his pocket, sawing deftly through the handkerchief and tugging the balled fabric from her mouth.

Emily wanted to cry again. She wanted to curl into his arms, sob into his shoulder, and beg him to take her away. She wanted to lie in his bed and feel safe and secure and forget this entire nightmare had ever happened.

But she could not. This time, she would not be selfish.

Mustering every ounce of theatrical talent she owned, Emily licked her dry lips and said with disdain, "What are *you* doing here?"

Chapter 48

Thank God, thank God he'd found her! When Zach had spotted her tied to the tree, her cheeks streaked with tears, his knees had nearly gone weak with relief. He'd begun to lose hope that he could hunt her down. He'd spent the entire night searching every abandoned house, church, and ruin along the northwest road from Northampton. Upon finding each dwelling empty, despair had widened in his heart like a gaping abyss. He could not imagine his life without Emily. She'd only been with him a short amount of time and yet he already knew he would never meet another woman as unique and precious as she was. He promised himself that if he found her, and he *would* find her, she was never leaving his sight again. He didn't care about the divorce anymore. He didn't care if he had to wait six years to marry her. He didn't care if they *ever* married. All he cared about was being with the woman he loved.

She opened her mouth to speak, and rather than sobbing out a declaration of love she said icily, "What are *you* doing here?"

He lifted a brow. What did the minx think she was up to?

"I have come to rescue my lover," he said, leaning back on his heels and scanning her over. From what he could see there were no bruises, no split lips, no torn gown.

She sneered. "Typical. You always have to be the hero. I do not need rescuing, Zach. I *want* to be here. I have been lying to you. My husband is alive, and I have decided to return home with him."

Zach gave a low whistle. He didn't know if Emily had truly lied to him or if she herself had been horrified to discover her husband was alive, but he had no doubt she was telling the truth. How it was possible her husband lived when he was supposed to be dead on the Indian Ocean floor he did not know, but the man's reappearance explained why Emily had unhappily gone with him instead of putting up a fight.

"I have gone back to Lionel," Emily repeated, her throat raspy. "He is my husband. Maybe I have said a few rotten things about him, but it is time I return home. Especially after you and I had—" She swallowed hard. "—such disappointing sex."

"Is that so, love?" He began sawing at the rope that tied her to the tree.

"Yes, that is so. Now if you will please leave..."

"Noodles, I hate to point out the obvious and ruin whatever it is you are trying to do here, but you are tied to a tree. In an abandoned castle."

"Yes. Well, I—I like it."

The rope frayed and split. Zach was so happy to have found her she could have told him to bugger off and he would have gladly kissed her face. He started on the rope cutting into the delicate skin of her wrists and felt stirrings of the rage that had receded beneath the weight of his relief.

"You like it? You like being tied up outdoors?" he asked.

"That is right. It's my fetish. It gets me hot and bothered."

"And the crying?"

"It is part of the fun. We, er, playact. We call it villain and the vixen."

Zach couldn't help it; he burst out laughing. It was remarkable how only fifteen minutes ago he'd thought he'd never be able to crack a smile again, and here she was already making him laugh.

The rope binding her hands split and he quickly unwrapped her wrists. As soon as she was free she shook her hands to return circulation and lifted her chin.

"Now that you have ruined my fantasy, please leave. My husband will return any moment and I do not want him to find my boring old lover here."

Even though she was telling him to piss off, she allowed him to grasp her wrist and haul her to her feet. She must've been stiff because she stumbled and he caught her to his chest to steady her. For a moment, just the barest moment, he felt her melt into his arms and breathe in his scent. Then she shoved him away and said, "Get out of here."

"Excellent idea. Let's go."

"No, I am not leaving. What do you not understand? I had my fun, and now I am done with you. I am going home where I belong."

"With me," he said, suddenly tiring of her game. "You belong with me. We belong together. I love you, Emily."

"Do not be absurd."

"Then tell me. Look me in the eyes and tell me you do not have any feelings for me."

She met his gaze with the same boldness she had the first night he'd seen her in the ballroom. "I—Zach watch out!" she screamed.

He whirled around just in time to dodge the dagger Lionel had thrust at his kidneys. Lionel, his face puce with rage, jabbed the dagger at Zach again, then swiped the nasty blade upward, trying to gut him. Zach continued to evade the strikes, cursing himself for leaving his pistol in his saddlebag.

Lord, Emily's husband was an ugly thing when he was angry. Built like a stocky bull and as enraged as one, it terrified him to think of her bearing the brunt of this man's anger.

"Listen," Zach said calmly, taking another step back. "I don't want to fight you. I am taking Emily and we are leaving. If you put the blade down now, I will not press charges and see you hang for abduction."

The blade whistled through the air again. "Can't abduct yer own wife," Lionel spat. Then he grinned, the action made even more malicious by the absence of several teeth.

"Lionel, stop!" Emily screamed. "Don't forget about the money! You've lost sight of what's important. He'll give you the money, won't you, Zach?"

"Whatever you want," Zach said, holding out his hands in surrender and fighting the murderous impulse to beat Lionel into the dirt. He didn't want to put Emily through any more terror than he had to.

"You can't take her. She's my wife an' I ain't never goin' to let her free. But now that I'm thinkin' about it, if ye pay me, let's say a monthly fee, I might let ye dip yer stick in her from time to time."

I'm never going to let her free. The words rang like a gong in Zach's brain, and suddenly he saw his and Emily's future laid out clearly: He would live in constant fear that Lionel would abduct her again and he wouldn't be able to find her in time. If they had children, he would fear for them as well. He would become overbearing, watching her every move and terrified each time she left the house. He didn't care about the money, not that he liked the idea of funding scum like Lionel, but it was nothing compared with the emotional havoc Lionel's threats would wreak on Emily.

Ice began flowing in his veins, and the eerie calm that overcame him in battle settled on him like a mantle. "No," he said flatly, his voice ringing against the stones. "You will grant Emily a divorce and you will never see her again. Your compensation will be your life. You will walk out of these ruins today with your heart pumping strong. If you do not agree, this will be your final resting place."

Lionel's beard quivered and his eyes became piggy slits. "I'm the one with the blade, unless ye've forgotten? Guess the bitch ain't worth the money, eh? That's okay. She can spread her legs for me customers."

Lionel lunged with the blade again. This time Zach didn't avoid it. He stepped into the thrust, whipping to the side at the last moment and slamming his palm into Lionel's wrist. The other man's fingers opened reflexively and the blade fell to the grass. With lethal precision Zach struck Lionel in the solar plexus, rendering him breathless. An uppercut to his chin sent him flying to the ground, and then Zach was on him, striking him in the face until Lionel's eyes glazed. He wrapped his hands around Lionel's neck and squeezed.

A soft hand fell on his shoulder. "Zach, that's enough."

The freezing rage dissipated enough to recognize Emily's touch and her calm request. Reluctantly Zach released Lionel's neck and sat on his heels. He wiped the back of his hand across his brow and stared at Lionel, teetering on the edge of violence.

At last he stood and Emily came to him, burying her head in

his chest. He wrapped his arm around her shoulders and they turned away. He wouldn't kill Lionel, because she'd asked him not to, but that didn't mean one of his men couldn't. A rat like Lionel could not continue to exist in the same world as Emily.

They'd reached his horse before Zach knew his feet were touching the ground. He was still caught in the drumbeat of battle, still fighting the impulse to turn around and sever the thread of Lionel's life.

He was so focused on not killing Lionel that he barely heard the man stumble behind him. Zach swung around in time to see the bloody bastard holding a heavy stone over his head, ready to smash it down on Zach's skull.

Quick as a snake Emily darted forward, the morning light glinting off the dagger she must've lifted during the fight. The blade disappeared, plunged into Lionel's soft flesh.

Lionel gasped, his mouth opening and closing like a codfish. He stared disbelievingly at the handle sticking out from his stomach. Then he staggered, dropping the stone to the side.

"Ye…bitch," he wheezed.

Emily said nothing, but her chocolate eyes burned with a tangle of emotions as Lionel sank slowly to the ground, never to rise again.

Chapter 49

Emily was silent as Zach helped her onto the horse behind him. He didn't try to talk to her, and for that she was grateful. The twin flames of relief and fear she'd felt when Zach arrived had blown out, leaving her empty and curiously detached, as if she were watching the trees pass and the blackbirds swoop through the eyes of an emotionless observer.

She clung to Zach's waist as they entered the tiny town of Wilmcote. When they passed the church, a memory surfaced. She, a child of ten wearing ragged clothes and bare feet, running past a stream of parishioners spilling from the double doors.

"There goes the laundress's daughter."

"Sinner."

"I hear the girls aren't any better than they have to be."

"Wild little thing. She must take after her mother."

She had kept running, pretending the words she heard and the scorn she saw on their faces didn't pierce her soul.

She realized with a start that Zach was speaking to a local. His words sounded distant and foreign, as if she were hearing them through a wool blanket. He nodded, thanked the man, and several minutes later they arrived at a tiny brick house with neat gingerbread molding. Zach dismounted and entreated her to stay with the horse. It hadn't occurred to her to get off. He went inside, where he could have stayed for five minutes or an hour; time ceased to exist.

When he returned, they left Wilmcote behind and returned to the highway. A mail coach passed going in the opposite direction, as did a lacquered carriage sporting a large gold crest of intertwined letters.

You did it again, a little voice jeered through the fog in her brain. *You're a murderer.*

She wanted to scream at the voice that she hadn't killed anyone before! She'd been an accomplice but she hadn't known. She hadn't understood what was happening.

That doesn't give them back their lives. And this time you really did kill someone. It's in your blood. Murderer. Murderer. Murderer.

"Emily!"

She lifted her chin. "What?" The words came out sluggish, as if she were drunk.

But Zach had turned around again, and she didn't have the energy to ask what he'd wanted.

Some time later he guided the horse off the road and down a gently sloping embankment, through a thicket of bushes, and across marshy grassland until they reached a placid pond in the shape of a Christmas-bell tea cake. Cattails and reeds the shade of sun-struck hay framed the little pond. The water was so clear that Emily could see the fish swimming in its waters. A gray heron, standing on long slender legs, cocked its beak in their direction but didn't move. Flies and gnats buzzed lazily about, seeming unable to exert too much effort in the beating sun.

Zach dismounted and helped Emily down. She thought about asking why they were at the pond, but the words seemed stuck somewhere between her brain and mouth.

"Strip."

She stared stupidly at him. He unbuttoned his shirtsleeves and yanked them off, then pulled off his boots and dropped his trousers. He really was a beautifully built man, she thought absently: tapered waist, defined arms and chest, thighs muscled from horse riding.

"Your turn."

She still didn't move, so Zach unbuttoned her wrinkled gown and tugged it off her shoulders until it pooled at her ankles. He went to work on her corset, chemise, and stockings, until at last she, too, stood entirely in the nude. She felt vaguely as if she should be embarrassed, or at least worried that someone might come along and catch them standing naked in broad daylight, but the worry seemed so far off, so distant, that she couldn't be bothered.

"Can you swim?"

She nodded.

"Good. Get in the water." When she remained still, Zach took her hand as if she were a child and walked her toward the edge of the water. The sun stroked every inch of her sweaty skin, the air so still that just standing without movement made her perspire. Her toes touched the cool water. Zach walked her farther and farther in, until the liquid slid over her thighs and to her belly. She gasped at the sensation. It was so sensuous, the water lapping at her bare skin, and so delightfully cool.

"Take a breath."

She did automatically, and Zach dunked her head under the water.

Emily fought against him until he released her. She shot above the surface, pushing her dripping hair out of her face and sputtering. "What the HELL, Zachariah?"

"Sorry, Noodles. Swim with me."

What she wanted to do was slap him across the face, but he was already cutting a clean line across the pond with strong, powerful strokes, and so she swam after him.

They must have swum and splashed and played in the water for an hour until finally, for the first time in months, Emily felt cold.

Laughing, they climbed out of the water and stood in the hot sun, droplets sluicing down their bodies. Emily was smiling like a fool. She hadn't had that much fun since she was a child. The water seemed to have had a shocking effect, knocking her back into the proper dimension so that she no longer felt distant and detached.

Suddenly the memory of Lionel's eyes growing dim and lifeless crashed into her happiness. Even in death, he had the power to dissipate her joy. Her smile faded and Zach tugged her close.

"I killed him," she choked. She couldn't cry, didn't know if she would ever cry over the loss of Lionel, but in some deep part of her she felt as if she'd been rendered in two.

He simply held her, skin to skin, until she stopped shuddering and they were nearly dry from the sun. Then they dressed and mounted the horse.

Once they were back on the road Zach said, "Are you hungry?"

Her stomach instantly growled. "Yes, surprisingly. Zach?"

"Hmm?"

"How did you know the water would help?"

"You had a shock. I have seen it a hundred times on the battle-field. After enough years of it, you learn to recognize the symptoms, and if you are lucky, you can snap someone out of it. Water is one of the more pleasant ways."

She'd left her hair down to finish drying, and it had soaked a patch on the back of her dress. She twisted it now and pinned it up, then buried her face in the back of Zach's shirt. He smelled of clean soap rather than pond water, and she suspected it was how his shirts were laundered.

"What will happen to his body?"

"The house where we stopped belongs to the local constable. He is seeing to the removal of the body and he took my statement that I killed Lionel in self-defense. Lionel will be buried at the church in an unmarked grave."

Even though she'd despised the man, she hadn't wanted to think of his body being left to wildlife. It was strange how full circle her relationship with Lionel had come: They'd been married in that church against her will, and their marriage had ended with his burial in that same churchyard.

"How did you know I was in trouble? Or where to find me?"

In front of her, his shoulders lifted with the rhythm of their mount. "Gut instinct, I suppose. I left London not long after you, and when I reached the inn the maids told me you'd disembarked the coach but never made it inside." He went on to describe his nightlong search for her, and Emily recalled the words he'd spoken in the ruins. *You belong with me. We belong together. I love you, Emily.* The declaration was precious, something to be taken out of the dusty box of her memory in her old age to cherish and warm her heart. Yet as lovely as his words were, Emily had learned long ago not to put too much stock in what others said. Actions, she'd discovered, spoke far louder. And Zach's actions last night told her that when he said he loved her, he meant it.

This handsome, funny, intelligent man loved *her*, Emily. The *real* Emily.

Euphoria inflated her heart as she realized she was officially a widow. She was *free*. Free of Lionel. Free of her mother. Free of her sister. Free of her past—

The euphoria dissipated. No, she was not free. She still carried her deepest shame with her, and even though Lionel was dead, her mother knew the truth, along with whomever else Lionel had seen fit to tell. Zach would never be safe from her.

"Now it is your turn," Zach said. "How on earth was your husband alive?"

Emily relayed how Lionel had missed his ship, and when it had sunk, his "clever" plan to start over with a new alias. She told him how he'd discovered that she worked in London, and how he had ascertained their relationship by spying on her.

"What did he intend? Blackmail?"

"Yes," Emily said miserably. "And if that did not work, he threatened to sell me at his new whorehouse."

Zach's body tensed between her arms. "If that was his destination for you, why did you try so hard to convince me you wanted to be there with him?"

"Lionel was a leech. I could not bear the thought of him draining you until you dreaded hearing the sound of his voice or opening a letter to see the shape of his script. I had no intention of being his whore; I would have escaped somehow. But I also could not tolerate him hurting you."

It was the truth. Every word. Just not the whole truth.

His body did not relax. "Zach?"

"Emily, I am trying hard not to be furious with you. I am more than capable of taking care of myself *and* you. You should have trusted that a man like Lionel would not best me. I have dealt with far worse."

She supposed that was true. "I am accustomed to making difficult decisions on my own."

The tension finally left Zach's body. "You do not have to shoulder that burden alone anymore. I know you are independent and entirely capable of taking care of yourself. Hell, you are stronger than most people I know, but there is also strength in learning to let go and lean on others. I am here for you. We are a team."

Emily choked on an unidentifiable feeling. Relief? Love? Safety?

Zach's voice, strong and steady, continued, "Emily, I do not know what is going through your mind right now, although I can guess. I have killed before, and the first time was the worst. You had no choice. You saved my life."

"I don't regret it," she said instantly. She would *never* let him feel guilty thinking she had exchanged her innocence for his life. "That is not what is on my mind. In fact, I would like to never talk about Lionel or hear his name again. It is over."

"Yes, Noodles, it is over."

Chapter 50

By midafternoon they'd arrived at the Chester Inn, fifteen miles from Brixton Hall. The inn was located in the center of town and had a sign in the window that boasted CLEAN LINENS AND ALE.

Zach signed the registry as Mr. and Mrs. Denholm and Emily didn't protest. Whether or not they were married, the inn owner would expect a couple sharing a room to at least pretend they also shared a marriage certificate.

Three maids were dispatched to lug a copper tub to their room and fill it with warm water, a luxury that came at an exorbitant expense. While they did so, Zach and Emily ate a hearty meal of mutton pie, potatoes, and roasted carrots, and washed it down with the advertised ale.

Some hours later Emily was properly stuffed, clean, rose-scented from a warm bath, and dozing lazily on the bed with Zach. She wore nothing but a sheer chemise in deference to the heat, and Zach's scorching gaze had traveled across her breasts and hips more than once but he made no move to touch her in a more intimate way. Instead, he simply stroked her back, up and down her spine, until Emily felt as soothed and sated as a beloved pet.

She'd written to the Brixton Hall housekeeper and explained that she'd taken ill in Northampton and had to stay behind for a few days to recover. She did not feel bad about lying. Lionel *had* been a disease, and Emily supposed anyone was due a few days of healing after committing murder.

The excuse gave Emily one last night to love Zach with all her heart.

She sighed and rolled over to face him, her curls falling over her shoulder and concealing the dusky shadow of her nipple visible through the fabric. A muscle twitched in Zach's jaw, and a secret smile tugged at her lips. He was determined not to touch her after what she'd been through, but at that moment the comforting, solid feel of his body was exactly what she wanted—no, *needed*. She needed to give herself to him, to meld with him and move with him as one, to feel his love and tenderness and return it with her own actions.

Because tomorrow morning she would leave him.

Forever.

Emily pushed on Zach's chest, and he fell back on the mattress. It was sunken in the middle, and he suspected the clean linens were the only clean thing about it. The room was small and mostly bare, with a chipped pitcher and washbasin perched on a rickety stand in the corner. The walls had recently been whitewashed but the effort wasn't enough to erase the evidence of pipe smoke. The floors creaked and the room smelled of the mutton pie they'd had for dinner, but it wasn't the worst place Zach had ever slept, and he was confident Emily could say the same. It would serve its purpose until the purchase of his Cheshire estate was finalized in a few days.

Emily straddled him and Zach's hands settled on her hips, stilling her when she would have rocked against him. "Let's rest tonight," he said, but even he could hear the gravel in his voice. He wanted her badly; he wanted to sink into her again and again, to hold her close and reassure himself that she was safe.

She smiled, leaned forward, and kissed his chest. Her hair fell across his skin in a tangle of silk as her lips lavished a line of open-mouthed kisses down his belly.

"Emily," he pleaded, this time somewhat desperately.

She lifted her head, looking up at him with those dark, sensuous eyes. "Zach, I am eternally grateful that you rescued me, so please do not take it the wrong way when I tell you to shut your mouth."

With that she unbuttoned his trousers, grasped him in her palm, and took him between her wet, hot lips.

Her exploration was torturously sweet. She experimented using her tongue, her lips, and even little nips of her teeth until she finally found a rhythm that had him bucking against her.

"If you do not stop, I will finish now."

She released him, a feline smile of satisfaction on her face, and she straddled him once again, this time slowly seating him fully inside her. She gasped at the sensation, and twin spots of color appeared on her cheeks.

"Take your chemise off," he ordered.

She did, pulling the thin fabric over her head and tossing it to the side, baring creamy breasts spattered with freckles and nipples already pebbled with arousal. Zach propped himself against the headboard and cupped the back of her neck, pulling her lush mouth to his. He made love to her mouth as she slowly began rocking back and forth on him. He swallowed her surprised sounds of pleasure, releasing her lips long enough to ravish each one of her breasts in turn.

Emily's head dropped backward and her eyes closed as she moved faster. Zach clasped her hips and lifted his own, deepening the angle. She moaned, her nails digging into his shoulders. She picked up the pace, riding him relentlessly and wildly, as if abandoning all awareness of herself. Time stood still, and Zach lost himself in her, in the act of becoming one with the woman he loved.

Her skin slickened with perspiration and Zach wasn't sure how much longer he could hold off when she cried out and tightened around him. He barely had time to lift her off him before he found his own release.

Panting, she lay beside him, one arm draped over his chest. After a few moments Zach reluctantly shifted her and rose to wet a cloth from the washbasin. After he washed her he re-wetted it and cleaned himself.

He returned to the bed and pulled the covers over them. Emily immediately tucked her head into his shoulder, and Zach felt complete and utter contentedness. This was exactly where he belonged and with whom he belonged. Every single thing about this felt right.

Even better, Emily was now *truly* a widow. He would have preferred it come about in another way, but fate had dealt its cards and Zach would be a fool not to play the hand he'd been given. He wouldn't bring marriage up tonight, but soon it would become his sole mission in life to convince Emily Leverton to marry him.

Chapter 51

Mrs. Hill listened to her lady's maid gossip, annoyed by the unending chatter and yet willing to tolerate it because the servants often knew the goings-on of the *ton* before anyone else did.

"And then my friend Rebecca, she's the lady's maid at the Charlestons' if madam will remember, she says the lord has made *two* passes at the nanny."

It was an interesting tidbit, but nothing Mrs. Hill had use for.

"Rebecca was walking back from fetching the post and she said she saw that upstart Mr. Denholm outside the Chester Inn. Then when she stopped in the kitchens on the way home she was telling me about this letter that—"

"Wait a moment," Mrs. Hill snapped, holding up a hand encircled with rings no longer set with real stones. "Mr. Denholm was at the Chester Inn tonight? She was sure it was him?"

"Oh aye, she's seen his likeness in the papers. She said he's a right handsome devil. Got eyes as blue as the ocean."

He'd arrived earlier than anticipated. Mrs. Hill sat in thoughtful silence as Miranda chattered on, the maid's words flowing over her head in a ceaseless cadence. A plot began to take shape in her mind. She had intended to force Jane into Mr. Denholm's path as often as possible while simultaneously discrediting his *cousin*, Emily, but perhaps she had been handed a golden opportunity to claim Mr. Denholm's name—and his riches.

Smiling, she called for Jane. When the girl appeared, Mrs. Hill told her to dress in her new gown and instructed Miranda to force Jane's rather limp, curl-resistant hair into a suitable style.

"Are we going somewhere, Mother?"

"Why yes," Mrs. Hill said, struggling not to sigh. What a stupid question! "And if you do exactly as I say, by the end of tonight, Jane dear, you will be engaged to Mr. Denholm."

Jane's perpetually pinched brow eased, and her thin lips curled into a wicked smile. "It sounds devious, Mother! Tell me all about it."

"In good time, girl. Now hurry!"

Jane did not hurry, but the hour was still early enough that Mrs. Hill didn't fret. Her plan hinged on Mr. Denholm having retired for the night. It would do them no good if he were still dining.

At last Jane was ready, and the two set out at a brisk walk. The Chester Inn was a twenty-minute stroll from their run-down house, and it was important that Jane's arrival went unnoticed, so they eschewed the carriage and went on foot.

"I am hot," Jane complained, tugging at her tight lace sleeves. She'd turned out nicely in an evening gown that approached the line of scandalous without crossing it. The material was sapphire satin, the neckline so low Jane's breasts swelled like two yeast rolls over the top. Miranda had done her best with Jane's flat, dull-brown hair, and it looked almost fetching piled atop her head. Although Jane's eyes were too close together and a weak, watery blue, the intricate silver filigree chain about her neck set with six paste sapphires drew the eye to her most admirable asset: her bosom.

"Oh, do stop fussing," Mrs. Hill scolded. What would her daughters do without her? Olivia was too stupid to survive on her own, and Jane was too lazy.

"Will you tell me what I am all tarted up for now?" Jane snipped.

"Mr. Denholm is lodging at the Chester Inn. According to Miranda's source he arrived only this evening. I am sure he will be hot and dusty and more than ready for an ale and his bed. When we arrive, I shall have you stand outside the window to the tavern while I go in and demand to know what room Mr. Denholm is staying in. When the innkeeper answers, I shall repeat it loudly. Once you have heard it you will hurry to the servants' entrance and find your way to Mr. Denholm's room."

Jane's eyes shone with glee. "Let me fill in the rest. I am to knock on Mr. Denholm's door, and when he answers force my way in, preferably crying about something. In the meantime you will gather the innkeeper and anyone else respectable in the establishment, claiming that your daughter has been led astray by an unscrupulous cad."

"Clever child." Perhaps there was hope for Jane after all. Besides, she had best play nice with the girl from now on if she was to be their future meal ticket. "We will burst into the room to discover you crying in his unchaperoned arms. It will be a most compromising situation, and Mr. Denholm will be forced to propose marriage to save your reputation."

She glanced over to find Jane's lips parted over her teeth. "Mrs. Denholm," Jane said dreamily. "I do not much care for the lack of title, but I will love the piles of money."

Mrs. Hill allowed her daughter to fantasize for a moment before issuing a word of caution. "The plan must go exactly or else we will ruin any chance you have of convincing Mr. Denholm to marry you otherwise."

Jane lifted a hand in dismissal. "He was not going to look at me twice anyway and we both know it."

It was true, and it was why Mrs. Hill was willing to take such a risk to entrap the bachelor.

Several minutes later they arrived outside the Chester Inn. Golden squares of light fell from the windows, and the scents of mutton pie, tobacco, and ale rode on the gently stirring breeze. There was a raucous cheer from inside, and when they approached Mrs. Hill saw through the window a dozen or more soldiers drinking themselves stupid.

"Excellent," she whispered. She couldn't have planned it better herself. "I shall enlist the chivalrous aid of that lieutenant to help me find my daughter. Mr. Denholm was in the military, and the presence of another ranking officer will only encourage him to do the right thing."

Jane clapped a gloved hand over her breast. "My heart is beating so fast. I cannot believe this is about to happen. *Thank you*, Mother."

Mrs. Hill preened. Yes, it seemed that she was in Jane's good graces, and soon she would be dramatically weeping in the chapel watching her girl marry one of the wealthiest men in London. Her empty pockets tingled at the very thought.

❦

The first part of Mrs. Hill's plan went exactly as she pictured. She stormed into the inn hysterical and demanding, *insisting* that her daughter had arrived with Mr. Denholm, a man she was able to describe to a T. She made a large, glorious scene, securing the help of the lieutenant, several soldiers already deep in their cups, and the innkeeper.

Together they marched up the stairs, a party of the righteous, ready to make Mr. Denholm pay for taking advantage of an innocent girl.

Outside Mr. Denholm's door Mrs. Hill took a deep breath, preparing herself for what was about to happen. She had done all she could; Jane would have to do the rest.

Little did Mrs. Hill know that Jane had knocked several times at Mr. Denholm's door, and when there was no answer, she had hurried down the servants' steps to warn her mother that he was out of residence, completely missing Mrs. Hill and her small army as they ascended the guest staircase.

The innkeeper rapped sharply on the door, and when there was no answer he inserted his key into the lock and turned it. Mrs. Hill, her heart pounding with anticipation and a look of shock already plastered onto her face, twisted the handle and burst into the room. Behind her, the lieutenant, his soldiers, and the innkeeper piled in.

Mrs. Hill's expression of surprise morphed into one of utter horror. Mr. Denholm was indeed in the room, but he was not holding her daughter. Instead he was in bed, bare from the chest up, his arm wrapped around a dark-haired woman who was clearly in the nude despite the sheet covering her to her chin. Mrs. Hill recognized the woman immediately as Mr. Denholm's "cousin," Emily.

"What is the meaning of this?" the lieutenant roared.

Mr. Denholm's expression was ice-cold and calm. "I will ask you the same thing. How dare you burst into my room?"

"Is this not your daughter?" the innkeeper asked Mrs. Hill.

"No," she said faintly.

"Well, whoever she is," the innkeeper said to Mr. Denholm, "I expect you will do right by the girl. This is a decent establishment."

Mrs. Hill's dreams crashed and flamed out like a carriage wreck. Instead of forcing Mr. Denholm to marry her daughter, she'd made public his compromising situation with the one woman she'd hoped never to see again.

Mr. Denholm smiled, and it was genuine in its joy. "Of course," he said. "Miss Leverton and I will be married within the week."

Chapter 52

A s soon as the party of onlookers left, Emily ducked her head under the covers and groaned.

"Mrs. Hill," Zach snarled. The moment she'd barged into his room Zach had understood her plan. The knocks that he and Emily had ignored earlier, whispering and laughing quietly as they cuddled under the covers, were no doubt from one of Mrs. Hill's daughters come to entrap Zach in marriage.

The woman's incessant scheming burned him. If she hadn't just been served the perfect dose of revenge, he would have sought out her brother and made it clear that should Mrs. Hill continue to pursue him, he would see to it Lord Moore's more lucrative social connections took a turn. There were powerful men who owed Zach favors.

That wouldn't be necessary. The look on Mrs. Hill's face when she discovered she'd inadvertently forced marriage between Zach and Emily was truly priceless, and if she weren't such a horrid woman, he'd almost be grateful for what she'd done.

"Why did she think you were here with her daughter?" Emily

asked from under the sheet, and if Zach didn't know better, he would have thought he detected a hint of jealousy in her voice.

Zach joined her beneath the covers and planted a kiss on her lips. "She has been scheming to have me marry one of her daughters."

"She is a rotten woman."

Zach touched the tip of his finger to her nose. "I *am* considered a catch, you know."

Emily sniffed. "I cannot imagine why."

He clutched his heart. "You wound me."

But Emily didn't seem to be in the same lighthearted mood as he. She was probably embarrassed by what had just transpired, but it could have been far worse: Mrs. Hill could have succeeded in her scheming.

"Do not worry," Zach said, lifting the sheet off their heads. Cooler air brushed across his cheeks. "I will procure a special marriage license from the archbishop."

"Do not be ridiculous." Emily slipped from the bed and searched for her chemise. "There is no need to marry simply because Mrs. Hill caught us indecent. I am a widow; I have done nothing wrong."

Zach frowned. How could she not see how necessary the wedding was? "Noodles, widowed women do have discreet affairs, but as far as anyone knows, including your employers, you are a young, unattached woman. You have been thoroughly, entirely compromised. Unless you marry me your reputation will be ruined, and so will any chance of respectable employment."

Emily tied the ribbon at the front of her chemise, refusing to meet his eyes. "I am not high society, Zach. No one gives two shakes about my reputation."

"Your employers will care."

"How will they hear of it?"

Exasperated, Zach said, "Darling, every house within a fifty-mile radius will have heard of this by morning. Servants talk. Soldiers talk. The innkeeper will tell this story far and wide."

Emily turned to face the window where stars slowly emerged on the ombre horizon and crossed her arms under her breasts.

"Emily, do you not *want* to marry me?" Zach pulled his trousers on and came to stand behind her, but she was straight-backed, her body language practically screaming for him to back off. "If I don't misremember, you said you would marry me if you could. Well, you can now. Not only that, you *should*."

At the ruins she had explained her protests about not wanting to be with him as an attempt to keep him safe from Lionel. Now, as she faced rigidly away, he wondered if there was more to the story. Her actions said she loved him and wanted to be with him. She made love with him, laughed with him, killed for him. Yet whenever the topic of marriage arose, unless it was hypothetical, she froze. Before, he'd assumed the reason was because she was still legally married, but she was truly widowed now and the freeze still hadn't thawed.

Zach yanked his shirt over his head, suddenly feeling angry and rejected. If she didn't love him, he wished she'd quit playing games. Either way, it was too late. If Emily was to keep any semblance of her reputation, they would have to marry.

He only wished his future wife was as happy about it as he had been.

Zach sat on the bed and it creaked under his weight as he tugged on his boots. Emily faced him and watched his actions dispassionately. "Leaving?"

"Yes."

"Where are you going? It is night."

"Questioning me is a privilege reserved for my wife." He looped his cravat around his neck and clenched his jaw. He was being an ass, so he added, "I am riding out to see the archbishop."

"For the marriage license." Her tone was dull.

Zach shoved his arms through his jacket. "Right. I will be back tomorrow."

With Zach gone the room took on a stillness that discomfited her. She paced for several hours, running through every possible scenario to escape the marriage. Ultimately, unless she wanted to leave England, Zach was right: They had to marry.

Emily sat down and considered how she might survive abroad. She did not speak French, and without the Dove's assistance, she did not think she would be able to find a governess placement outside of England. She didn't have enough money to travel farther than the immediate Continent.

No matter how she examined the issue there was only one feasible solution: to marry Zach and pray he never discovered what she'd done or who she really was.

A large part of her thrilled at the idea of marrying the man she loved, but she tamped it down. She didn't deserve to be excited, not when she was putting him in such an untenable position.

It was very late when Emily finally went to bed. She tossed and turned, her thoughts bouncing between Zach and the leering face of Lionel. At last she fell into an exhausted, dream-haunted sleep.

The next morning Emily washed, dressed, and ordered a tray of sweet rolls and tea. While she munched on the cakes she sat down to pen a letter to the Eastmorelands to resign her post. If Zach was right, then they were already aware of the scandalous position she was in and would have terminated her anyway.

After she sent the letter with the morning post she went for a walk to explore the town, but she felt as if every person who passed her had heard about last night. Was she imagining the frowns on the decorated ladies who drove by in fancy carriages? Were the maids' titters about her?

Meanwhile she thought and worried and ruminated. Would Zach manage to secure the license? They were generally reserved for peers, and there was no way she would survive the public humiliation of having the banns read for three weeks if he could not. What would she wear to her wedding? Who would they choose as a witness? Where would they live?

After a cold-plated luncheon, the countess's response arrived. To Emily's surprise the countess requested she return for a few days to settle the children while she contacted Perdita's to find a replacement. She must not have heard of Emily's predicament after all. Emily felt returning was the least she could do since she was leaving with such short notice. She wrote back that she would arrive the day after morrow.

There was one more person she had to write to, and Emily couldn't fathom why she was so reluctant to send off this letter. At last she sat down and forced herself to pen her resignation to the Dove. She explained that she was getting married, but that she was returning to Brixton Hall for a few more days before leaving her post permanently. She thanked the Dove for the opportunity and then signed and sealed the envelope.

Emily caught the post headed for London just in time, and it was only after she reached the inn that she remembered she had forgotten to mention Frankie Turner's mathematical theory. She would tell Zach when he returned.

But when she walked in and found Zach waiting for her in their room, his eyes heavy and speculative as he looked her over, her intentions vanished. He was windblown from having ridden most of the night and day, and he smelled of horses and fresh summer air.

He looked delectable. Emily wanted to run into his arms and kiss him all over. Instead she planted her heels and clasped her hands in front of her. "You're back."

"Yes." He didn't offer any other information.

"Did he grant you the special license?"

"Yes. We will marry tomorrow at the chapel. I spoke with the priest an hour ago. He will provide witnesses."

Dread and elation tangled in an uncomfortable sensation in her breast. This was her moment to go to him, to break the ice that had formed like a thick sheet between them, but her throat was dry and she couldn't seem to make her feet peel off the ground.

Zach studied her for a moment and then turned his back. With that, the moment was gone.

Chapter 53

The next morning Zach wrote to London. Although Emily was a reluctant bride, he would have her wear his ring. A jeweler was to send a dozen rings, and Emily could choose the one she liked best.

While he penned the letter, all he could think of was how he hated that she was being forced into marriage again. She'd been sold into matrimony before by her mother, and now for the sake of her reputation, she was once again being coerced into taking vows. He was heartsick with the knowledge that she did not want to be his wife, but every part of him chafed at the idea of his courageous and spirited Emily being bridled by marriage when she so clearly wished to remain free.

He and Emily bathed separately and re-dressed in the clothes they'd worn the day before. They had been pressed and brushed, but were far from formal clothes: he in the clothes he'd ridden halfway across England in, she in her navy-blue governess gown. It was not going to be a fancy ceremony, and for that Zach felt a pang of regret. Emily deserved a ceremony with flowers and a gown decorated with gold thread. She deserved to have her hair arranged by a lady's maid, to have jewels at her throat. For his part, he wanted his friend Wright present. He wanted to give her all of those things, not a slapdash wedding because they'd been caught in bed together. But Mrs. Hill had taken that choice from them.

When she was ready, even though she wore her governess gown and a frown, she was still the most enchanting woman in England. Zach's heart squeezed as he took her arm outside the inn. It was a short walk to the church and early enough in the morning that the sun had not yet begun its persistent crush of heat. The sky was clear with not a cloud in sight, and birds trilled from the copse of trees behind the inn. The weather was a good omen, Zach thought, even if their stilted silence was not.

They'd taken only a dozen steps when a carriage driving up a cloud of dust and going much too fast came to a sudden halt before them, the horses breathing heavily and their coats glistening with sweat.

The driver hopped down and opened the carriage door. Out swept Mrs. Hill, her lips pursed in smug righteousness, her eyes black with glee.

Zach went cold with anger. He stepped forward to lambaste the woman and he didn't care who witnessed it, when he realized she was not alone. Two other women had followed her out of the carriage and were flanking her on either side. There was something oddly familiar about them. One of the women was quite a bit older, with gray-streaked black hair, wrinkles that spread from the corners of her eyes and mouth, and a clean yet poorly made gown of brown satin. Her sun-spotted bosom was on display, and she wore more makeup than good taste dictated. Her dark eyes were devoid of emotion except for a smattering of malice and greed.

The other woman was a slighter replica of what was clearly her mother, except her hair was the color of damp hay, her eyes light brown. She would have been beautiful if it were not for the obvious wear on her, as if life had trodden on her time and again. The girl glanced at Mrs. Hill, and Zach could almost read the desperation in her eyes.

He turned to Emily to see how she was taking in this odd ensemble and found her staring stricken at the two women. Her cheeks were white and her lips pale and stiff, as if she were staring at two spirits instead of flesh-and-blood women.

Then Zach saw it. His gaze bounced from Emily to the older woman and the girl, then back again.

Holy God. Now he knew why they looked so familiar.

"Mrs. Leverton and Miss Leverton, I presume," Zach said to Emily's mother and sister.

Her mother's lip curled. "Is that the name she uses? Too good for the Lewis name, eh girl?"

Emily said nothing.

Lewis, Zach thought. He'd once told Emily he didn't need to know her true identity, but he had a feeling that if he'd pressed, whatever was about to happen could have been avoided.

"Come to witness our nuptials?" Zach asked coolly, his gaze directed on Mrs. Hill, who couldn't hide her delight over the awkward scene she'd orchestrated.

"Mr. Denholm, I trust that once these two women speak their piece, you will be most eternally grateful for my intrusion," Mrs. Hill announced with a grand sweep of her arm.

"No," Zach said, "I can promise you I will not." He took Emily's elbow and started to guide her past the women. "I have no interest in what you have to say. Do not contact me or my wife again or I will have you all arrested for harassment."

Mrs. Hill gasped, but Emily's mother seemed unfazed, as if she'd been threatened by the law more than once in her life. Mrs. Lewis glanced quickly at Mrs. Hill, saw her payment slipping away, and shouted after Zach, "I would want to know if I was marryin' a murderer."

Emily stiffened.

"Lionel was killed in self-defense," Zach said.

Emily's sister made a noise that was a cross between a mourning lament and a stuck rat. "He died in a shipwreck," she wailed. "Ye never loved him, ye nasty whore. Ye didn't deserve him!" She pounced after them and grabbed Emily's hair, ripping her head back.

Emily swung around and shoved her sister. Her sister went reeling and fell to the ground, sobbing hysterically. "I loved him! I loved him!"

Zach witnessed the spectacle with disgust. A small crowd had begun to form, and he snarled at the onlookers to get on with their errands.

Mrs. Hill turned up her nose. "This is what happens when you consort with common filth."

The interested passersby scattered, or at least had the good sense to look occupied elsewhere, and Emily's mother assessed the situation with morbid interest. "Lionel's death is not what I was talkin' about," she said.

A chill crept down Zach's spine, and a metallic taste filled his mouth. He knew that taste—it was how foreboding felt.

"Don't ye know?" Mrs. Lewis displayed a mouth of rotten

and missing teeth. "*Emily* is responsible for the deaths of eight women."

Zach scoffed, but Emily was staring at her mother with an unmoving face. Why wasn't she denying the outlandish claim?

Mrs. Lewis strolled closer, swinging her hips as only a trained prostitute could. "That there is Esther Lewis, not Emily Leverton. What other lies have ye told, Esther dear? Does yer betrothed know yer a bastard?"

"No."

"Does he know yer the product of an affair with a marquess?" She circled Emily, her gaze raking over her daughter, who stood as if being whipped. "Have ye told him yer adoptive father went to jail for connin' and thievin'?" Mrs. Lewis grinned. "That was my husband of course," she said to Zach. "I married him after I had Esther. Marla is the product of that union. Esther later claimed him as her father, and I would, too, if I were hidin' the past she is."

"Stop," Emily said quietly. "I will tell him on my own."

Mrs. Lewis peeled back her lips. "But my pockets get filled if *I* tell him." She turned to Zach, who stood mesmerized by the scandal unfolding before him. "Ye see, when we moved to the city my darlin' little Esther worked in Mayfair sellin' flowers. No one pays attention to an urchin girl sellin' blossoms, and the *ton* would talk around her as if she didn't exist at all. At the end of the day Esther would run to her real father's house, tap on his door, and tell him all she'd heard. She weren't allowed inside of course, bein' a filthy bastard and all, but she wanted to please I suppose. And what did Daddy dearest do with that information, Esther?"

Emily's lips parted slightly but no words escaped. Her eyes

were dark and fathomless pits as she relived some sort of nightmare from her past.

"Why, Esther, don't be shy now." Mrs. Lewis cackled. "Ever hear of the Silk Stalker, Detective?"

Zach flinched involuntarily. No...surely what Emily's mother implied was ludicrous.

"I see ye have." She tapped Emily on the shoulder. "The Silk Stalker is Emily's real father, and she helped him choose all his victims."

Emily's lips parted on a breathless exhale. "I did not know."

"Does it matter? Ye fed him that information. Ye fairly selected the young women he would strangle. Yer selfish, Esther. The missus has told us all about the detective. He's supposed to be findin' that Evangelist. How could ye marry him knowin' what you are? How would it look if he were to marry the *blood relation* of the Silk Stalker? Folks would question if he was even sane. Why, it would ruin his career."

Zach swallowed something thick in his throat, praying Emily would deny the accusations even as he knew her mother told the truth.

Holy God, Emily was the daughter of one of London's most notorious killers. She'd been actively involved in her father's crimes. Zach had been fine with the thieving, the lying, the knife-wielding, and the cons, but this was an entirely different matter. As much as he despised Emily's mother, the woman was right: He'd been tasked with hunting down a murderer, and the implications of Emily's past could have dire consequences not only for his investigation, but for the integrity of the entire case. He wanted to forgive her for keeping this part of her past a secret.

He wanted to feel the same assurance about marrying her that he did even five minutes ago.

But he wasn't sure he could.

Emily turned snapping eyes on Mrs. Hill. "Why have you done this?"

The other woman seemed taken aback by the venom in Emily's voice. "How dare you speak to me in such a manner? You are nothing but a dirt-poor, murderous bastard." Mrs. Hill lifted her chin with the full force of her class behind her. "I have done my duty and saved a valued member of our society from your scheming and lies. You ought to be thrown into prison for what you have done."

"Get out of my sight," Zach said quietly. He felt fully frozen, inside and out, the way he did after a violent battle.

The women stilled, no one sure who he was talking to.

He met the gazes of Mrs. Hill, Mrs. Lewis, and Miss Marla. "You three, get out of my sight. Do not *ever* let me lay eyes on a single one of you again, or I swear to all that is holy and mighty I will not stop until I have destroyed everything you hold dear."

The Lewises were streetwise enough to hurry back to the carriage, but Mrs. Hill was not used to being spoken to in such a manner. "Surely you jest, Mr. Denholm. I have come here out of the goodness of my heart—"

"You have come here out of spite. You are a twisted, sick woman and I pity the world for having you in it. Tell me how you tracked down Emily's family."

She pursed her lips in defiance, fine lines radiating from them like the creases in a drawn pouch.

"No? Then I shall see to it Lord Moore takes poor investment advice. You will be living in squalor within the month."

Fear erased the defiance in her eyes. "Last night you called her Miss Leverton. My maid knew an Emily Leverton worked for the Eastmorelands as a governess. After that it wasn't difficult to have Craven trace her back to her roots. I–I don't know his full name."

"I know who he is," Zach snarled, and the primal part of him was satisfied when she flinched. "Leave."

Mrs. Hill seemed to receive the message this time, because she spun on her heel and returned to the carriage with an undignified trot. A moment later the horses took off, leaving him and Emily as they'd been found, even if the course of their lives had been irrevocably altered.

"Zach—"

He held up a hand. Just the sound of her voice felt like betrayal scraping across his nerves. "I need to think about all this, Emily."

The vulnerability in her eyes quickly disappeared. As a street thief, she would have learned to conceal her deepest emotions at the drop of a hat. She didn't run to him, cling to him, or beg him to hear her out. He almost wished she would force him to listen to her now, before the ice completely encased his heart.

Instead she said with a far-too-steady voice, "I am going to Brixton Hall for a few days. It has already been arranged with the countess. If you wish to speak with me, you know where to find me."

When she started to turn away, he said, "Do not think I will not come for you, Emily." He heard the harshness of his tone, and yet he could not seem to thaw the barren wasteland that had become his soul. "I need time, but rest assured I *will* marry you. I compromised you, and I will not turn my back on my duty."

She sucked in a breath. "You will still marry me, even though my past might destroy your career and derail the case?"

He gave a sharp nod. "I gave you my word, and your reputation is equally at stake."

"I see." She took a step back. "You are an honorable man, Mr. Denholm."

Something seized Zach's throat at the flat look in her eye, something that felt suspiciously like panic. Yet when she turned her back to him, her shoulders squared, he didn't go after her.

Chapter 54

When Emily arrived at Brixton Hall, she was shown her room by the head housekeeper, who, seeming to have no knowledge of what had transpired that morning, appeared unfazed that she had arrived a day early.

Like a straw-stuffed version of herself, Emily carried on with the motions of small pleasantries until she was safely locked in her room. She was not expected to start the children's lessons until the next day, which left her most of the afternoon and evening to think.

It was an unwelcome prospect.

Emily set her hat on the small, unvarnished table and unpacked her bag, which had remained in the Eastmoreland coach after her abduction and was waiting for her in the room. She took off her dress, hanged it carefully on a peg, and began to brush her hair.

The room was sweltering hot even with the window open, and yet Emily didn't mind the heat. In fact she felt cold, her skin clammy to the touch.

It's over, the voice in her mind whispered.

"I am aware of that," she said aloud. Zach had looked at her that morning as he never had before, and it had felt as if she were a child all over again when the neighbors had stared at her as if she were scum. No matter what she had revealed about her past, Zach had never seemed to find fault with her. He had loved her unconditionally.

Until conditions had arisen.

Who could blame him for being less than thrilled about tying himself to the Silk Stalker's own daughter? Deep down Emily had known it would change how he saw her, that it was one of the few things that would turn him away. Wasn't that why she'd never told him the truth? There were plenty of times when she could have sat him down and told him the story from her perspective, but fear had held her back. Fear that she would see in his eyes exactly what she had seen today. Fear that he wouldn't believe she'd been unaware of what her father was doing. Fear of rejection.

So instead she'd held tight to her secret, preferring to leave him than face his disgust. That was until Mrs. Hill had intervened.

Unwittingly Mrs. Hill had righted her wrong. The woman had nearly forced Zach and Emily into marriage, and in the nick of time had saved him from it, because although Zach would not abandon Emily, *she* would not marry *him* now. He was willing to honor his promise even though it would ravage his reputation and career, but Emily could not allow him to do that now that her shameful secret had been brought into the light. She would not be the duty that hung about his neck, his personal albatross and constant reminder of what had been stolen from him. She was worse than tainted goods. She was, as Mrs. Hill had so aptly described her, nothing but a dirt-poor, murderous bastard. And since she'd killed her husband, the words were more accurate than ever.

Everything that she had feared might happen if her secret were exposed, had. The only blessing was that it was not too late to save Zach.

Emily would stay the three days she had promised the countess and then she would leave to find work. Perhaps one of the factories would take her. She could not show her face as a respectable governess anywhere on the Continent now that she'd been compromised and had her past dragged into the present for every passerby on the street to hear. She was sure Mrs. Hill would make certain the story spread far and wide.

Emily sat on the bed and tried to cry. She thought she might feel less cold, less like her lungs had been crushed if she could only sob for a few hours, but nothing came out.

After half an hour she stood, dressed in a fresh gown, and headed for the kitchens for a cup of tea. She was passing the library when she nearly mowed down the dowager countess exiting with a book.

Emily squeaked in surprise, narrowly avoiding the collision, and then curtsied. "I beg your pardon," she said breathlessly.

The dowager was a tiny woman with thin fingers and knuckles that bulged with arthritis. She resembled her son not in the slightest. Where Lord Eastmoreland looked like a frog wearing a cravat as a noose, the dowager was ethereal and fairy-like. Her russet hair was streaked with silver, her eyes a shimmery gray. Emily thought she must have been quite beautiful when she was young.

"Child," the dowager said, reaching forward and grasping Emily's arm. "I am so sorry."

Emily's mouth parted with uncertainty. Was the dowager confusing her with someone else? Would it be impolite to ask her what she meant? Emily didn't have long to wonder before the dowager spoke again.

"I have heard the gossip. This is a terrible world for women, is it not? You were caught in a compromising position with a man and then he abandoned you. What repercussions will he face? None. It is our sex that must carry the burden."

Emily was sure she could taste her heart in her mouth. How foolish she had been to think the news had not reached Brixton Hall! The head housekeeper had not known of it because she was so stiffly respectable that no one had dared gossip to her. The dowager, on the other hand, was a known sympathizer with prostitutes. Her maid would have been eager to share the news with her.

Emily could not allow Zach's reputation to be impugned. He had not abandoned her; it was she who would leave him. She had to make sure, for his own sake, that when the time came for her to disappear, everyone knew she'd called off the engagement rather than he.

"Something about my past came to light," Emily said stiltedly. "Mr. Denholm needs space to come to terms with it, but he is still willing to marry me. I must make that point clear, especially for when... especially for when the wedding does not happen."

The dowager nodded, her misty gray eyes sympathetic. "And when the news breaks that *you* ended the engagement, his reputation will remain intact while yours will be shredded."

Emily nodded and swallowed hard. "I have not always done the right thing. This time I will."

"I am sorry you find yourself in such a way. You may or may not know that I am the benefactor of a halfway house for prostitutes. We provide women with an education and then we find them positions with decent salaries."

At Emily's look of surprise she chuckled softly. "When I was a young woman, my husband, the late earl, and I promised we would do what good we could with our unearned wealth. Unfortunately Robert did not inherit our noble intentions. If the rumors are true, he takes advantage of the very same class of women my husband and I strove to help."

Unsure what was appropriate to say and what was not, Emily stuck to the truth. "That is very progressive of you, my lady."

The dowager countess waved her arthritic hand, releasing Emily with the motion. "Women have been cast an unfair lot in life. I am simply trying to even the score. Now you listen closely, Miss Leverton. If you should need anything at all, do not hesitate to ask me for help. No doubt Lady Eastmoreland will hear the gossip soon and she will have you out on your ear. You will need someplace to go and some type of occupation to support yourself. I may be able to help you."

For one of the few times in her life Emily felt the tenderness of maternal concern, and it touched her in a way she found hard to describe. If she ever had a child, she would want him or her to feel this way every single day. "Perhaps," she said hesitantly, "you would write me a letter of recommendation?"

The dowager smiled beatifically. "Consider it done. I shall have the letter delivered to your room before the night is out."

"Thank you, my lady. You are very kind." Emily curtsied again, and the dowager continued down the hallway, her footsteps as light as a true fairy's. When she was gone, Emily returned to her room. There was no way she was showing her face in the kitchen now, even if it meant going hungry.

Chapter 55

The next morning the children were delighted to see her and saddened when she told them she would be leaving.

"Will you not miss us?" Charlie asked, his four-year-old face drooping into a pout.

Emily tapped his chin and said, "Well, of course I will. You have been my favorite family. However, my mother is ill and I must take care of her. Otherwise I would never step foot away from you!"

Minnie met her eyes over Charlie's head, and they were sympathetic and worried. So she had heard the gossip. Surely the countess would be next.

Emily worked the children through their lessons, making sure to leave each child with a kind memory of her, praising them and telling them lovely things about themselves until all six of the children, and she herself, were nearly in tears.

Minnie snuck a tray of tea and biscuits to Emily after lessons were over, saying in a confidential whisper, "I imagine the kitchen is a viper's nest right now."

Emily hugged her hard. "Thank you, Lady Minnie. How is Miss Winegartener?"

Minnie smiled and brushed back a strand of fine blond hair. "She has been scared straight. She has not wanted to go slumming since that night."

"Good. You are smart, my lady, but more important you are kind. I wish you the best."

Minnie's allergy-red eyes watered, and she and Emily embraced again before Emily headed upstairs to her room. She wasn't certain the countess would dismiss her that afternoon, but she thought it was likely based on the speed with which the gossip had spread.

So she was not surprised when later that night, after Lord Eastmoreland had left to visit their neighbor's estate for a nightcap, Lady Eastmoreland requested she join her in the library.

Emily's bag was packed and ready at her bedroom door. She surveyed the room to ensure she hadn't forgotten anything, lifted her chin, and made her way to the library.

When she arrived, a fire was crackling and popping in the Caen stone fireplace, warming the cavernous space when even the oppressive sun could not. Candles were lit in the candelabras and cast the room in a warm, golden glow. It was a remarkable library with rows and rows of books so high that one needed a ladder to reach them. The impeccably kept furniture included a brocade sofa and three massive leather-and-mahogany chairs that must have weighed a hundred pounds each, positioned in a semicircle near the windows. Velvet drapes were drawn over the same high-arching windows, and family members memorialized in oil paints and gold frames stared down at the library's visitors. The smells of expensive liquor, burning wax, and old books filled the space. Emily would have felt entirely at home had Lady

Eastmoreland not been standing with her back to the fire, the flames silhouetting her body and her expression etched in stone.

Emily was about to step forward when the countess's voice rang across the room in a clear command. "Lock the door."

Emily grimaced but did as instructed. Once the key turned, she walked to the countess and curtsied. "You requested my presence, my lady?"

The countess, always an imposing sight, appeared even colder and more formidable than usual. Her pale hair was affixed tightly to her scalp, and she was turned out in a dark-green gown with a matching emerald earring-and-necklace set. Her silver eyes, unlike those of the dowager, were flat and predatory.

"Miss Leverton, I have heard some very unpleasant rumors about you today." Lady Eastmoreland's voice, normally chiseled from a block of ice, sounded... *excited*. Emily thought perhaps she enjoyed verbally lashing her employees.

Emily remained silent, and the countess arched a pale brow. "You have nothing to say for yourself?"

Emily thought of what the dowager had said about women bearing the burden of scandal. She doubted anyone was demanding Zach explain his actions. The double standard was maddening.

Refusing to grovel, Emily said, "I apologize if my actions have impugned the character of this family. I shall leave the grounds immediately."

The countess studied her for so long that an unexpected chill ran down Emily's spine. Why wouldn't she just scream at her and be done with it?

"This is not the first time you have acted like a whore, Emily."

Emily jerked as if having been slapped. A warning bell jangled softly in the back of her mind. Not only had the countess called her a whore, she had used her given name. "I beg your pardon?"

The countess's cream-white teeth appeared. "I spotted you walking home a few mornings ago, disheveled and in the same gown you had worn the day before. I knew you had been giving yourself to a man."

Emily remembered the fluttering curtain in the second-story window the morning she'd walked home after spending the night with Zach. She'd thought it had been due to a breeze.

"You are a whore, Emily. You are no better than the women who sell themselves on the street. You lead men astray by spreading your legs and acting as if you are in a position of authority over them, when real power lies in the hands of a wife—not a mistress."

Although listening to the countess castigate her was great fun, Emily had had enough. The warning bell had grown louder, and her street instincts were telling her to get the hell out of there. There had been a subtle shift in the countess as she spoke, a burgeoning energy. Her cheeks had flushed and her eyes had grown bright with fever.

Emily curtsied again, never taking her eyes off the countess, and backed toward the door. "I will be gone within minutes," she assured her.

"No, Emily. You are not leaving."

Emily froze when the countess lifted a wicked, seven-inch knife from atop the writing desk and tilted it this way and that, watching the flames of the fire reflect off the blade.

In an instant the puzzle pieces Zach had talked about flew together to form a terrifying picture. The prostitutes' warnings of the predator in green; the countess's rage when the dowager invited a woman of ill repute to the house; the framing of Lord Eastmoreland—who routinely visited prostitutes; the countess's plain-dressed presence the night Minnie had gone slumming, and the stymied attack on the prostitutes in Bethnal Green that very same evening. Information that had seemed to swirl in a disordered kaleidoscope suddenly fit into a horrifying visual.

The governess, Frankie Turner, had been right. Only *Lord* Eastmoreland wasn't the killer.

"My God," Emily whispered. "You're the Evangelist."

Chapter 56

The day Emily left, Zach took up position in an armchair and drank brandy straight from the bottle. When he was properly soused, he opened a letter from Wright. His friend and superior wanted to know if he had finalized the sale of the estate. He added that there was no news of the Evangelist to report; in the time since Zach had left the city, no further prostitutes had been attacked.

Zach tossed the letter on the floor. If there was no news, why bother writing to him?

A contingent of soldiers entered the inn later that evening and Zach listened to their tales of bravery without contributing any of his own. The deeper into the bottle he sank, the more morose and silent he became until at last he stumbled into his room and passed out, fully clothed. His last coherent thought before the alcohol overtook him was that he desperately missed Emily.

The next morning, through a raging headache, he bathed and dressed. Over breakfast he flipped through the mail and was surprised to see a letter for Emily. The handwriting on the envelope was decidedly feminine, and stamped in red ink at the top was the word: URGENT. Emily must have written to someone in the short time she'd been in residence, and this was her correspondent's reply.

Zach tapped the envelope on his palm. Emily had no family to write to and no acquaintances that he knew of. Then again, it appeared he didn't actually know her very well. For all he was aware she could be running a brothel.

He knew it was an unfair thought, but he was still angry. If the letter was urgent, he should ride to Brixton Hall and deliver it to her, except he wasn't ready to face her. He could open it and read it, but he wasn't sure he wanted to know any more of her secrets.

Instead he tucked the letter inside his coat, finished his cup of tea, and rode out to sign the papers on his estate.

The entire time he toured the massive estate he thought of Emily. She would rejoice in the little pond during the hot summer months, and she would adore the cool forest and charming cow path that wound through a field of daisies. The library would be her favorite room, or perhaps the little breakfast nook with so many panels of glass that it was bathed in sunlight. She'd hate the overbearing bed frame in the master bedroom, as did he. In the twenty-horse stable he stroked a gray mare with a spunky temperament that matched Emily's perfectly.

By the time he'd signed the paperwork and the transfer was complete, he was in a horrid temper. She was everywhere, even in a place she'd not once visited, this woman he loved who'd lied to his face.

Did she lie to his face? When the solicitors had cleared out, they'd left Zach alone in the den, a refreshing evening breeze tinged with pollen blowing in through the open window. He sat in a leather chair and did his best to recall his past conversations with Emily. Aside from omission as a form of lying, had she directly lied to him?

No, he didn't think she had. In fact, she'd been forthcoming about not wanting to marry him even after her husband had died a second time. Could her reluctance have been because she wanted to protect him? It was the first time the thought had occurred to Zach.

He tried to put himself in Emily's shoes, tried to imagine what it would be like to discover he was a powerful peer's unwanted bastard. How desperate would a young woman in her impoverished circumstances be to please her father, to find a sense of belonging? Sympathy for the innocent girl she'd once been expanded in his chest. When she fed that information to her father, could she have known what she was doing?

The moment he asked himself the question he knew it was absurd. How could she have known her father was secretly murdering young women? Emily had a violent side cultivated from necessity, but she also adhered to a personal moral code. She'd taken on three men in an alleyway in Bethnal Green to save her young charges even though it had meant certain assault or death for her. Would a person willing to do that also be someone willing to help her father murder innocent women?

Of course not. Shame licked beneath his skin. Had he let her leave believing he thought her a true accomplice?

Ultimately what had been Emily's crime? She'd omitted sharing a truth that had humiliated and ostracized her for her entire life. Could he really blame her for that? Look how he'd reacted when he found out.

She had probably known that if discovered, her past would affect his career, so she'd resisted marrying him even though he had pushed and pushed, until at last Mrs. Hill had left her with no choice. In effect, he'd put her in a terrible situation. She cared for him—of that he was certain—and yet she'd been held back first by her marriage, and then by the circumstances of her past.

With crippling clarity Zach realized how much of an idiot he'd been. Instead of listening to Emily when she was at her most vulnerable, he'd turned away, and she'd been too proud to insist.

He would explain Emily's background to Wright, and if his friend asked, he would resign. He was passionate about justice but there were a great many other ways he could contribute to society. And there was only one Emily Leverton. When it came to police work or the woman he loved, it was no contest.

Zach reclined in the chair. When Emily had finished her remaining days at Brixton Hall, he would fall to his knees and beg her for forgiveness. He could only pray she would find it in her heart to overlook his stupidity.

The breeze had died down, turning the study into what felt like a stuffy, airless coffin. Zach reached into his pocket for a kerchief to wipe the back of his neck, and his fingers brushed against the envelope for Emily. He withdrew the letter and the hair on his arms stood straight when his eyes again fell on the word URGENT.

Fear suddenly squeezed his heart. He ripped open the envelope and tilted the letter toward the single candle burning on the desk.

Emily,

I have just received your missive and I am writing to you at once. I beg of you, do NOT return to Brixton Hall. I do not have time to explain if I want this letter to make it into the next post, but I truly have strong reason to believe the Evangelist resides within the Eastmoreland family.

Write to me as soon as you have received this to let me know that—

Zach was already running out the door.

Chapter 57

Lady Eastmoreland smirked. "The Evangelist. It is not a bad name, is it? I am indeed scrubbing London clean, giving immoral women second thoughts about their whoring ways, and glorying the church with my commitment to marriage."

"Why not murder the men who visit the prostitutes?" Emily asked, her eyes darting about the room, searching for any type of additional weapon with which to defend herself. The candlesticks seemed heavy enough to cause damage. "They are the ones breaking their marriage vows, not the women."

Rage flickered in the countess's eyes. "You sound like Robert's dear, stupid mother, who adores the whores. If the women were not taunting and flaunting, the men would better control themselves. Men are weak and easy prey."

"Like your husband?" Emily asked, edging closer to the candlestick.

The countess's hand flexed around the hilt of the knife. "He is the weakest of them all, preferring a woman who dominates him to a wife who respects him and has carried his six children. If all women had the same morals that I do, affairs would not exist."

Right. If everyone had the same morals as the countess, there would be a whole lot of dead people.

"Is that why you tried to frame him?"

"It was a stroke of genius, but the execution was botched. That is what happens when you hire a drunk, I suppose. If it had worked, my ungrateful fool of a husband would have been blamed and jailed, leaving me free to continue my missions work."

Deranged. That was the only word Emily could think of to explain the countess's belief that she was doing society a favor.

"Do you think I am unaware of who you have been opening your thighs for, Emily?" the countess asked, tilting her head to the side like a parrot. "The great Detective Constable Denholm! The man who assured the public he was closing in on the Evangelist, when in truth he is as in the dark as every other bumbling policeman. You did well. He is quite wealthy, not that you will see a farthing of it. You were letting him bed you without vows, just like every other bunter. And when he was finally forced into offering marriage, your filthy past emerged." Lady Eastmoreland advanced a foot. "Is it true? Are you the daughter of the Silk Stalker?"

Emily's heart sank. She'd known news of her postponed wedding had reached the Eastmorelands, but she had not known if her Big Secret had as well. She gave a tight nod.

"Monster," the countess hissed.

"And you are not?"

She reared back as if Emily had slapped her. "How *dare* you compare me to him! He killed from dark lust. I work for the angels."

Emily was a few feet from the candlestick when the countess leapt forward, swiping at Emily's midsection with the knife. Emily screamed and backed away, narrowly avoiding the wicked tip of the blade.

"No, no, dear. I do not want you to even think of fighting back. Truly, it only excites me. How delicious is this going to be?" Lady Eastmoreland licked her lips, the candlelight catching in the moisture and making them glow. "I am about to sink this blade into the breast of Detective Constable Denholm's very own whore. It is too fitting, too just."

She advanced, backing Emily into the corner. She stretched out the knife and settled the tip at Emily's breastbone. Emily stilled her breathing, afraid her panicked breaths would inadvertently cause the knife to pierce her. Despite her efforts, the blade was so razor-sharp that a thin red point appeared on her skin. A drop of blood welled and dripped into the valley between her breasts.

Lady Eastmoreland swiped her finger inside Emily's dress, caught the drop of blood on her fingertip, and touched it to her tongue. Emily shuddered with revulsion.

"Is this how you charmed him, Emily? With your ripe fruits? I shall have to slash them when I am done. Or perhaps I will do it *before* I run you through. I think I shall enjoy the agony on your face while I scar you. He will not even want to look at your body when I am finished."

Emily's hands were slick with sweat. She discreetly wiped them on the skirt of her gown. "I do not think it was my breasts that drew him to me," she said.

The countess lifted a brow. "No?" Her gaze drifted lower.

"No, not that either."

Lady Eastmoreland chuckled. "Enlighten me. I am eager to hear what personality trait you will claim captured his interest."

"Well," Emily said slowly, "I think it was when he discovered I'm a violent street bitch."

The countess's eyes widened as Emily struck her palm, sending the knife flying. Before the countess could recover Emily thrust her shoulder into her belly, knocking her to the floor and falling on top of her. The countess slapped Emily across the face, and Emily returned the favor with a backhand, splitting the countess's lip and spraying blood on the rug. Emily withdrew her trusty dagger and pressed it to the woman's throat.

"Do not move, my lady, or you shall discover how it feels to have your flesh opened by a blade."

The library door handle rattled and the countess's eyes turned calculating. "Help!" she cried out. "The governess has gone mad!"

A foot slammed into the lock and the door burst open, wooden shards flying. Emily didn't remove the blade but her heart sank when she realized how the tableau must appear.

"Emily!" It was Zach. He sprinted forward and dragged her off the countess.

"Thank God!" the countess exclaimed. "Arrest this woman!"

Emily fought him. "No, it is not how it looks, Zach."

He took her by the shoulders and looked her in the eye. "I know, love. I trust you."

He turned and helped the countess to her feet.

"I am so grateful you have arrived, Detective." Lady Eastmoreland's voice quavered. "When I dismissed her from her position, she went insane. She attacked me in my own home. You ought to—what do you think you are doing?"

Zach had slapped a metal bracelet on her hand. He spun her

around, locking the second cuff on her other wrist. "You are under arrest, Lady Eastmoreland, for the murders of four women and the attempted murder of a fifth."

Lady Eastmoreland gasped. "Are you out of your mind? I will see you hanged for this impertinence, Detective!"

"The only person who will be swinging from the end of a rope, my lady, is you."

Chapter 58

2 Days Later

The arrest of the Countess of Eastmoreland made headlines across the nation. There were many who whispered they *knew* something had been off about the woman; she'd always been so *frigid*. Still others doubted it until the papers printed damning evidence, once again proving they had a source in the right place.

An anonymous benefactor had mailed the police a dossier of circumstantial evidence collected from a who's who of sources, including a tip that Lady Artice, the Black Widow, was aware of the Evangelist's identity and had been blackmailing Lord Eastmoreland for an astronomical sum. While the countess had been plotting to incarcerate her husband, he had been trying to protect her.

The Black Widow's testimony, along with Lord Eastmoreland's and Emily's, was enough to seal the countess's fate. The discovery of snippets of the prostitutes' dresses in Lady Eastmoreland's embroidery basket was simply the punctuation on the execution order.

When they had arrived back in London, Emily had questioned Zach's timely entrance at the library. He'd handed her the letter from the Dove.

"I suspect she is the Metropolitan Police's anonymous source," Zach had said, "but you know better than me. Will you tell me her identity?"

"I do not know it, and that is the truth," Emily had replied. "I know her only as the Dove."

"What of your connection to her?"

Zach had been amazed when Emily had explained how the Dove had ties with almost every governess in London and beyond, and that she used her network of spies to collect information on crimes that went unpunished among the wealthy. It was an entirely clever setup, and Zach had been vastly impressed. He'd told her that one day he hoped to meet this extraordinary woman.

Emily stayed with Zach at Stanford House while he took care of the case details. He told her he needed her nearby for any questions he might have, and as she had no other place to go, she agreed to a short visit. She slept in the guest chamber and they saw each other at meals, and although they were cordial, there was a stiffness between them that could have stood without legs.

And still she soaked up every awkward moment with him, because soon she would leave. Soon she would sever the one source of light and joy in her life. Although the Evangelist had been stopped, there would be more murders. More cases. More whispers and public doubt that a detective constable married to the Silk Stalker's daughter could do the job right.

On her second day back in London, Emily slipped out of the house while Zach was in a meeting with the police commissioner and walked to Willoughby House. She rapped on the side entrance and waited until a maid opened the door.

"I wish to see Miss Turner, the governess," Emily said.

"That odd duck?" The maid wrinkled her nose. "She en't here anymore."

She began to close the door, but Emily slapped her hand against it. "Do you know where she has gone? Has she found a new situation?"

The maid sighed heavily. "Wait 'ere. I'll ask around."

She did not invite Emily inside, so Emily paced the dirt-worn patch in front of the door until it opened again. Before her stood the head housekeeper, holding a crisply folded sheet of stationery.

"What is your name?" the housekeeper demanded. She was a severe woman with a severe hairstyle that gave Emily a headache just looking at it.

"Miss Leverton," she answered, praying the housekeeper would not recognize her name from the papers.

Apparently she did not, because she handed over the note without a word and slammed the door in Emily's face.

"Well!" Emily exclaimed. She turned her back on the Willoughbys and thought Frankie had had every right to be miserable at the place. She unfolded the note, which had been addressed to Miss Leverton. The script inside was spiky and, judging by the number of ink blots, seemed to have been written in great haste.

Miss Leverton,

I have left in search of my sister, and as I do not know how to contact you now, I can only leave this letter behind and pray you will visit. I have recently learned more of the Dove, and if you are reading this, I beg of you to pass her the message below.

—*Frankie Turner*

Emily read the brief message Frankie had written for the Dove and frowned. She had come to the Willoughbys to thank Frankie for trying to save her life, only to discover that now she was worried for the other governess. She did not understand Frankie's message, but if she wanted the note delivered to the Dove, Emily would make it happen.

Chapter 59

Zach set down the newspaper and glanced over at Emily, who was playing with her toast. Her brow was creased in thought and he wanted to smooth it with his thumb. Instead he cleared his throat and said, "I would like to take you somewhere."

She let the toast fall to her plate. "Where?"

"It is a surprise. Fetch your shawl and we will be off."

The oppressive heat had finally blown out to sea, and cooler air had filled its place.

They took his carriage even though their destination was within walking distance. Zach didn't want any distractions in the form of men stopping to congratulate him or women giving Emily the cut.

When they pulled in front of Exeter House, Emily couldn't hide her surprise. "Have we come to call on the marquess?"

"No."

She eyed him suspiciously but accepted his hand when he offered to help her out of the carriage.

The butler greeted them warmly and took Emily's shawl, then

a maid led them to the ballroom where Zach had first set eyes on Emily as she slipped alongside the wall, stopping long enough to laugh at his predicament with the Hill sisters.

When they stepped inside, Zach was pleased. Wright and his sister, the marchioness, had followed his instructions exactly. The chandeliers were lit even though it was broad daylight, and a hundred bouquets of hothouse tulips were arranged in glass vases on the floor. Petals lay sprinkled among the vases, giving the impression of a sea of blooms.

Emily gasped, slowly taking in the effect until she faced him, her eyes luminous. "What is this, Zach?"

"This, Noodles, is my apology. I wish you had told me your secret earlier, but considering how I acted when I found out, I cannot blame you for not doing so. I was an ass. Never, not for one second should I have doubted you, and I swear that for the rest of my life I never will again."

Emily hurried to him and clasped his hands. Those beautiful, unmanageable black curls of hers were already slipping from their pins, framing her freckled face in soft tendrils.

"No, I'm sorry, Zach. I'm so sorry I did not trust you enough to tell you."

Zach could have happily drowned in her deep, joyous eyes. "I have done a lot of telling you I am going to marry you, so this time I shall ask and the decision will be entirely yours. Emily Leverton, will you do me the honor of becoming my wife?"

She slowly shook her head. "Zach, you know that soon the truth about my past will reach London, and it will ruin your reputation as a constable."

"I am not concerned."

She withdrew her hands, regret clear on her face. "My mother and sister cannot be trusted. Neither can Mrs. Hill."

"No, they cannot be," he agreed. "But I am untouchable. I handed in my resignation last night."

"Zach! No! You love your work."

"I love you more." He held up a hand. "Before you protest, know that I have given it some thought and have decided to open my own consulting detective business. Without the constraints of public money and expectations, I think I shall be quite happy, especially if the partner I have in mind agrees to join the agency. She has keen senses, and it is the police force's loss that they do not accept women into service, but it will be my clients' gain."

Emily pointed her thumb at her chest and mouthed, "Me?"

Zach's eyes creased. "Yes, you."

Tentative hope returned to her face. "You promise that is what you want?"

"I promise."

"Then Zachariah Denholm, I have another secret I've been waiting to share with you."

He grinned. He had a feeling it was a secret he'd been waiting to hear.

"I love you!" she cried, throwing her arms around his neck. "Yes, I will be your wife, *and* your partner."

They tumbled to the floor, and in the very spot where they first met, they made love among a sea of blooms.

Epilogue

The Dove closed the society pages with satisfaction. The impending nuptials of Emily Leverton and Zachariah Denholm had made the front page, as they had every day for the past week.

Abreast with the news, she returned to the task at hand. Spread on the desk before her were over a dozen letters from governesses that had caught her eye. There was a pattern in them, hidden in the daily descriptions and mundane interactions. A picture had begun forming in her mind: a ring of noblemen purging their fortunes at gambling hells, a spate of hasty weddings, and whispers of blackmail.

Propped beside the letters was the note from Frankie Turner, the governess who had reached out to her with a simple sentence:

St. James's Street, JJ, forced marriages?

Indeed, the Dove thought as she scanned the governesses' letters again. *JJ* stood for "Jasper Jones," the darkly mysterious owner of Rockford's—the rising star of gaming hells located on St. James's Street between Piccadilly and Pall Mall. Frankie seemed to suspect his hell of something more nefarious than emptying the pockets of the *ton*.

When Emily had given her Frankie's note, Emily had mentioned how the other governess had used math to determine the identity of the Evangelist. The Dove had already tracked down Frankie Turner's location, and she was *very* interested in meeting the woman she suspected was a mathematical genius.

She allowed her gaze to fall on one of two framed portraits she kept in her study. The portrait was of a young girl with flaming-red hair. Her name had been Eleanor, and she had been far too clever for her years; pigheaded and full of conviction, she'd gone after what she wanted, unable to see the shades of gray within the blacks and whites. She had not believed in the twin gods the Dove worshipped: redemption and retribution. Eleanor had been too focused on the narrower details in lieu of the larger picture.

Still, the Dove had loved her sister fiercely, and her sister had been taken from her far too early, suffering the fate of being the Silk Stalker's final victim.

Emily Leverton, or rather Esther Lewis, had been unwittingly instrumental in her father's success as a murderer. The Dove had watched Emily closely over the past six years as Emily had borne the shame and guilt of her actions. The Dove had judged Emily's true character as the girl had fought off her mother's johns, stolen from the wealthy, and struggled to survive.

Despite Emily's role in her sister's murder, the Dove had believed in her. She had found her worthy of redemption, and so she had posted advertisements for governess positions where Emily would see them day after day.

The seed had been planted, and Emily, with her sharp intelligence and gritty determination, had flourished with the ruse.

The poetry of the Dove's plan was that as a young girl Emily had assisted a killer by spying on the *ton*. As an adult, the Dove had given Emily a fitting way to atone for her guilt: spying on the *ton* to *stop* a killer.

The Dove touched her fingertip to the painting, trailing it over her sister's hair. At the time of Eleanor's death, her sister had not understood who the Dove truly was. Eleanor had thought her boring and common. Eleanor couldn't have known that her death would turn the already fearsome Dove into what she was today.

Now the Dove would spend her remaining years delivering redemption to those who deserved it, and swift retribution to the monsters who felt above the law.

She would do it for Eleanor. She would do it for her husband.

The Dove pulled down a fresh sheet of paper and dipped her quill in the stone inkwell. Something evil was connected to Jasper Jones's gaming hell, and she was going to root it out and banish it.

It was time she and Frankie Turner became acquainted.

Don't miss the next book in the
Secret Society of Governess Spies series,
coming Spring 2025.

Acknowledgments

Publishing this book was my greatest dream come true, and it never would have happened without the hard work of so many people. Thank you so much to:

My agent, Emily Sylvan Kim, who was the first person to give my writing a chance. I'll never forget reading THE E-MAIL in a shopping parking lot and bursting into tears of happiness. Your belief in my writing career is what started everything, and for that I will forever be thankful.

My editor, Junessa Viloria, who loved the concept of governess spies and gave me this amazing opportunity. I read your offer e-mail while doing laundry and dissolved into tears (of joy, not because I had to do laundry). I am thankful for how your insights and commentary have made this book so much better.

The Forever team: Dana Cuadrado, associate marketing and publicity manager; Sabrina Flemming, assistant editor; Luria Rittenberg, production editor; Laura Jorstad, copyeditor; and Daniela Medina, cover designer.

Kaye Publicity: Dana Kaye, Katelynn Dreyer, Hailey Dezort,

and Eleanor Imbody, who have made the launch of this book so special.

My close friends, especially Victoria, who became my own personal cheerleader when I finally admitted to my secret writing life.

My mother and father, for buying me books, taking me to the library, and encouraging my writing. Heather, Matt, my amazing in-laws, and extended family members—your unending support means the world to me. An extra shout-out to my mother's romance book collection, which is the entire reason I'm obsessed with this genre.

My children. When you have questions about relationships, I'm probably going to point you toward romance novels.

Lastly, my husband. Not once did you lose faith that one day I would be published. For years I spent every spare moment typing away, and even when I felt like a failure, you stood steadfast in your encouragement. Thank you for picking up the slack when I needed to write. Thank you for listening to all of my book talk, and for being there for both the low moments and the high moments. Thank you for being my own real-life romance hero.

About the Author

Lindsay Lovise writes historical and contemporary romances with quirky heroines and a dash of mystery. Although she earned degrees in English and teaching, she always knew she wanted to write stories about love. When she's not writing, Lindsay is reading (probably romance), drinking coffee, and avoiding laundry. She currently lives in New York, but she was born and raised in Maine, where the winters make for perfect reading weather.

You can learn more at:
LindsayLovise.com
Instagram @LindsayLovise
Facebook.com/LindsayLoviseAuthor
Twitter @LindsayLovise